My
JOURNEY
IN AND OUT OF
COMMUNITY
A NOVEL

KATHERINE ZYCZYNSKA

MY JOURNEY IN AND OUT OF COMMUNITY
A NOVEL

Copyright © 2015 Katherine Zyczynska.

All rights reserved. No part of this book may be used or reproduced by any means, graphic, electronic, or mechanical, including photocopying, recording, taping or by any information storage retrieval system without the written permission of the author except in the case of brief quotations embodied in critical articles and reviews.

All Bible quotations, unless otherwise indicated, are from the New American Bible (Revised Edition) (NABRE).

iUniverse books may be ordered through booksellers or by contacting:

iUniverse
1663 Liberty Drive
Bloomington, IN 47403
www.iuniverse.com
1-800-Authors (1-800-288-4677)

Because of the dynamic nature of the Internet, any web addresses or links contained in this book may have changed since publication and may no longer be valid. The views expressed in this work are solely those of the author and do not necessarily reflect the views of the publisher, and the publisher hereby disclaims any responsibility for them.

Any people depicted in stock imagery provided by Thinkstock are models, and such images are being used for illustrative purposes only. Certain stock imagery © Thinkstock.

ISBN: 978-1-4917-7442-7 (sc)
ISBN: 978-1-4917-7443-4 (e)

Library of Congress Control Number: 2015913221

Print information available on the last page.

iUniverse rev. date: 12/03/2015

Acknowledgments

To God be the glory for whatever good comes out of this book.

I want to thank, Dr. Frank and his wife who through their prayers, and encouragement, helped me heal physically and emotionally. I am deeply grateful for Danielle who sacrificed her own peace of mind, to help in the process of this book. To all the wonderful people at iUniverse publishing who truly care about their authors. Thank you to all my Catholic church family, who love me with all my faults.

Chapter 1

Looking for Love

We had all gone astray like sheep,
All following our own way;
But the Lord laid upon him
The guilt of us all.
—Isa. 53:6

At eleven and a half years of age, my life changed forever. My dad—the only man our mom ever loved—died in a traffic accident. My shock and sadness were deep. I desperately wanted and needed a daddy—*my* daddy—to love me, teach me, and help me feel safe and secure. I knew my mom loved me, but she was unprepared to deal with this sudden tragedy. As a family of eight, we all suffered in our own ways, trying to deal with our loss. The oldest son, Bill, went back to college, keeping his pain inside. Susa, the oldest daughter, was in college as well. My other older brother and sister tried their best to be emotionally supportive, while I shut myself in my room and the youngest brother, five-year-old Phil, said, "I hate God for taking my daddy!" I didn't know at the time, but my longing for parental love set the stage for this story.

On May 2, 1972, I turned sixteen. Now, instead of babysitting to earn spending money, I could get a real job. After school, I walked into our local family-owned bakery and greeted the owner. "Mrs. Knapp, do have any job openings that I might apply for?" I asked.

"This is unusual," she responded. "We haven't even advertised yet, but Cindy, our cashier, is leaving next week to go to college. Could you come in this Saturday to train?"

"I certainly can," I answered excitedly. "Thank you!"

Now I could finally drive myself to school, and I also had a job! I went home thrilled, and my mom was so proud of me. She planned on giving me her old Dodge Coronet. The dealer who wrote up the title transfer needed an amount for sale, so we agreed on one dollar.

I loved working, having a car, and looking forward to the future. By my senior year of high school, I was working after school and on Saturday mornings at the bakery. I was also taking a 7:00 a.m. nursing class during the week. To this I added a 3:00 p.m. to 11:00 p.m. weekend shift at the Masonic Nursing Home as a nurse's aide. In our family there were many medical people. My mom and aunt were retired registered nurses. My grandma was a retired licensed practical nurse, and a sister and a brother worked in respiratory therapy. I figured I should follow their example.

This frenetic schedule occupied my days but still did not fill the empty feeling I carried with me every day. Sunday church and youth group did not fill this emotional hole in my heart either. What I needed most was to know I was loved. Although I didn't realize it at the time, God heard the cries of my heart.

"There is a Billy Graham movie at the theater this weekend, Kata. Do you want to go with the youth group?" my friend Tina from church asked me.

It sounded interesting, so I agreed to go with the youth group. The plan was to have a potluck dinner at church during our normal Sunday meeting and then go to the movie together in our church bus.

The movie, *A Time to Run*, was a story about a college-age man who had to choose which direction his life would head: toward God or being a fugitive from the law. When faced with a decision to accept Jesus and ask forgiveness for his sins, he tried to run away and hide from God, but there was no running away from him. He found himself outside a Billy Graham crusade. After hearing God's word, his heart felt broken, and he was ashamed of the life he was living. He stood up, as if in a daze; he was walking with a large group of people who searched for a free space to kneel at the altar and accept Jesus as their Savior. When he knelt at the altar, he felt a rush of emotion come over him. He was free at last of the guilt that pulled him down; Jesus had forgiven him his bad choices.

When the movie ended, a pastor came out on stage and asked if anyone in the auditorium wanted to make the same choice for Jesus as the young man in the movie had made. He invited people to come to the front, ask forgiveness for their sins, and accept Jesus as their Savior.

Tina and I held on to each other, weeping as we walked down to the front, and prayed to accept Jesus in our hearts. There was a counselor present to guide me in my prayers and give me a Bible and further information to learn more about living with Jesus. Mary, my counselor, asked me if I had been baptized. "I don't know; I assumed that I had, but I was never told about it."

"If you haven't been baptized, then your first assignment is to be baptized," encouraged Mary.

That night when I returned home, I called my mom. "Mom, let me tell what I did tonight!" I shared with her my experience of feeling Jesus change my heart from that of an unhappy teenager to that of a young woman who felt the forgiveness of my sins through the gift of Jesus dying on the cross. I asked her if I had been baptized as a baby, like my little brother had been.

She explained, "When you were born, your dad had stopped going to church. He said he had a conversion. He stopped smoking, read his Bible every day, and gave up going to the Presbyterian church, because he felt the church was only getting together as a social meeting, not a place to study the Bible and live out the teachings from the Bible. He was a different man. He also didn't want you to be baptized until you made a decision to live for Jesus; you had to make the choice."

On Easter Sunday, April 1973, at the age of seventeen, I was baptized into the family of God in my Presbyterian church. My search for the love that I'd missed with no dad was fulfilled by the glow of my new life in Jesus.

I did not seek out Mary, the counselor from the movie screening. I looked for someone at church, but as my dad had found out, the church was a great place to socialize, not a place to be fed spiritually. I was more comfortable having a smoke outside with my godfather and his friends, rather than visiting with the other members at coffee hour. No one was to blame but me; being a Christian takes hard work, daily prayers with the Lord, and choosing to live for Jesus every moment. A person may be born with a gift to run, but he or she will only become an Olympic gold medalist by daily training, hard discipline, many sacrifices, and, most important, a great coach. I had none of these in my life.

After graduating from high school in 1975, I was eager to get out on my own. My first apartment was a small studio, sharing the bathroom with an older couple. In the convalescent hospital where I worked, I made friends with women who were older, divorced, and loved to "party." I was an inexperienced eighteen-year-old. These women became mentors to my new independent lifestyle. They would invite me to go along with them to the local bars after work for dancing, drinking, and meeting men. Dancing was lots of fun, but they would take off for a while with men they had met, and I had to wait until they came back so that I could go home. The schedule worked out well since I did not have to be at work until two thirty in the afternoon. These late nights still left time to sleep off the alcohol from the night before.

Still looking forward to my having a nursing career, my mom arranged for me to take LPN classes through a community college held at our local hospital during the day, which would not interfere with my work at the nursing home. The same women who were my partying coworkers were also going through the classes to become licensed practical nurses. As I continued to join my friends at bars for drinking and dancing, they instructed me that I needed to protect myself if the opportunity opened up to have sex with any of the men. "Go to the doctor, and ask for birth control pills so you can be safe," they insisted.

When I went to our family doctor, he asked me happily if I was getting married. I told him I was not. He was disappointed but wrote the prescription without further questions. The only knowledge I had of sex was that when I was thirteen, my mom told my older sister to take me in her room to explain "things" to me. My dear sister nervously drew an anatomically correct picture of the male sex organ and the female sex organ, but she never told me how the two got together.

The following weekend when I went out with my friends, I was prepared to have my first sexual experience. I was scared to death. As I chatted with the bartender, a man asked me for a dance. I was still frightened, but the feeling of having a man seek me out to dance and hold me in such a gentle way was exhilarating. His name was Harry. He made his living as a truck driver and lived with his parents when he was home. As we talked, my fears diminished; he seemed very kind. He volunteered to take me home, so I accepted his offer. My friends giggled when I told them Harry was taking me home. The first stop was to his house to meet his parents. They were friendly farm people, just like their son, Harry. Later, when we arrived at my apartment, I invited him in for a beer. He asked straightforwardly if I had ever "been" with a man.

"No, I have not, but I'm open to try," I told him.

He promised that he would not force himself on me but said it would be an honor if he could be the first. We slept together on the floor in our clothes all night so I could get used to a man sleeping next to me. Harry led me through my sexual experience, but the next day he was gone, and I have never seen him since. I wrongfully thought that he loved me. Unfortunately, I learned the hard way that this kind of sex has nothing to do with love. I came to detest the term *making love*. It didn't feel that way to me when it was outside of a marriage commitment. It was just sex, something that every animal engages in for the sole purpose of reproduction. When we feel we have a right to do it for pleasure outside of marriage, in reality it causes pain and separation from God. Free sex is not love, nor is it free. This realization didn't change the path I was on, however.

One day just for fun, my friends and I visited a palm reader. They went regularly. I was skeptical but went for the experience. As we arrived at the palm reader's house,

I had the strange feeling that I had been there before. Once we entered the front room, I remembered clearly. I had accompanied my dad on one of his calls to repair her refrigerator! I recalled the smells of incense in her house and the pictures of Jesus hanging on the cross. There I was, in that same house again. When it was my turn, she asked me what I wanted. I blurted out the first two things on my mind: "I want to find my uncle Jimmy, and I want to know Jesus!"

I clearly caught her off guard, for, after a significant pause, she responded, "Well now, as for your uncle, he will show up when you least expect him. For your other request, he will find you."

I left there with a big smile on my face and a light heart. My friends asked me what happened, but all I could say was, "I am happy." If I had told them about my requests, then my wishes might not come true. Funny, though—both requests eventually did occur.

I won't go into all my exploits searching for love except for the moment when I hit rock bottom. I had driven home from the bar alone one Saturday night and gone to bed, when there was loud knocking at my door and I heard two men giggling loudly. When I opened the door, I recognized the two men whom I had met at the bar that night. They asked if they could come in for some fun. Wanting to keep them quiet because of the neighbors, I let them in. That was a huge mistake! The next thing I knew, I was on the floor with nothing on, and these two naked men were having their way with me sexually. All I could do was to be passive.

I have no idea how long they were there. I felt so terribly helpless and filthy. When they finally left, I took a bath, but I discovered that soap and water would never cleanse away the damage done on the inside of my soul. This experience changed my attitude toward casual sex. It was definitely not pleasurable. But what other option was there? I was without direction, so I continued this lifestyle, thinking that by searching in this way, I would find the one man who would love me for who I was, rather than just for sex.

Chapter 2

Failure at Nursing

For I know well the plans I have in mind for you—
oracle of the Lord—plans for your welfare and
not for woe, so as to give you a future of hope.
—Jer. 29:11

Clearly it was impossible to keep up my schedule. In the mornings I had the nursing class at the hospital, and I worked at the Masonic home as an aide from three to eleven. After work, I went out with friends for drinks and then headed home to bed after the bars closed at two in the morning. On the weekends I would work Friday nights, go to bars with my coworkers, and hook up with men. On Sunday morning I was at church like always, thinking no one would even suspect what I had been up to the night before. Somehow I sensed Mom knew, but she never let on. For about a month, a man lived with me. He was in his thirties and divorced; he had no place to live but with his parents. I brought him with me one Sunday, and then we had dinner at my mom's house.

I did not care that he was older than I, but to my mom it made a big difference. A man in his thirties dating her eighteen-year-old daughter was not an ideal relationship in her opinion. My mom decided to call my oldest sister, Susa, who lived in California with her husband and two children, to tell her that I was dating an old high school boyfriend of hers, who she felt was a worthless bum. She pleaded with my sister to do something about my loose lifestyle. She knew I needed a change and to get away from the friends who were a bad influence on me. By this point I had lost my vision of nursing, which should have been my top priority. I just could not handle work, school, partying, and so on all at one time.

June 1976 was when I would find out how well I was performing as a nurse. The moment that ended my nursing career was about to occur. I was assigned two patients, an elderly woman with leukemia and a younger man with an abdominal wound. When I went in to give the woman her bed bath, everything went well. I even took the time to rub her back with lotion. I talked to her and made her happy. What I dreaded was taking care of the young man. I was very embarrassed to change his dressing. When I went in to change it, my supervisor came in to observe me. I got so nervous that after I changed the bandage, I threw away the old dressing and then put my hands in my pocket to write down my notes.

My supervisor, Mrs. Miller, immediately called me out to the corridor. "After you have done any procedure, never, ever put your hands on anything until you have washed them thoroughly!" Back in the seventies, we did not use gloves, as is the practice nowadays everywhere.

I made no excuse; she was right, of course.

At the end of the first semester, Mrs. Miller and the nurse in charge of teaching, Sister Patricia, called me in to the office to explain that I had failed and had no aptitude for being a good nurse.

I then turned to Sister Patricia in all sincerity and asked, "How could I become a nun?"

She was dumbfounded by the question but finally responded, "I don't think you would make a good nun."

I believe that there are no coincidences. Our lives are a series of coordinated events put together by God. The priest at my church once said in a sermon, "Coincidences in life are really God-incidents." My God-incident was failing at nursing. This door had just closed. I needed another direction, another door for my life. Finding that door was going to be up to God.

CHAPTER 3

Cancer Scare Leads to a New Journey

[To him] Jesus said, "No one who sets a
hand to the plow and looks to what was left
behind is fit for the kingdom of God."
—Luke 9:62

Shortly after this my mom called. Her doctor had told
her the x-rays he ordered at her last checkup showed signs
of cancer in her uterus. He wanted to operate as soon as
possible. My siblings and I rallied to support our mom. I
gave up my apartment and moved back home to help Mom,
anticipating chemotherapy.

On the day of Mom's surgery as we gathered in the hall of
the hospital, my sister Susa said, "We need to pray for God
to heal Mom right now!" We huddled together, and Susa
prayed a powerful prayer, asking God to go into Mom's

body, clean her of all cancer, and guide the doctors as they operated.

We waited for what seemed like hours before the doctor came out with a strange look on his face. He said, "I don't know what happened. I checked and double-checked the x-rays. When I opened your mom up expecting to see cancer in her uterus, there wasn't any cancer. I can't believe it!"

To the doctor's surprise, Susa said, "I can! God healed her!"

We cried tears of joy and relief. God had answered our prayers.

As Mom was recovering, Susa presented a plan she had been thinking about since Mom's earlier phone call: "Do something about Kata!" she had pleaded. "Kata needs a change; she is getting too wild." Susa offered to me, "Why don't you pack your things, and we could drive across country together so you can meet this Christian group called the Olive Tree Community. It is an extended family of men and women, married and single. It's not too far from where I live. You might meet a nice Christian man there. Write to them asking if you could make a visit sometime."

Mom thought this was a great idea. I was torn. One part of me felt like my mom planned a cancer scare just to get Susa back home to get me to go back with her. But the other part thought maybe God had this plan in his mind as he watched me make wrong choice after wrong choice.

Susa first met two of the members of the Community at a church function while both their families were in the navy stationed in Millington, Tennessee. Danielle and her husband, Gary, were newlyweds spending three months there while Gary attended a naval school. They met at church. Danielle was drawn to Susa because she had a young baby, and Danielle was looking forward to starting a family of her own when they returned to the Community. When both couples finished their naval duty in Tennessee, they returned to California and renewed their friendship. Susa pushed me again: "Kata, you should write to Danielle, asking if you can come for a visit."

I sent a letter with a simple explanation of my problem areas, asking if I could come for a visit. Danielle wrote back stating that if I was ever in California, I should call to arrange a visit to see if this kind of life would work for me. This was the open door God provided. We planned to leave in a few weeks. The only stipulation Susa had about driving across country was that I must promise not to smoke in the car with the kids.

The day before we were to leave, Susa wanted to take a small test drive to get the feel of how my car handled. We headed over to visit her Polish in-laws, taking a back-alley shortcut to their house. Suddenly a car coming from the opposite direction drove in front of my car, smashing her driver's-side window and denting her door. My Dodge hardly had a scratch. I cannot recall how the sheriff showed up, but as we were standing there, Susa realized she had left her purse with her license in it at the house. He asked where she lived, and Susa explained that she was staying at her in-laws' house, the Przybyz. A flash of recognition crossed the sheriff's face. "Yes," he said, "I know them very well. So you married their son Antonin! I cannot believe he is married with two kids. Go ahead and run home for your license, and I'll wait for you."

There were no injuries in the accident. The sheriff determined that we had the right-of-way and that the other driver should have yielded to us. When we returned to the car, I asked Susa whether she knew the sheriff, for clearly she was quite friendly with him. She laughed and shared that they had dated in high school, so they were recalling old fun times they had together.

When we returned from this incident, Susa's mother-in-law, Klara, had wonderful food prepared, especially her borscht. Dessert was her "secret Russian torte," an eight-layer, whipped cream, creamy chocolate and raspberry fillings cake! Susa gave me permission to share this secret recipe at the back of this book, Olga Przybyz' Russian Torte*. Always have one of these cakes in your freezer; you never know when company will come.

Leaving home this time was bittersweet. The idea of moving to California sounded exciting. But leaving Michigan meant the realization that I would no longer share special weekly jaunts with my mom to explore restaurants, flea markets, and sales. I made the choice to leave my past behind and only look forward.

Chapter 4

Journey West

So whoever is in Christ is a new creation: the old things
have passed away; behold, new things have come.
—2 Cor. 5:17

We started out early in the morning of July 26, 1976. I was
filled with great anticipation of what lay ahead, while Susa
and her two children, Fiona and Stanislaus, were looking
forward to going back home to their normal routine.

We spent the first night in St. Louis, Missouri, in a quaint
little motel decorated to feel like forest cabins. We Americans
need at least once in our lives to take the time to travel across
our country to appreciate the people and land we live in.
When we arrived at the border of Texas, it was nice for a
while to be in cattle country. But after a day and a half of
the same thing, we were very tired of the cattle and the
signs that advertised, "If you can eat a one-pound steak in
an hour, you can have it for free!"

When we arrived in Laredo, Texas, we stopped to get gas and switch drivers. It was my turn. I made a left turn when it should have been a right turn, which put me on the freeway going south. Looking up, I saw a sign that read, "Bienvenidos a Ciudad Juarez, Mexico." I shouted, "Oh my God, Susa, we're headed for Mexico. What do we do? We do not speak Spanish!"

Susa laughed and responded, "No problem. Make a U-turn and head back the way we came."

We left Mexico without any problem, but being there, although for only a very short moment, left a lasting impression on me. As we continued west, away from flat Texas to the deserts and mountains of New Mexico, my sister jokingly assured me they spoke English.

We stopped at a place called Carlsbad Caverns. To go from ninety-degree weather to the cool underground caverns was delightful to say the least. Being inside the caverns was like descending into another world with stalagmites and stalactites, dripping steadily and creating unique formations above and below. They looked like icicles going both directions. Off in the distance, if you listened carefully, you could hear the chatter of bats signaling to each other as they captured their prey. Of course, you also heard the chattering of other people walking in the cave, with the occasional child calling out to hear his or her echo. We wanted to put out our hands to see how cold the "icicles" were, but the ranger leading our group said, "Please, do not touch anything, because your fingerprint will make a mark that will forever blemish this place." We immediately put our hands into our pockets to resist the temptation to touch anything, for fear of ruining it for future people to enjoy as much as we had.

We crossed the desert as best we could, thanks to my sister, who packed cold drinks and delicious crisp green grapes to keep us cool since my poor 1973 Dodge Cornet did not have air-conditioning. Driving through the desert felt as if we were part of the western movies we watched on television as kids, with their tall cacti and sandy hills. All we needed were cowboys on horseback to come galloping by to make our memories real. The heat was real, however, and we continued to make the best of our drive by singing cold winter songs while we sprayed each other from a bottle. My sister Susa has always been able to bring frivolity into any situation. Then again, she got it from our dad, who always made us laugh.

We arrived August 1, 1976, in California, to her small apartment. Fiona and Stanislaus ran out of the car as fast as they could. They were so happy to be home again after a long trip. Susa had plans for the month of August. We visited all the theme parks, the zoo, and the beaches. She even took me to a Tupperware party, hosted by a Filipino woman. The food was a feast of all Filipino delicacies. By August 10, I figured I had better call the Community and schedule an appointment to come for a visit.

Now lay my opportunity for a new life, in the form of a letter from Danielle at the Olive Tree Community.

CHAPTER 5

Visiting the Olive Tree

All you peoples, clap your hands; shout
to God with joyful cries.
—Ps. 47:2

On August 26, 1976, I pulled out the letter from Danielle and read it again: "If you are ever out here, look us up. Here is our phone number." All I had to do was dial the number. "Just dial it, Kata; get it over with," I had to keep telling myself, but I was extremely nervous. I thought about the fun I had with Susa and the kids driving across the country, making a U-turn in Mexico, going to the amusement parks and the zoo. But I knew this was just a vacation trip. I couldn't live like this forever.

I finally made the call and asked for Danielle.

"Who are you?" a male voice asked, so I explained who I was and why I was calling.

"Please hold on a minute, and I'll see if she can come to the phone."

It was the longest minute of my life, but finally Danielle was on the line.

"We knew you wanted to visit sometime, but we didn't expect you so soon! We will have to get back to you to see when you may come," Danielle said firmly but kindly.

The next day, August 27, I got a phone call from Danielle stating that I might come on September 7. Her husband would pick me up on his way home from work. When I got off the phone and shared the news with my sister, I was surprised to see her sad face. The seventh was the day her husband, who had been deployed for six months, was coming home, and she thought I'd really enjoy seeing his ship dock in port. I called back and explained the situation to Danielle. There was some discussion in the background, but she said I could come on the ninth but not to change it again. I was certain they believed me to be a typical irresponsible teenager. I could hardly blame them.

That night as I lay down on the sofa in the small living room of the apartment, I thought about the fact that my brother-in-law, who had not been with his wife for six months, might like the privacy of the apartment and his family alone, without a sister-in-law in the way. I planned to call the Community back when Susa stepped out of the house to explain about the situation and ask if I could change the date back to the seventh.

At the first chance, I made the call. Again there were muffled sounds. I waited and waited. Finally Danielle came on the phone and in a firm voice explained very clearly, "We had thought that very same thing, but you were very insistent, so the date remains the same. We told you not to change it, and we are sticking to our word."

"Yes, I understand," was my sheepish reply. "However, it is very embarrassing to think I will be in the next room when they are, you know, having sex." There was a pause.

Then the reply came: "You made the decision. We agreed and will pick you up on the ninth." Click. That was their second impression of Zdzislawa Katarzyna Zyczyaska. First was my surprise phone call announcing my arrival in California with no warning. Danielle had said in her letter, "If ever you are in town, give us a call!" She just did not know that I was going to be in town in a couple of weeks, with the sole purpose of making a visit to the Community. Second was my instability about the day to visit. I could only imagine they were not amused.

Anton, my brother-in-law, stood proudly on the ship as it came into the port. Five thousand sailors were lined along the rim of the ship, looking sharp in their white Cracker-Jack uniforms, saluting the crowd. Everyone must witness the event of men and women returning from deployment at least once. It is a splendid feeling to know that these people lay down their lives for our freedom every day.

Finally the afternoon of the ninth arrived! Susa prepared me for Gary by telling me a tall handsome naval officer would be picking me up. He was prompt, just as Danielle said he would be. He put my things in the trunk of the car, and we started up the freeway. There a nervous silence until I asked some questions about where we were going and about the family.

After a long trip down winding roads, we arrived. I saw a large property with an ample garden, chicken coop, two goats in a pen, ducks and quail roaming around, and a hutch filled with at least twenty rabbits. As I looked down a dirt pathway, people were going in and out of the house. I thought, *What am I getting myself into?* I wondered if this was such a good idea. I felt relieved it was only a weekend visit.

Danielle met us at the gate, gave her hubby a big kiss, and then gave me a tour of the property. She had long hair and wore an ankle-length dress. She was talkative, quite the opposite from her quiet husband. All the ladies were wearing long dresses, so I felt very out of place in my hip-hugger pants worn out at the hem, tight T-shirt top, and my brown curly perm.

As Danielle showed me their expansive garden, which provided vegetables year round, and their rabbit hutch, I asked, "Why do you keep so many rabbits? Are they all pets?"

"You'll soon find that out," explained Danielle. "We are having a celebration dinner tonight for a couple wanting to formalize a relationship with our Community."

I was to sleep in a small unattached cottage that contained two tiny rooms. Each room had two twin beds, but not much room for anything else. The door to the bathroom was a strange shape, cut off at the top—I guess to let air in, although there was a window at the head of the built-in bathtub that opened out onto the trash yard, not a nice smell when the trash cans were full. Everyone had to walk through the bedroom to get to the bathroom. In addition there was what looked like a kitchen area, but instead of a stove there was a washer and dryer. The cottage was heated by a large electric space heater in the middle. A unique feature was a lovely brick window in the shape of a rainbow, with slats that opened and closed.

Two other women shared one of the small rooms. One was Valerie, a blonde-haired twenty-year-old woman whose focus was on her upcoming wedding. She seemed nervous, needing to keep her hands busy doodling, knitting, or crocheting. Valerie's roommate was Dee, a short woman with black curly hair and a peaceful demeanor. Dee was a naval officer like Gary; they carpooled with him to their jobs in San Poncho. I slept alone in my little room. The other bed was for a young woman named Renée, who was away at a trade school. There was a little window by my bed; I could see a small round mushroom-shape table with two mushroom-shape stools on either side. Very cute and inviting.

We walked down a dirt path along a fenced-in yard to the main house, passing through a side door into the very large dining room. "We do not have a front door to this house. The other door"—Danielle pointed to a door about ten feet away—"leads to the kitchen." There were four large dining tables, each about six feet by four feet, with twenty chairs in total. Each place setting had a placemat, with silverware and cloth napkins. There were two doors on one side of the dining room; one led to a laundry room, and the other led to a room where Hans and Evelyn slept. I learned that everyone called them Mom and Poppa. "You will meet them later, along with all the other members of the family," Danielle informed me.

The living room had three long sofas, two easy chairs, an organ, a rocker in one corner, and a television in another corner, yet still some people sat on the floor.

"Hey, everyone, this is Zdzislawa. I hope I didn't kill the pronunciation." Danielle laughed.

"Most people can't pronounce it. I go by my nickname, Kata, which is short for Katarzyna; it is a Polish family name," I explained.

We walked through the living room down a long hall. The first room on the left was a small bedroom with a bunk bed, where two of the single men slept. One was the third elder of the Community, Uncle Basil, an Episcopal priest, a man in his late forties, bald on top with a cute ring of curly red hair framing his head. L. T., short for Lawrence Thomson, was Uncle's roommate, a tall skinny man in his twenties with a large bushy black Afro. When he smiled he showed a silver tooth right in front, which gave him a playful character. I never found out how he got it. L. T. was a talented artist who wrote Christian songs, played guitar, and drew illustrated Bible stories in cartoon form.

Across the hall from their bedroom was a large bathroom, with two sinks and a five-foot-long bathtub. All the men who lived in the main house shared this one bathroom.

The only other room upstairs was a massive bedroom, with a separate dressing room filled with mirrors. It had one bed, lots of furniture, and a private sliding glass door to the outside. This room belonged to Anne, the owner of the house, a widow in her eighties. I did not meet her as she was away on a trip with a friend.

Downstairs was a basement, used for car repairs, woodworking, and other projects. There were two rectangular freezers. One was filled with meat and the other with bread. In one corner there were several shelves filled with jars of canned fruit, tomato sauces, jams, and pickles.

I asked Danielle, "What is that large machine?"

"That is our mill. We grind our own wheat flour, cornmeal, and oats. We try to live simply by planning our meals around what we grow ourselves," she explained. "One of our favorite bread recipes is Two-Tone Bread*."

The rest of the single men slept in a room downstairs, directly under the living room. Of the single men, there was Robert, a man in his late twenties, tall, strongly built, with wonderful brown curly hair. He worked at an elementary school as an accountant. His university education was to be a doctor, but illness sidelined his plans. He put his studies to good use, teaching himself to use scalpels for his woodworking.

"Robert likes to work with wood," Danielle said. "He's very talented."

Tony, who was engaged to Valerie, was a dark-haired Italian American man in his early twenties. He was studying for his nurseryman degree and always had a joke to tell or found humor in any conversation. Larry was Renée's brother, a blond-haired, quiet, stocky man in his middle twenties who attended classes to learn how to paint cars. Carlos, a dark-haired Mexican American, who had a distinct Chicano accent, loved to eat Mexican food. His hobbies were making stained glass artworks and playing the harmonica. L. T. and Carlos were best friends, having grown up in East Los Angeles together. The two of them had formed a Christian musical group that performed at local churches, spreading the gospel using songs written by L. T., who sang and played guitar, with Carlos singing and playing the harmonica, kazoo, and assorted other percussion instruments.

I realized each person came to this Community for his or her own particular reasons, but all shared a desire to change the direction of their lives and to improve their relationship with God.

Outside a loud bell rang, signaling everyone to come in for dinner. There was a lot of activity. People were running around bringing dishes to the table, putting ice cubes in glasses, and so on. I stayed out of the way, not knowing what to do to help. Everyone had a task to do, and everything was getting on the table for dinner quite efficiently. Danielle showed me where to stand. Everyone gathered around all the tables and held hands to pray.

Before praying, Evelyn, or "Mom," as everyone called her, announced, "Everyone, this is Kata. She will be spending the weekend with us. Kata, we are going to tell you all our names—one, two, three." Everyone shouted their names simultaneously. It was obviously meant to be funny, but all I could think was, *Great. I will never get to know anyone now.*

After praying we sat down, but before they passed the food, there were several rules to follow, including pass the food to the right and wait to pass the water and milk until all the food was passed because—in their peculiar use of language that used fractured Bible verses for fun—"Where two or three are gathered, someone always spills the milk." Dinner was homemade bread, plenty of garden vegetables, some sort of jelled salad, and a casserole with pieces of meat over rice covered with aluminum foil, called "Souper Chicken/Rabbit*."

I asked, "What kind of meat are we eating?" I looked for a wing, but all I found were small leg or breast portions.

Danielle said, "Just try it; it's like chicken."

I took a bite, and yes, it tasted like chicken. It was only after I took my first bite that they told me it was rabbit meat butchered right on the property.

While we sat at the dinner table, I had more time to observe the new family I hoped to live with until I found a new direction for my life.

I learned that the three elders—Father Basil, Hans, and Evelyn—founded the Community to reach out to young men on drugs. A vivacious personality, Evelyn seemed to lead the conversations at the table and kept the dialogue moving along so everyone had a chance to share. I could tell everyone deferred to her. She was in her forties, with shoulder-length wavy brown hair, young-looking, with a trim figure. Evelyn insisted that everyone call her Mom. Evelyn's husband, Hans, was a quiet man; he was known as Poppa. He managed the Community finances and ran a home-repair business. I liked him because he reminded me of my father. Like my dad, he was of German ancestry and had a short stocky physique and a dry sense of humor; he was in the navy during World War II. Father Basil, known as Uncle Basil, was an Episcopal priest, forty years old, with a gentle demeanor. He was slightly hunched over, bald on the top of his head, with an encircling crown of reddish hair. He was as comfortable in his priestly robes as he was in his overalls, tromping through the mud both at work in the garden or milking the goats.

After dinner, during cleanup, I sat with Danielle, and we went through Olive Tree photo albums as Danielle explained the Community's history. She told me how she arrived when the Community ran a beach ministry in Los Angeles.

When cleanup was done, they pulled the television out from the corner, where it was normally covered with a cloth; it was only brought out when the whole group would watch programs together. That night the program of choice was *The Waltons*. Afterward Danielle informed me of the next day's schedule. I went to bed trying to remember all the rules, schedules, names, and who called whom what.

The next day I had to get up earlier than I had ever gotten up—six thirty—to empty the dishwasher, pour the juice, and put out the milk in preparation for breakfast at seven o'clock. They'd set the breakfast table the night before according to whatever Valarie decided to prepare. She planned and prepared not only the weekday breakfasts but also the sack lunches for those who worked or went to school. She was up before dawn to make breakfast for the men who left early and to spend time with her fiancé, Tony, before he left for work. That Friday morning we had hot oatmeal and juice, served with goat's milk, raisins, and brown sugar. Goat's milk tastes like the animal at first, but more creamy. I got used to it after a while but never drank a full glass of it as Robert did every night with his graham cracker snack. He would eat a cracker in an unusual way. He put the whole unbroken cracker in his mouth, flipped it with his tongue, and then broke it perfectly in half with his teeth.

The last day of my stay, they held a church service in the living room, including Communion. This was unusual for me. Having grown up in the Presbyterian Church, for me Communion only happened at Christmas and Easter. Danielle played her guitar, leading us in songs. Everything was so new to me. Even though church was in the living room and informal, everyone was expected to be well dressed: no jeans and T-shirts. I did not own a dress or skirt, but one of the women loaned me a dress she got from the "missionary barrel."

"What is a missionary barrel?" I asked.

Every so often they would get a donated bag of clothes. It was called a missionary barrel since that was the term many overseas missionaries called donations from the States. The women would open a bag together, and Evelyn would hold up one piece of clothing at a time to see if anyone would like to try it on. My borrowed dress that day came from one of these bags.

After church some of us helped in the kitchen to prepare brunch: Crazy Pancakes*, with sausages and fruit cups. We set the table, served the food, and then when everyone gathered, we sang a hymn as our prayer before the meal. Anyone who helped prepare the meal beforehand was exempt from cleanup afterward.

In the afternoon I joined a small group of members to play a "getting to know you" game called Ungame (used by permission www.talicor.com). The way this game is played is each person in the group chooses a colored piece and then rolls the dice, moving his or her piece the correct number of spaces according to whatever number is thrown on the dice. Depending on the place on the playing board where the piece lands, he or she may have to pick a card and answer a question such as "What is an ideal marriage?" or "Who has influenced your life the most?" There is no loser or winner in this game. The goal of the game is to learn about each other, or in our case, it was a nonthreatening method to expose troubled emotional problem areas in players' lives.

There are set rules for playing, such as you cannot talk while someone is on his or her turn. You can ask a question or make a comment only when you land on a green space. On a green space you can make a comment on someone else's question, ask a question to someone, or share a personal statement. Other times the player rolls the dice and lands on a space that says, "Have you gossiped this week?" If you had gossiped, you had to move your piece to the "get on the treadmill" square, where you had a time-out.

When I landed on a green space, I earnestly stated, "I have only one problem."

At that point a couple of the people stood up cheering and clapping loudly.

Turning red in the face, I asked, "What was that for?"

"That's a first!" Evelyn smiled; "You said you only have *one* problem! We were amazed you had only one, so we all applauded you. So what is your one problem?"

"I do not think I can call Evelyn Mom or Father Basil Uncle," I replied.

There was no response, a complete opposite of their previous actions. I didn't realize I still could ask what they thought.

On my next turn, when I got another green space, I asked if I could stay, possibly forever.

Evelyn said, "We will have to discuss your request. We will get back to you tonight."

Having to wait was difficult, so I walked around the property until L. T. called me into the house to find out the decision. Finally, after the members came out of that little room off the dining room, they decided I could stay for a month's trial. Living here would mean I would have to live by their rules of the house and do my share of the daily chores.

A normal day began at a quarter to six in the kitchen to help get breakfast on the table by seven. Breakfast always ended with a devotional and prayer. After cleanup we had free time until formal morning prayer from the Episcopal Prayer Book at a quarter after eight. When I had free time, I usually took a walk. After morning prayer we had nine o'clock prayers in the living room for singing and intercessory prayers. Immediately following prayers, the females gathered in the kitchen to sign up for the daily chores: cooking, cleaning, and any extra work according to what produce came in from the garden. Housecleaning was done weekly, each of us changing the jobs we did monthly. On the day we had housecleaning, if all the teenagers finished their jobs before lunch, we would get to go to the beach, a great incentive for getting the jobs done. Before dinner, Hans and Basil turned on the television to watch the news. After dinner we played games, read, or just went to bed.

During the day, besides work, there were games, walks, Bible studies, free time to read books, and prayer times. Several of the women would sew their own clothes; it was very popular for women to wear long skirts or dresses. I tried to learn but lacked the patience and enjoyment that the other women had.

While I was there, the Community was practicing for their "Olive Tree Review." It consisted of various types of musical Christian skits and dancing, ending with the Gospel message. Valerie taught me Israeli dance steps she had designed for the review. At first, I had a difficult time learning the steps with the circle of women, since this kind of folk dancing was so different for me. We held hands, moving our feet together to the rhythm of the song. We also wore costumes sewn by the women in the Community: long skirts, blouses with puffy long sleeves, and headscarves.

The review was performed at different venues, such as schools, churches, and public halls to present the message of the Gospel in this humorous, winsome way. The first time I participated, the Community performed in a large church auditorium before several hundred people. In one skit Evelyn dressed in a long sexy backless dress, holding a microphone and singing, "Jesus Still Loves You, Even If You Have Warts." L. T. wrote this song and played guitar. I was a backup singer with two other women, singing doo-wop-a-doo in rhythm. Evelyn descended the stage while singing so that she could sing to people in the audience in the style of Marilyn Monroe. As she got to the line, "He loves you even if you have no hair," she kissed a bald man on top of his head; his face turned a dark pink.

Another skit was a cancan dance. L. T., Robert, and Gary—all tall, thin men—wore shorts showing off their skinny hairy legs and danced to the melody from "High Hopes."

The words were changed to, "High faith, he's got high faith." They certainly kicked high, which brought quite a lot of laughter and applause from everyone.

Another skit was performed by Robert and Danielle, with L. T. playing guitar. In this skit Danielle approached her "boyfriend" Robert, singing, "Popeye, I really must talk to you about this Jesus who forgives sins." At first he does not understand. He just replies, "Oh, Olive, I don't know about this Jesus, but something about you is different." When she tells Popeye that knowing Jesus has made her happy and maybe he would want Jesus too, Popeye asks Jesus into his heart, making both of them happy. At that point a pregnant Danielle puts her hand on her belly and sings to Popeye, "Now that we both know the forgiving love of Jesus, maybe we should get married." This brought roars of laughter from the crowd. At that time, in the 1970s, having a baby out of wedlock was uncommon.

We ended with the Israeli dance (with original words and music) I had practiced with the women. The plan was to end with everyone repeating the ending phrase of Alleluia to encourage the whole audience to sing with us, and then the dancers would go down among the people dancing, singing, and clapping hands. When we went down, filled with the joy of the Spirit, I kept dancing around, not noticing that the rest of the dancers returned to the stage.

Evelyn had to call over the microphone, "Has anyone seen Kata? We lost Kata. I believe the Holy Spirit got hold of her. Please come join us back on stage, Kata."

Everyone laughed while I ran back on stage to join the group, feeling very embarrassed. This was the first time I experienced this kind of happiness. It felt so good! Although I did not know it at the time, I was experiencing the joy of the Holy Spirit.

CHAPTER 6

The End of the One-Month Trial

The trivial round, the common task,
Will furnish all we ought to ask.
Room to deny ourselves a road,
To bring us daily nearer God.
—"New Every Morning," John Keble, 1822

After my one-month trial, I asked to stay longer. As per their decision-making style, the discussion took place in a private meeting to decide if I could stay on at the Olive Tree. After about an hour, the members came out of the room, having decided I could stay six more months to "see how it goes." So now I joined in this family's lifestyle in earnest. It definitely was a complete change of life for me. I continued with the daily routine that I had become accustomed to.

The one thing that I never could seem to feel comfortable with, however, was our time of morning prayers. Nine o'clock prayers could be a nerve-racking experience because one never knew who might be in the hot seat that morning. The hot seat, I soon learned, was if someone needed correction, it was Evelyn who took the lead in the discussion—or, as we called it, "the working out" of whatever problem the person was having. These "discussions" somewhat leaned more toward Evelyn asking questions of the person, and if that person did not answer correctly according to Evelyn, then the subject was either dropped or that person had an assignment from Evelyn, to be handed back to her on her personal clipboard.

I was always busy doing something in the kitchen. When prayers were over, we girls worked together to plan the day's chores. One would sign up for lunch, two people were assigned to make the casserole for dinner, and the other jobs—salad, vegetable, bread, and dessert—were given to the rest of the girls. One of our favorite meals was Corn Patch Casserole*, an easy dish to make for a large group. I didn't realize how much work was involved to support so many people from the food we grew on our land! The goats needed to be milked twice a day. Our fowl needed to be fed and their cages cleaned. Eggs were gathered. We would pick and clean vegetables from the garden, grown seasonally, dividing them for dinner or food storage. We cooked our plums, boysenberries, and strawberries into jam (see Grandma Merle's Strawberry Jam*). I helped grind wheat flour, cornmeal, and whole oats in an electric stone mill for our flour, cornmeal, or oat cereal. Uncle Basil would bring in wheelbarrows loaded with seasonal vegetables such as cabbage. We would make sauerkraut, coleslaw, and cabbage casseroles. With zucchini, we would make relish, zucchini bread, casseroles, and Zucchini Pizza*, utilizing zucchini, eggs, and cheese as the crust.

With my bakery background, I always volunteered to make desserts! Planning and making dessert became my favorite kitchen job.

I hadn't forgotten my sister's comment that I might find a Christian man here to be my husband, so I would pay attention to the kinds of desserts the men in the community liked.

The ladies housecleaned once a week. We each knew our jobs for the month through a chart that was posted on the refrigerator. We rotated through the different tasks this way. The kitchen floors were mopped. All the carpets were vacuumed. Bathrooms were cleaned. Furniture was dusted. Every six months the hardwood dining room floor needed to be hand waxed and polished. This hours-long manual project usually meant all the ladies on our hands and knees, singing and laughing as we scrubbed and polished. While we worked all morning, Uncle Basil would usually head into town and bring home a big bag of hamburgers for lunch as a treat for the family.

When planning meals for so many people, Evelyn would call in an order for a quarter of a cow from a butcher, who divided the beef in various cuts or grinds to serve our needs. We would fill up the van with the nicely wrapped meat, bring it home, and put in our large horizontal freezer; it would last us about six months.

The family members met on Sunday nights during what they called the LIAHO family meeting, which stood for "Let It All Hang Out." This was where anyone could say anything about household problems or complaints, ask to buy a new pair of shoes, consider taking a class at the local community college, and so on. Once a week everyone received a weekly allowance of five dollars to buy the occasional treat or buy a birthday gift for someone. That amount did not change in the whole thirty-two years I lived in the Community. Finances were shared from those who had outside jobs, meaning whether a member made $5,000 a year or $25,000 a year, all the monies earned by members went into the Community coffers. Every purchase had to be registered in a ledger found in the locked cash box, with the combination lock known only to the permanent members.

Monday night after dinner was Bible study. Evelyn was the teacher. Each week she would bring out her recipe card box filled not with recipes but with questions she had handed out to each of us the week before. We would search different translations of the Bible or look in study guides, found in ample supply on our library shelf, to find the answers to her questions. We usually studied Scripture along thematic lines, such as "living by faith," "the role of women," "true manhood," or "Jesus and forgiveness." One evening the Bible study focused on the "Raising of Lazarus." Evelyn took me in the bathroom and wrapped me up from head to ankles in white sheets. The only way to move was to scoot my feet. "All you have to do is scoot out into the living room and stand there after I go sit down. I want to see how long it takes for someone to get the idea of what to do," instructed Evelyn.

She went back to the living room and sat in her rocker. I listened to hear Evelyn begin talking, and then I slowly scooted out to the living room. Being wrapped up, I could not see where I was going or what expressions were on the faces of those around me. It felt like no one would do anything until I heard the heavy steps of Robert's shoes coming over to me to unwrap my "grave clothes." Evelyn's point? Jesus did not remove the clothes; he called someone else to do it. Every person's life task is to hear Jesus when he gives an order and then carry it out. Many of our Bible studies were very creative like this one.

In addition to our common meals, cleanup schedules, work on the property, and Sunday worship, once a month on Wednesdays, we held a prayer-and-praise evening, beginning with a potluck dinner we shared with friends who came to fellowship with us. After dinner cleanup we gathered in the living room for singing, dancing, and praying. At some point the whole group started singing in some unique-sounding language. I would sit back with eyes tightly closed, wondering how I might be able to learn this wonderful way of speaking, yet too afraid to ask.

During my six-month trial, my roommate, Renée, came back from trade school. I found in her a wonderful friend with whom to spend many fun hours walking in the hills behind where we lived. There was one very memorable walk one day when we decided to walk near the creek just to see what was down there. As we descended through the thick brambles, we discovered a completely different world. We found ourselves in cool darkness. Above our heads were intertwining branches, which had woven into each other as if they were arms and their hands were tightly clasped together, never to let go. The sun shone through the underbrush like twinkling lights, rather than the hot rays that burned our arms just moments earlier before we crept down into shade. We followed along a well-worn path next to the almost-dry but still-flowing creek. I have no idea how much time passed or how far we walked, but we arrived back in time to help prepare dinner.

Within a week from the time we had our little adventure, my arms started to itch terribly. Then a rash with blisters formed, and the itching got so bad I had to show it to Evelyn, who said I needed to go to the doctor.

Uncle Basil took me to the family doctor, and when he examined my arm, he said with a straight face, "Well, you either have syphilis or an allergic reaction to poison oak." He thought he was making a joke, but I did not think it was funny, knowing what kind of lifestyle I was carrying on just a few months earlier back in Michigan. Fortunately it was an allergic reaction to the poison oak I walked through down by the creek. I spent the next week or so with a nice pink coating of the anti-itch lotion.

Another walk we took was on Easter Sunday, when all the festivities and church services were over. We packed our drinks and snack, and headed off to the hills. About three miles behind the Community house were several hills that had some paved roads, but many were either rocky paths or dirt paths worn deep from walkers, bike riders, horseback riders, and the many Mexican workers who passed through there on a daily basis. Some lived in the orchards. Others just took the shortest route to find work. We found a path that wound around one of the mountains, so we decided we would find out where it would lead us. We kept walking and walking until we realized we were all the way on the other side of town when we came to a main road. At first we did not recognize where we were until a car pulled up alongside of us asking if we wanted a ride. It was Gary and Danielle returning from a church service they attended across town. We had no idea how far away we were from home, so we were very grateful for the lift back.

Living in the tiny home with the ladies was fine. We shared well, with only one small bathroom among all of us. Dee even found time to take a book into the bath with her, where she would relax for an hour or two.

As the days moved into weeks and months, I began to sync with this new Christian community lifestyle. I learned that living in this manner meant everything needs planning and organization well ahead of time, or else disaster and confusion result. The best way to avoid this was to have clear expectations and plans. Hence, I began to understand the reason for all our meetings and discussions.

Once in a while, as a break from the normal schedule, those of us who were home would load up our fifteen-person van and go up the mountain for a day hiking, picnicking, and best of all, buying bread from the well-known bakery. It was fun choosing the several loaves to bring home and serve at Sunday breakfast. When it got hot, one of my favorite outings was to the local soft-serve ice cream stand. We would all pile into the van and line up to order our favorite fattening treats. At that time we did not think about fat or calories, so we would order large shakes, such as my favorite: peanut butter chocolate chip shake. This place was a favorite hangout for lots of people, so there were always lines to get your ice cream. The owners always looked forward to serving us when they saw our van pull up. Another inexpensive form of entertainment was the town's only movie theater, which showed movies for one dollar a ticket. Although these movies were not recent films, the price was right for a movie, and treats were inexpensive too.

One downside of living this way, besides all the house rules, was that when we left the property, we had to inform someone else where we were going, how long we would be gone, and when we would return. This kind of accountability was something that I found difficult to adjust to.

Each Friday morning the girls who did not have jobs outside the Community met for Bible study, Ungame, or simply discussions, depending on the circumstances. As I described before, Ungame was no ordinary game. It advertised itself as a way to communicate with others. Evelyn used the cards in the game to solve spiritual and emotional problems among us. I found it difficult to try to figure out what answer Evelyn was looking for.

For example, one particular morning my first question was "What makes a happy marriage?" I answered, "A happy marriage is a couple who commit to each other for life, promising to be faithful to each other."

Evelyn's turn was next, and she landed on a green space. "I knew God would answer my prayers for a green space," she began. "Kata, how do you think a person is supposed to find the perfect husband to achieve a happy marriage?" This became an invitation for me to come up with another answer. She then had the freedom to continue asking me questions in the direction she wanted me to go so I would discover her real motive, which was for me to say that it was wrong to flirt with guys.

I wanted to say, "When I flirt it makes the guy think only one thing: sex." But I was too embarrassed to bring myself to say the answer directly. I had been trying very hard not to flirt with the guys, but when I baked cookies in the kitchen and a guy walked in smelling the odor of baking, it was difficult not to be thrilled with the compliment when he asked for a nibble and thanked me with a big smile. Evelyn's stern voice reminded me that even that kind of "flirting" was unacceptable.

The men had their weekly meetings on Saturday mornings, since many of them worked or went to college during the week. I do not know what went on in these meetings, but the nervousness of the wives when the men met signaled to me that whatever went on in those meetings resulted in anger and tension among the men. A few times I could hear one or two men yelling.

CHAPTER 7

Birthdays and Celebrations

They celebrate your abounding goodness
And joyfully sing of your justice.
—Ps. 145:7

October was the first of many birthdays celebrated within the Community. The established tradition in Community was that the birthday person picked his or her favorite food for the dinner as part of the celebration.

October 22 was Mabelle's birthday. Mabelle was a special education teacher at a school for handicapped children. She lived up the road from the Community, and she was a good friend of Anne, former owner of our house. Mabelle had met Evelyn and Basil while she visited Anne one afternoon. When Gary and Danielle got married in 1975, she offered them her spare bedroom with a private bath so they could have some privacy as newlyweds. In exchange for the use of her spare room, she ate dinner every night with the Community when she got home from working all day. Mabelle always looked elegant, even when she wore her neatly pressed blue jeans and sweatshirt. She had a tall, straight stature and a kind, gentle voice, whether talking to her "special" children, teenagers, or old folks. She used to call everyone either "honey heart" or "lambie-pie"; that way she didn't have to remember names.

Another birthday tradition was the singing of a song dedicated to the birthday person; we found a familiar tune and changed the words to fit the person. Then, between dinner and dessert, everyone participated by singing the song we secretly practiced. After the song, presents from family members and a larger one from the Community were opened. The festivities ended with everyone back at the table to enjoy the dessert and coffee.

Mabelle—deciding that as a senior citizen she had arrived at the ability to enjoy life in creative ways—asked to have a "desserts only" dinner. We all thought that was hilarious, but Evelyn decided that after a long school day, she needed to have something nutritious first, so we came up with Baked Chayote with Cheese*. A chayote is a squash-like vegetable that grows on a vine, similar to grapes. In addition, instead of Mabelle choosing desserts, Evelyn suggested that family members form teams. Each team would pick a dessert to make together, and then Mabelle would judge, picking her favorite from all the desserts served.

Uncle Basil and I paired together to make dessert. It was easy to be paired together since we both liked chocolate.

After looking through a few recipe books, we decided on a Kraft Peanut Butter & Swirl Pie*.

The kitchen was busy all week with various combinations of people secretly making their concoctions to please Mabelle's palate. We all looked forward to presenting our desserts at the table, so the chayote course was eaten quite rapidly. As it turned out, the winning dessert was *ours*! The sweet taste of victory really is "delicious." I soon learned that celebratory meals happened quite often, whether it was a birthday, a special guest for dinner, or any good reason to celebrate.

Halloween was coming up, so Evelyn came up with the idea to have a party, with each person dressing up in homemade costumes and playing games. We filled a big tub with water and floated apples on top for "dunking for apples," and then we tied doughnuts with string and hung them from the branches of the plum tree. With our hands tied behind our backs, we had to bite a doughnut.

We ended our celebration with hot apple cider or chocolate, sitting around the dining room table talking, sharing how each person celebrated Halloween in his or her childhood.

Because the dark pathway to our house was quite a distance from the street, no children came to our door, especially since we did not have a traditional front door to the house. We always bought candy for the bowl "just in case" someone should show up, but no one ever did, so we ended up enjoying the candy.

Poppa's birthday came in November, and once again the birthday traditions were repeated. Another fun perk: the birthday person was excused from cleanup.

My first late autumn/winter in Southern California was a shock since I was used to cold weather and leaves turning bright yellow, orange, and red colors, all in anticipation of winter snow. The weather here, however, was hot and dry, with strong winds, known as Santa Ana winds. Everything appeared as a dull single color of brown. I kept waiting for the weather to cool down, but it never did.

November preparations for Thanksgiving began more than a week early. We had the task of looking for recipes to try out for the meal so that the meal could be special. Evelyn, who managed the kitchen, would listen to all the ideas, and then after planning a menu that seemed to go together, she would take one or two of us shopping. Going shopping with Evelyn was always an adventure, because even though there might have been a menu plan at the beginning, she would find a sale on some food or other or see something else that might be appetizing, and she would substitute the item she found for something already planned. She never checked to see if she had enough money; she always knew when she finished her purchases the money always worked out.

Clearly, Evelyn was the driving force of decisions made within this large family. I had no idea the terrible consequences this would bring in my future.

CHAPTER 8

My First Thanksgiving and Christmas

Give thanks to the Lord for he is good,
His mercy endures forever!
—Ps. 107:1

I grew up having the same Thanksgiving meal every year, so it was new territory for me to try out different recipes. Meal planning can get contentious when each person is used to his or her own family traditions. Living in the Community supplies each person room for growth to adapt to others. Who would have thought that there were other ways to make a green bean casserole besides with mushroom soup with french-fried onion rings on top? How many people put honey-coated walnuts on top of pumpkin pie?

Never had I worked so hard on a holiday meal before—special table settings, candles, and so many bowls with serving spoons, each dish divided into three serving dishes to go on the table. We had at least two turkeys to carve in the kitchen by two men, so they took up the kitchen table space. Even among the men, when it came to carving the turkey, each man had his own way. How to carve the turkeys was different for each man. One had to have all the cutting boards set out with the carving knives. Others preferred the electric knives, and then carving forks, platters to put the specific slices for serving, foil, and separate containers for the bones. Some of the men would get upset if one of the women would come by to nibble on the meat before dinner.

Poppa would say, "Nibble, nibble, like a mouse. Soon you'll be as big as a house!" But we couldn't help it! The smells coming from the kitchen were irresistible!

When all the food was on the table, candles lighted, and wine poured, we gave thanks to God for all he had provided for us, and then we would eat. Everyone talked at the same time as we passed the food to the right as always, but once the clanking of all the serving dishes discontinued and everyone had plates full of both familiar and unfamiliar foods, we would restore our "one person talking at a time" rule. The second time around meant more clanging and chatting, but this time there was a bit more groaning from being overstuffed.

We would then take a break to clean up, put food somewhat away, and then serve coffee and dessert. With the hustle and bustle of cleanup, everyone was able to make room for dessert, with often two different kinds of dessert for those who liked variety or those that did not like pumpkin pie.

One dessert that was served as an alternative was Persimmon Pudding with Secret Butter Sauce*.

The biggest task came at cleanup both before and after dinner. The amount of dirty dishes was unbelievable, and fortunately, everyone helped on cleanup until it was finished. After cleanup, everyone retreated to his or her own bedroom to sleep off the feast, or some of us would stay and play a game at the kitchen table from the wide assortment of games available in a long side cupboard in the dining room.

Friday after Thanksgiving was a free morning to sleep in, take a long walk, or drive somewhere. The Community mandate for individual families was that when there was a holiday, everyone in the Community was required to be at home for that holiday. In the situation such as Danielle's, whose family lived close by, she, Gary, and their children went to her mom's house to celebrate the day after the holiday.

On the "free" day, Renée and I opted for a long walk with our lunch in a backpack. We decided to walk up to the radio tower, situated at the highest elevation in town and only about an hour's walk from our house. The road leading up to the tower was a windy switchback road. Our legs felt the strain when we got to the top, but the effort was worth it. The panoramic view of the valley and the snowcapped mountain ranges in the far distance were majestic. Below us we could see a dairy, with black-and-white spotted cattle grazing in the fields; we saw the ocean to the west and all the beach cities—such a spectacular scene, only about two miles from where we lived.

When we got back, everyone wondered where we had gone and why we were gone so long. We explained we had walked up the road to the radio tower, which was the highest peak in our neighborhood, so we could see the ocean to the west and snowcapped mountains to the east! We ate lunch with the snowcapped mountains in view.

With Thanksgiving behind us, the focus of the Community was not only on Christmas but also the January wedding of Valerie and Tony. They had grown up together in the same neighborhood and graduated from the same high school, so they knew each other quite well. Valerie was Hans and Evelyn's biological daughter, the only real blood relative in the Community at this time. During the day she worked as a babysitter and then came home to work on wedding plans.

With December came the celebration of Advent, which begins four weeks before Christmas. The hymns, Scripture readings, devotionals, and a wreath adorned with three purple and one rose-colored candle all proclaim Christ's coming into the world and his returning again as King and Judge. A purple candle is lit for the first, second, and fourth weeks. The rose candle on the third week symbolizes not only the expectation of Jesus coming into the world the first time but also his second coming at Judgment Day. The wreath, shaped in a circle of evergreen, represents everlasting life. I learned so much about the Episcopal Church this first year at the Community; I began to love all the traditions and practices of this religion, which has endured for centuries.

About the third week of Advent, decorating the house and setting up the tree with lights added to our Christmas spirit.

Poppa put the lights on the tree; he always had all the lights neatly wrapped around boards specially made to keep the lights in order to make unwrapping simple. I had never seen anyone so well organized. There was some freedom to decorating the house, with the exception of certain decorations. These were for Evelyn or her daughter to put out because they were family heirlooms or had emotional memories.

Decorating the house took all morning. Playing Christmas music while working together made the work more festive, but for me, there was so much stuff! I felt that way since for me growing up, the Christmas tree plus our stockings were the most decorations we had. Later in the day after a light dinner, the whole group gathered in the living room. Evelyn would sit in her rocker taking charge of passing out the decorations as each one of us lined up to receive an ornament to hang on the tree.

Like Thanksgiving, the Christmas menu, as well as the extra events such as open house, Christmas caroling, and Christmas Eve service took advance preparation. Cookie baking began with everyone trying new recipes or bringing out old family favorites. The freezer would end up full of plastic containers with delicious assortments of treats. We needed a lot of treats!

We celebrated with

- a party after Christmas caroling;
- a party for decorating the Christmas tree;

- the open-house party for all our friends and neighbors;
- a party for the anniversary of the beginning of the Community (December 21, St. Thomas the Doubter day);
- the Christmas Eve opening-presents party after midnight Mass;
- Christmas brunch;
- Christmas dinner; and
- The New Year's Eve party.

We also had to have plenty of cookies to make up gift plates for people like the United Parcel Service driver, the postman, and even the garbage men. We were prepared at any time for guests, because at this time of year, we would get surprise visitors. We knew we would have cookies to serve with coffee and tea. There would need to be a separate book to include all of the cookies, brownies, and snack recipes that we prepared over the last thirty-two years, so included at the end of this book are only a few of our favorite well-stained recipes from family, friends, and books. I hope you enjoy the few I have added.

Christmas Eve began with a mushroom soup made by Valerie, her own special recipe that changed each year depending on what ingredients she decided to use, served with homemade french bread. Everyone got dressed up for dinner to be ready for our church service after dinner. We put candles around the living room, sang Christmas songs, read the Christmas scriptures, and finished our glorious worship with Communion. We quickly set up the table with food we had prepared for snacks, since we passed out the gifts later. Then we changed out of our best clothes to pajamas and bathrobes to be comfortable while we opened presents until late into the evening. Everyone helped clean up the debris so that those of us who had preparations for the Christmas Day brunch could go to the kitchen to make sure the food was ready to cook the next morning.

My dear mom had sent several gifts for me to open on Christmas since this was my first Christmas away from family. I missed her and the Michigan snow, but I believed this was where God had brought me to get away from the unwholesome influence of some of my friends. I was learning to grow into a woman of God.

I made sure I was up early to help in the kitchen so that the brunch was ready on time. With so many people in the kitchen going different directions, we were usually running late because with more than one item in the oven being baked at the same time, the oven door kept being opened and closed, which lengthened the cooking time. Finally, all the prepared dishes were on the table. We gathered to pray, and a peace came over the dining room as we thanked the Lord for his gift of Jesus in our lives, the greatest gift of all. After brunch, no one who helped before had to help afterward, but those of us who had food to make for dinner needed to figure out how to get our tasks done to be on time for dinner. For this size family of approximately eighteen to twenty-eight people, we prepared at least three bowls for each dish to assure everyone had the opportunity to receive a serving.

One requirement for all in the Community was that all of the members had to be present for the Community Christmas holiday meal. If you had biological family living in close proximity to the Community, they could spend the day with us. If the family lived farther away, you waited until the day after Thanksgiving or Christmas to celebrate the holiday with the members of your family. Several members who had family living close by would go visit them at this time. Evelyn explained that this would bond us together as an intentional family, by celebrating the actual holiday at the Community first.

Only much later did I learn that this concept never sat well with any of the small family groupings.

The week between Christmas and New Year's was peaceful and casual, with some preparations for the meals for New Year's, but not as complicated as Christmas. A tradition the Community had for New Year's Eve was the choosing of a Bible verse that became "your verse for the year." The next year you'd write a short essay about how God used that verse in your life throughout the year. This was repeated annually. I did not have a verse to share, so Evelyn told me to write about a favorite verse, and then I would get my new verse for the New Year. The day before New Year's Eve, a group gathered at the kitchen table to choose appropriate verses for the next year, and then they carefully cracked open walnuts, took out the nutmeats so that the folded-up verses could fit in the nutshells, and glued them back together.

On New Year's Eve, we ate snacks of leftover cookies and chips and dip, and drank sparkling cider and champagne to toast the New Year. After New Year's we women took down and neatly put away all the Christmas decorations. I enjoyed watching Poppa take down the Christmas tree lights in his very particular way.

For the whole thirty-two years of my time in the Community, this was how we celebrated the Advent/Christmas season.

CHAPTER 9

From Extended Family to Monks and Nuns

How good and how pleasant it is,
When brothers dwell together as one!
—Ps. 133:1

Early in the new year, Anne, the owner of the main home, announced when she came back after her vacation that she would be moving out to live with a friend close by. My first thought was alarm. It was because of her that we were living in this large house. How could twenty-some people live in the little house? I realized I hadn't remembered that God was in charge of our lives! The answer soon came that she was willing to sell her house to the Community. The six members prayed and felt God would somehow provide the means to pay a second mortgage on her house and property. They were already paying a mortgage on the half-acre where the little house stood. That meant the Community would own two half-acre properties with two houses, which we had affectionately nicknamed the little house and the big house.

Besides this first dramatic change, there was Tony and Valerie's wedding at the end of January and the announcement that Danielle and Gary were expecting their first child in June. He or she would be our first official "Community child." But these huge changes didn't come close to what came next—a change that would completely alter the course of our lives forever.

When Uncle Basil had his annual meeting as a priest with the bishop of the Episcopal Diocese, the bishop asked that the Community consider being structured as a religious order, rather than simply function as a legal, nonprofit ministry. In some ways the Olive Tree was already functioning in this manner. We had a legal status, an established way of life, and common finances. But unlike traditional single houses of monks and nuns, where members take vows of poverty, chastity, and obedience, we consisted of married *and* single members. In regular religious orders, a vow of chastity means celibacy. However, we interpreted a vow of chastity as purity—fidelity for the married couples and celibacy for single men and women.

Hours and hours of meetings late into the evening continued among the Community members. There were so many ideas to consider, always trying to catch the vision of what God had in store for us. I longed to become a member and sit in on those discussions, but since I had not lived even a year with the Community, that simply wasn't possible. Fortunately, I had something to look forward to.

I had received a wonderful Christmas gift when Dee gave me the gift of a plane ticket. She had orders to work in Memphis for her last year in the navy and asked me if I would drive with her and then fly back home. We would stay with Gary's sister, who had a home there. What a thrilling adventure! I had never been on a plane before, and having just driven across country a few months earlier, seeing a new part of the country would be exciting. Once the members' discussions about becoming a religious order were solidifying, Dee decided she would return after she left military service to take her temporary vows to the religious order.

Shortly before we left, Dee introduced the Community to a young single mother, Peggy, whom she knew through her job in the navy. Peggy's daughters were ages three years old and six months old. This mom had no close family in the area and was looking for a place away from an abusive ex-husband. It was decided that Peggy could move in for a while until she got a "heading" from the Lord as to what she should do with her life. With Dee moving out and Valerie getting married at the end of the month, the Community agreed that the young mom and her daughters could move into the little house. Therefore, Renée and I moved out of the little house and over into the small bedroom in the main home.

The decision-making process that in the beginning had seemed so mysterious was now clear to me. The Community members made decisions by what they called "being in consensus." Believing that the Holy Spirit had one will and following the example of the first Christians, on major decisions everyone had to agree completely. If one person felt any doubt or serious concerns, the decision was delayed. These meetings always happened behind closed doors in Poppa and Evelyn's room. Sometimes the members would be in the room for hours. When that door closed, not one person could interrupt unless there was an emergency. The rest of us stayed in the living room playing games or watching television.

Dee and I left in her car the second week of January for our adventure across half the country. We had a wonderful time driving through the desert, unlike the trip with my sister Susa, when the temperature was 110 degrees. In January the thermometer was in the sixties. We made one side stop at an old mission in New Mexico. It was located in the middle of almost nowhere, was very well kept, and was still in use by the people of the area.

As we entered Texas, I remembered how boring driving across the state had been with Susa, but this time the difference was Dee. She had so many interesting experiences in her life. As a naval officer she shared her travel adventures, including time in Europe. She grew up in Chicago with a mom who was a teacher. She spoke lovingly about her kind father. We passed away the hours getting to know each other.

When we were hungry, she suggested that we stop at a truck stop in Texas, because if one sees lots of trucks parked at a restaurant, it is a sure sign they have delicious food. "No trucker will eat poor-quality food," this city-bred girl informed me. When we arrived at our table, I noticed a bowl of what looked like a vegetable soup. A spoon was next to the bowl, so I decided to taste this "soup." What a surprise—or rather shock—when I put the spoon in my mouth and it burned terribly. Dee just laughed, saying, "Welcome to Mexican salsa. It is meant to be a topping for a taco and contains hot chili peppers."

"How can I cool down my burning mouth?" I gasped.

The server soon brought us some tortilla chips to eat with the salsa. That helped.

Gary's sister Natalie greeted us at the door when we arrived, tired and ready to stay in one spot. Her house was empty of furniture since she and her husband were getting ready to move to Oregon. We immediately dove in to help pack dishes into moving boxes. Several years back Dee and Natalie roomed together while both of them were attending naval school, so they had catching up to do, talking until late in the evening. We slept on the floor that night, a little uncomfortable, but at least we had a place to stay.

The next morning Dee dropped me off at the airport with a good-bye hug and said she would be back in a year. The feeling of the plane lifting off the ground was exhilarating. I realized that my life with the Community so far had provided me with so many new experiences.

I wondered as I looked around the plane at the other people buckled in their seats as the plane lifted off the runway, *Are they feeling what I am feeling? Is it so normal that they forget that they are putting their lives in the hands of the pilots and all the technicians involved in making sure this plane arrives at its destination safely?*

The landing was smooth but a little unnerving since we were flying between buildings so close I thought I could see people in the windows of the tall office buildings. It is funny when you fly for the first time. The people seated around you can tell by the look on your face that it is your first time. I met some very compassionate traveling companions on that flight and marveled at what a wonderful world we live in.

CHAPTER 10

Pause for a History Lesson

But if we walk in the light as he is in the light,
then we have fellowship with one another, and the
blood of his Son Jesus cleanses us from all sin.
—1 John 1:7

We are frequently asked by visitors, "How did this Community begin?"

The story began during the era of what was known in the 1970s and '80s as the Charismatic Movement. In many mainline churches, as well as small independent Christian churches, people began experiencing what was referred to as the baptism of the Holy Spirit. This usually was accompanied by signs and miracles in the group and the speaking of tongues (a heavenly prayer language). This was the story of Pentecost, found in the first chapter of the book of Acts in the Bible.

Katherine Zyczynska

Hans and his wife, Evelyn, lived in San Poncho with their teenage daughter, Valerie. They had two older children, who were married with their own families but lived in the same city.

Hans and Evelyn attended the local Episcopal church, where they became good friends with the pastor there, Father Basil.

Evelyn had an acquaintance with Anne W., who led Bible studies and held charismatic prayer meetings in her home. Evelyn was very skeptical of this new charismatic movement, but she and Father Basil went to Anne's house one evening to talk to her about the Holy Spirit. Anne kindly explained about the baptism of the Holy Spirit, referencing each fact with scriptures to support her explanations. God works in his own ways and timing, and they both left with hearts full of joy, filled with the Holy Spirit.

In time, Hans, Evelyn's husband, learned about the Holy Spirit and became baptized also.

Father Basil and Evelyn saw a great need to give the young people at church a place to have fellowship outside of church, especially the young men who found themselves getting involved in the drug culture of the early 1970s.

Young men received love and a firm hand, surrounded by a vibrant Christian lifestyle of prayer meetings, Bible studies, and youth activities. Soon word of mouth brought more needy teens than they could accommodate. They prayed for a solution. Then an anonymous gift of $4,000 arrived with a note that said, "To add on a room for the boys." For two years this ministry flourished. Many of these young adults, now off drugs and fervent Christians, added vitality and renewal to their church and neighborhood.

Word of their success spread one day to a priest from another parish, located in Los Angeles. The Episcopal priest, Father James, asked Basil if he would consider bringing his community to Los Angeles to minister to the young people as a beach ministry near his church.

Following the logic of the world, such a move would be ridiculous. This priest offered no financial assistance. There were no job guarantees and no housing. God did not expect them to drop everything and move, did he? As they prayed for guidance, Basil and Evelyn took a trip up north, "just to look" at the situation. As they drove back to San Poncho, they felt the same elated urgings, much like when the Holy Spirit told them to open their house up for young men on drugs.

When they arrived home, Hans was sitting at the kitchen table staring at a layoff notice he had been handed that very afternoon. Rather than be disappointed, they cheered: "This is God answering our prayers for direction!" Evelyn proceeded to explain what she and Basil had felt during the day.

The next day, with a $1,000 loan from a friend, confident they were responding to the call of God, the three of them traveled back up north to Los Angeles. They discovered a perfect location. There was a house on oceanfront property at the extremely high cost of $90,000! (Roughly three times the property values of a typical middle-class home at the time.) Undeterred, they contacted the Realtor, and after telling him their story, against all odds, their offer was accepted! They put up their San Poncho property for sale, bidding farewell to all that was familiar.

The local newspaper printed an article with an interview with Father Basil. Father Basil shared, "Somehow the Lord paid the rent each month, put food on the table, and sent us people in need. How did I feel? As though I were in limbo. As a priest I saw myself with nothing to do. We had no church. Not even a yard where I could busy myself. Plus the twenty-four hour tumult outside was not pleasant." By tumult, he meant dopers, drunkards, prostitutes, drug dealers, and all the normal happenings in a tourist/university beach town. The family policy was open door. Anyone, at any time, could come in for a place to experience Christian loving care, sleep off whatever they were on, get a bite to eat, and leave with a Bible.

"Leave your switchblades at the door" was a verse from a catchy, humorous song Danielle wrote that was actually based in fact. Danielle, a college student from a nearby university, a new Christian, and working on her degree in mental health, found the Community during this time. For twenty nonstop months, hundreds of people passed through their doors, including undercover police officers making sure they weren't a front for anything illegal, college students on hand for the worship services, surfers who wanted to meet some of the cute young women, neighbors invited for a meal, and a growing number of people God was pulling together for his future plans. Three of the students wanted more from life than the typical path most people take. Six of the college students asked the elders, Father Basil, Hans, and Evelyn, if they could stay and be part of the ministry. After much prayer they made promises to each other to be part of the Olive Tree Ministry.

Once again God had a change of plans in store. One fall day they received a letter from a woman who knew somebody who knew somebody else who knew of the ministry. She wrote, "I have been praying for you to move to Viejo, California. Would you please consider coming down here?" This request came out of the blue, and once again, the growing group of Christians choosing to live and work together as the Olive Tree took it to prayer. At the same time, Danielle was feeling that God wanted a stronger tie with this ministry, so she asked Evelyn, Poppa, and Uncle Basil if they would think about establishing some sort of more-permanent commitment among those called to serve others in need there. They too were feeling the need to formalize some kind of structure, and with an attorney's help, they formed a nonprofit corporation.

Evelyn suggested that all who were living at the Olive Tree write a short letter sharing what they wanted from the ministry. The letters were quite revealing. Several of the college-age Christians stated a desire to live and work together, to pool their resources to live in common, and to commit long-term to the ministry. Therefore, in addition to the original founders—Hans, Evelyn, and Father Basil—this group included Robert, a young man who studied medicine in college and worked with wood; Gary and Danielle, who were engaged at the time; and one other married couple,

Derrick and Kerri. Several foster children, including Renée and her brother Larry, and the biological teenager of Hans and Evelyn, Valerie, were part of the family who would live wherever the ministry located.

Shortly after this, history repeated itself. Property in a semirural corner of north San Poncho County became available. With resources from this fledgling group, coupled with many God-incidents, the ministry left behind their frenetic beach lifestyle and moved to a bucolic property nestled against hills far from the center of town. One photograph from the move is of Danielle in pigtails, red-checkered shirt under overalls, taking furniture out of the rented van into the kitchen. It is a small but revealing picture of what the poor neighbors saw out their windows with this unusual collection of people moving into their quiet neighborhood.

Almost immediately, as a friendly gesture, the women of the kitchen made homemade cookies and took them to all the neighbors to introduce themselves. Shocked would be the best description of how this retired age group of neighbors responded to very energetic young hippie-looking people dressed in either overalls or long dresses, greeting them with big smiles and cookies. *What did they put in those cookies to make them so friendly?* must have been the thought going through their minds at the time.

This strange collection of adults were about to embark on a brand-new adventure. They had a steep learning curve as they learned how to raise goats for milk, chickens for eggs, a huge garden for vegetables, and even rabbits for meat. By the time I arrived in September 1976, this motley group had become a functioning Christian community, living successfully largely off their land. This was when the bishop recommended they consider becoming a religious order.

CHAPTER 11

Becoming a Religious Order

We must consider how to rouse one another to love and
good works. We should not stay away from our assembly,
as is the custom of some, but encourage one another,
and this all the more as you see the day drawing near.
—Heb. 10:24–25

To become a religious order, in addition to nonprofit status,
you also need a "rule of life" and a constitution. This meets
both the church requirements and the IRS regulations as
a 501c. I recall many days where Father Basil and Evelyn
would banter back and forth on how to write articles of the
constitution and what vows to the rule of life each member
would profess. As I write this, I looked over the vows written
for the original six members on March 27, 1977. I realized,
as I reread a newsletter explaining the meaning of the vows,
that they sounded to me a lot like a prenuptial agreement.

As a result of [the vows], six of us will become permanent members of ROCF (the Religious Order of Christian Families). This term needs to be distinguished from lifetime members. In the past, many traditional religious orders made irrevocable lifetime vows. We are not making our vows for life or on a renewable basis. Instead, we have chosen to make our permanent commitments to each other for as long as God chooses. If anyone leaves, it is with the bishop's and the Community's approval.

The rule of the Community was written as: "To live out the Gospel as an Intentional Family with Jesus first, others second, yourself last. (J-O-Y) and to 'Walk in the light as he is in the light.'"

Much discussion took place over the making of habits for our order. Since our new order would consist of naval officers, working men, and mothers with children, it was agreed to wear habits only when the members functioned as a religious order. The women would wear blue dresses below the knee with three-quarter cuffed sleeves, and a blue cap. The men would wear a dress shirt with a tunic shirt over it, cut in the same style as the women's dresses, at hip length. The temporary habit would be the same style as the blue habits only in brown, and all would wear a cincture around the waist, as well as a custom-designed silver dove necklace and ring. The women in the family had the fun of shopping for the material and then measuring and sewing the habits for each person.

After arranging all the details, making plans with the local Episcopal church to be the place for the service and reception, the day arrived. The church filled up with family, friends, and those who intended to take an associate vow to the Community. These associate vows, put simply, are vows to be "formal friends," supporting the Community in prayer and living the rule of the order in their own families as closely as possible.

The Institution of ROCF
Bless the Lord, my soul;
All my being, bless his holy name.
—Ps. 103:1

The processional hymn began as the six members marched down the aisle, followed by Dee, who would take a vow of intention to become a permanent member; L. T., who would take a temporary vow; then Pastor Raymond and Father Ward; and lastly, the bishop. The bishop asked Father Ward to intone the solemn hymn, saying in a letter to Pastor Basil, "You really do not want to hear my voice."

"Veni Creator Spiritus"
Words: Attributed to Rhabanus Maurus *circa* 800

Father Ward's clear tones filled the sanctuary so powerfully with the Holy Spirit, I got holy goose bumps.

"Magnificat"
Text taken directly from St. Luke's Gospel 1:44–55

Danielle (being six months pregnant) had to get up and leave in the middle of the ceremony to go to the restroom. Normally one could sneak out unnoticed, but in Danielle's case, since the members were seated in the front choir loft, she had to stand up, move in front of the others, and walk out. Probably this was the first case in history that a woman about to say vows of poverty, chastity, and obedience had to excuse herself due to pregnancy bladder-overload.

"A Mighty Fortress Is Our God"
Text by Dr. Martin Luther, 1483–1546

Two of the men in this new order were raised as Lutherans. Since they were giving up their Lutheran church to join the Episcopal church as members of the Episcopal Religious Order, we thought it would be a nice addition to sing this hymn by Martin Luther.

After the service everyone moved to the reception hall for an abundance of sandwiches, cookies, vegetable trays, chips, and dips. There were two large, beautifully decorated cakes, provided by Peggy, who insisted on asking a friend of hers to decorate them. She was determined that Evelyn had to be the one to cut the first slice.

Everyone asked, "What kind of cake is it?"

"It is a very special sponge cake recipe," she responded.

It took quite a while for Evelyn to get to the hall. She is a very sociable person, eager to chat with everyone. When she finally arrived, she then insisted on waiting for the bishop and his wife to be at the table also.

"Why not let all the members gather to cut the cake, since this is our celebration?" asked Evelyn.

"No." Peggy was certain that trying to get six people around the cake would be too crowded.

Evelyn paused just a moment before making the actual cut. She had a funny feeling inside. As she began to make the cut, the knife would not go through the cake. She pushed harder, but still there was no cut. At that point Peggy burst into laughter, and so did everyone else.

"I told you this cake was a special sponge cake, but what I didn't say was that it was a *real sponge* cake!" she told Evelyn.

Fortunately, the second cake was real, and there was plenty of cake for everyone.

Through the years ahead, March 27 became a very special Community celebration. We always planned a special meal and a time of reflection and sharing for all God had done in our lives. We were in our heyday. If only we could have held on to that kind of togetherness and trust.

CHAPTER 12

Ministry, Healing, and the Holy Spirit

God blessed them and God said to
them: Be fertile and multiply.
—Gen. 1:28

That June we looked forward to our first Community child. Danielle enjoyed babies even more now that she was expecting her own. Danielle and Gary rearranged their tiny bedroom in Mabelle's home to accommodate their queen-size bed, bassinet, and changing table. Their baby would be not only the first Community kid but also the first grandchild for Danielle's mom and Gary's parents.

With delivery day approaching, Danielle kept up her normal work in the Community kitchen and housework. One effect being pregnant had on Danielle was the constant need to clean. She is a naturally neat person, but while pregnant, her nesting instinct went into overdrive. One day she chose the kitchen task of cleaning the two refrigerators in the main house. This meant taking out all the food, all the shelves and drawers, bending down to clean from top to bottom, and then putting back everything. In the middle of the cleaning process, Danielle's mom called to ask how she was feeling. Danielle took the telephone back to where she was working so she could clean and pulled over a chair to put the telephone on and talk at the same time. I offered to take over for her, but she wanted to continue.

Her mom inquired, "So are you having any pain?"

"Yes, Mom, I am having some pain, but it comes and goes," responded Danielle.

"What are you doing now?" her mom asked.

"Oh, I am only cleaning the refrigerator. I feel fine."

Her mom's voice grew concerned. "How often are you feeling that pain?"

Danielle calmly replied that the pain came about every two minutes. She had not told us about her pains because the pain was not very painful.

I could hear her mom's voice on the other end of the telephone almost screaming, "You get to the hospital; you are in labor! I'll drive down as soon as I can get away!"

I finished cleaning the refrigerator so Danielle could leave. Within an hour, with our love and prayers, Gary and Danielle were on their way to the hospital. Later that evening we got the call that Gary and Danielle were the proud parents of a boy, Michael. Elation is the best way to describe the birth of our first Community kid.

It so happened that my sister Susa, living on the naval base, was pregnant at the same time. The following week, after the newborn Michael came home from the hospital, I packed my bags for a one-month stay with my sister to take care of her two children when Susa gave birth to her third child, due in July. I enjoyed the stay with Susa, her husband, Anton, Fiona and Stanislaus, in their trailer home on the navy air base.

Susa had a bicycle, so I often went out bicycling around the base to watch the planes and all the good-looking men in uniform. The jets would look as if they would land on the runway, but instead they would descend, touch, and fly back up to the sky. There was a swing set in walking distance from the trailer, so I would sit out there at night, watching the planes. One of the times on a bicycle tour, I stopped in to the base chapel. I heard a voice speaking, so I was very quiet as I walked in. A priest was standing in the pulpit practicing his homily. I quietly stepped back out so as not to disturb his time. On July 4 Susa suggested that we go to the bay to watch the fireworks; she explained how beautiful the fireworks were when they burst over the water. She was right. It was twice the light and color to see the reflection of the fireworks in the water.

My sister has always been the kind of person who finds the best in any situation. She has lived in so many places that no one is a stranger; they are just friends whom you have not met yet. Even nine months pregnant, she spent the whole day rambling around the zoo or the park with me. No wonder she and Danielle became friends while the two families lived in Tennessee. The two women are similar in personality. I thank God he brought the two of them together.

Susa woke up the night of July 9 with labor pains. Having given birth to two children, she pretty much knew what to expect. She had decided on a name for her baby son. He would be André, although she would wait until he was born to be sure. Labor went on until the next day, and on July 10, 1977, Sasha Anton Chwastek was born. She later shared that when she saw him, she knew he was not an André. He looked Polish-Russian like his Polish grandpa, so she determined "he looks like a Sasha," which when translated means Alexander.

Being on base for the month was a nice break from all the daily chores and conflicts of living in Community, but when it came time to go back, I prepared myself for getting back to the routine.

CHAPTER 13

My "Growing" Activities in the Community

But grow in grace and in the knowledge
of our Lord and savior Jesus Christ.
—2 Pet. 3:18

God was in the process of preparing me for the next step in my spiritual journey. I was growing up from a flighty teen to a responsible adult.

Dale had lived in the Community for the summer while she attended a horse-training school at a local ranch. One day she asked if I would like to go and get a tour where she worked. I love horses, so I looked forward to seeing what kind of work she did at the ranch. She took me to the indoor arena, where they worked the horses for competitions. The ranch had an area where they rehabilitated horses with injuries. They also gave riding lessons and had camps for children. The very last area that she took me to was the breeding barn. It just so happened there was a breeding in process in front of us. This was my first time witnessing such large animals mating right in front of me. It was not an experience for the faint of heart.

Dale also was a licensed beautician, and she cut hair for everyone in the Community. Before she moved to Texas to pursue a career as a horse trainer, she worried about how everyone would get their haircuts. Evelyn suggested she make an inquiry to see if anyone would like to learn how to cut hair. When she made the offer, I jumped at the chance. Once I got started cutting hair, considering all our family members and their varied hairstyle requests, I was kept busy all the time!

When people came for a visit, often at the dinner table Evelyn asked each one of us to share what jobs we did in the Community.

My response would be, "I work in the kitchen and cut hair."

"Oh, could you cut mine?" the guests would ask. This happened often.

Our ministry and its outreach to troubled teens began to become more known in church circles. For instance, a priest from another church in the diocese called about his problem son, who had a drinking and drug problem. Greg was a self-confident young man and did not know why his father wanted him to come to this Community. Evelyn pulled out the infamous Ungame to learn about this young man. The biggest impression she got was that he did not see he had a problem. After the game Evelyn told all of us to keep an eye on him.

I watched him walk outside to the porch swing located under a pepper tree we had out back. I was in the kitchen on that warm July afternoon preparing a Frozen Strawberry Yogurt Pie* for dessert that night. I felt a gentle breeze from the west come in the window, yet I also smelled something else wafting in. I had a sinking feeling. This smell was familiar to my nose. I went to find Evelyn. As soon as she came to the window, she recognized the scent as well.

"I am pretty sure the odor is pot," I told her. "Is that what you smell too?"

She agreed, and the two of us marched right out to the swing.

In her authoritative way, Evelyn surprised Greg with her firm voice. "Young man, what do you think you are doing?"

He tried to cover up his reefer, but we caught him fast enough so he had no excuse.

Evelyn called his father to pick him up, explaining that his son did not want to face up to having any problems although we caught him smoking marijuana on the property.

The father was clearly disappointed that he had to pick up his son without being fixed.

Sometimes we had close friends ask us for help with their teens, but for completely different reasons. Father Tom, a neighbor and priest at another local church, asked if his teenage daughter could stay a week with us while he and his wife went on a cruise.

"Absolutely. We will take good care of her while you are gone," responded Evelyn.

Katie was a wholesome blonde teenager, soft-spoken and top of her class at school. She happily participated in all the regular activities, such as learning how to make homemade jam and grinding whole-wheat flour to make homemade bread. She was such a joyful addition to the family.

On the last day, Evelyn had the idea of returning Katie to her parents in less-than-perfect condition. "Take her outside, get her really dirty, and take some clothes out of the missionary barrel—and mess up her hair too," suggested Evelyn.

When her parents came to pick her up, Evelyn said, "I am so sorry, but we had a problem with Kaitlin. She went wild, and we just could not contain her."

At that point she walked in looking dirty and disheveled. No one could keep a straight face, and we laughed so hard we had tears in our eyes. This scheme was one of Evelyn's great ideas that ended in success. She frequently claimed that she only said aloud about a quarter of the ideas that ran through her head. As the years progressed I believed her.

For example, Evelyn suggested I make a farewell cake for a young man in the navy who was about to leave for his first naval deployment on a light aircraft carrier named the

Belau Wood. "You should make him a cake!" exclaimed Evelyn. I liked making desserts but realized it would be a monumental task to decorate a cake to look like a ship. Gary found a picture I could use as a model, and I found some plastic helicopters to put on top. With Evelyn's help the cake actually came out looking somewhat like the aircraft carrier, much to our sailor's delight.

Evelyn was the first to wear her habit away from home, when she attended an Inner Healing Conference in Colorado. When she got back, she shared how much she had learned about the healing power of God. "He is always ready to heal spiritually, emotionally, psychologically anyone, anytime, anywhere—we only need ask!" she enthusiastically reported.

After dinner several of us were eager to experience this inner healing power.

"Come into my room, and I will pray with you," offered Evelyn.

We lined up, hearts beating with anticipation for our turns to get healing prayer. As each got their turn to be healed, I waited for my turn, not sure what kind of healing God could give me. I had so many bad things in my life that needed healing. I started to shake inside for fear of what God would bring up from my many past sins. When it was my turn, Evelyn put her hands on my head and prayed in that heavenly language I would hear at our prayer and praise meetings. I began to weep uncontrollably, but my mind was dark. I had no thoughts other than feeling like I could not breathe. I hurt so much my chest felt heavy inside.

Evelyn said, "I see a baby in darkness. That baby is you, Kata. You are still inside your mother's womb, and you don't want to come out."

I cried out, "It will hurt, and I am afraid."

"You can come out. Everything will be all right. Jesus is standing outside to catch you. Do you see the light?" Evelyn encouraged. Evelyn told me to relax and let whatever happened, happen. She asked me to imagine Jesus holding his arms out to me. I let myself be born into his arms and his light. A weight lifted from my chest. I felt free!

When I finally stopped crying, I shared about my birth. My mom had once told me the umbilical cord was wrapped around my neck and my face was blue. That evening, when I asked for healing, I never expected God to heal me of a frightening birth experience.

So many of the family members requested prayer, it was three o'clock in the morning before we went to our rooms to contemplate all that took place in that tiny space of time filled with such Holy Spirit's power.

CHAPTER 14

The Holy Spirit

And they were all filled with the Holy Spirit
and began to speak in different tongues, as
the Spirit enabled them to proclaim.
—Acts 2:4

After that long night, I longed for more of the freedom and power that God had given me through my inner healing. I didn't yet understand the Holy Spirit was waiting for me to recognize that I had a need only he could fill.

A few days later, I shared the desire to know more about the Holy Spirit. When we sang songs of praise, lifting our arms up toward heaven as a sign of submission to God, I felt a burning sensation in my heart for more of God's power. Evelyn gave me a book to read: *Nine o' Clock in the Morning* by Dennis Bennett. The book tells the story of how Dennis, an Episcopal priest, and his wife experienced the baptism of the Holy Spirit. As he shared his experience with his congregation and prayed for his parishioners to also receive this baptism, a powerful movement in his life, his family, and his church began spreading throughout many other congregations as well. Evelyn suggested more books about the baptism of the Holy Spirit, with testimony after testimony of its effect in people's lives.

One does not simply go to a friend or pastor and ask that person to pray for baptism in the Spirit as if it were a prescription. Baptism in the Holy Spirit happens in God's timing, which can be anytime, anywhere. For example, one person who asked for the Holy Spirit in a prayer meeting went home dumbfounded because she did not feel anything. The next day she went to put some muffins in the oven, opened the oven door, and immediately began to cry uncontrollably, speaking in tongues. When she finally settled down, she called her friend, who had prayed for her, and asked, "So I opened the oven door and felt a rush come over me so powerful. Is this how everyone gets baptized in the Holy Spirit, by opening the oven door?"

The two friends had a good laugh, and then her friend explained what the next steps were to learn more about the Holy Spirit by digging deeper in the Bible for evidence of the baptism of the Holy Spirit.

Needless to say, after hearing about this lady's experience, I went in the kitchen and opened the oven door just to see if maybe the Holy Spirit was in there. All I found was a cold, empty oven.

That evening I made the frosting for a Poke and Pour Jell-O Cake,* which we would enjoy after our prayer and praise meeting. About twenty other guests joined us. After communion, Evelyn asked if anyone wanted specific prayers. Silence filled the room. My insides were shaking so much I blurted out before I could think, "How do I become baptized in the Holy Spirit?"

"All right. Sit on the stool in the center of the room, and anyone who feels led, lay hands on Kata," Evelyn replied.

Sitting on the stool in the middle of the room with my eyes tightly closed for fear that no one would lay their hands on me was very nerve-racking. Finally I felt hands on my shoulder, and then my back, head, and arm. All the tension left my body.

Evelyn guided me along the next steps. "Hold out your hands as if I am about to give you a gift," she said. She told me to empty my mind of any distractions and just picture Jesus because he had a gift to give me. "Thank Jesus for this gift; keep thanking him, praising him for the Holy Spirit, and let go of yourself. Now, open your mouth and breathe. Start speaking as if you were talking baby talk, learning to talk. Let it go; just let go … Someone hold her; she is falling back. There you are, Kata. You have the Holy Spirit!"

I remember both laughing and crying at the very same time. I felt as if I were drunk, but I knew I was completely sober! I felt unbounded, pure joy. I laughed all the way to bed, opened my Bible, and read the verses in Acts where the disciple Peter preached to the crowd, who were all baptized in the Holy Spirit. That night it seemed as if the words on the page glowed. Things were different after that night. The Holy Spirit filled me with a new perspective on the people around me, the air I breathed, and everything I touched. I still had problems getting angry, and self-pity hit me like a slap on the face. But now, the Holy Spirit gave me the gift to know that I was forgiven.

CHAPTER 15

After a Year, What Was the Next Step?

Come to him, a living stone, rejected by human
beings but chosen and precious in the sight of God.
—1 Pet. 2:4

September 9, 1977, marked the end of my first year of living in the Community, and I had hoped to have a celebration to mark this anniversary. When I asked Evelyn if I could do something special, she responded, "If we had a celebration for the anniversary of everyone, we would never get anything done. I don't think we need to do something special."

Embarrassed that I had said anything at all, I walked to my bedroom feeling dejected. She was right: if we celebrated every anniversary, it would get out of hand. Picking myself up off my bed, I went to the kitchen to do my chores for dinner: Scalloped Chayote Casserole*.

It was a normal meal. Everyone shared what he or she had done for the day. Gary came in a little late, and we had coffee while he ate his dinner. Then L. T. got up from the table and blindfolded me. He led me by my arm, as I could hear everyone move their chairs out from the table. I was told not to take off my blindfold until I had permission. We went outside because I could feel the warm air and heard the dogs barking.

"Step up well; now sit down," L. T. commanded.

I felt the van fill up with people and then drive until we stopped a short while later. L. T. guided me down again.

Then everyone shouted, "Take off the blindfold! Happy one-year anniversary!" We were at the local ice cream stand!

I thanked Evelyn and everyone else for this special surprise trip.

A few days later at the Sunday night Community meeting, Evelyn asked, "Does anyone have anything else to bring up?"

I had expressed before my desire to be a Community member, but the answer was always, "We'll pray about it." Here I was again with that same burning in my stomach, thinking, *I really want the security of being a member of ROCF.* I knew in my heart this lifestyle of serving others, with Jesus first, others second, and myself last, was God's will for me. I squeaked out, "I know I brought this subject up before, so here I go again. May I please become a member of this Community?"

I looked around at Evelyn, Poppa, Uncle Basil, Danielle, Gary, Robert, and Dee. A deafening silence filled the room, and then in unison, they all shouted, "*Yes*! First you will say temporary vows for six months; afterward we will see where we go from there."

Tears filled my eyes; I was happy and very relieved to know I had a vision for my life. I called my mom and sister Susa. We planned the ceremony for my temporary vows at a time my sister's family could share the moment. We had a celebratory dinner of baked chicken, potatoes, vegetables from the garden, and two-tone bread, and for dessert I made the delicious eight-layer Russian torte.

"I, Zdzislawa, do promise to live out the rule of life of this Community as it applies to me, as a temporary member, with Jesus first, others second, and myself last. I choose to live under the vows of poverty, chastity, and obedience and do sincerely seek God's purpose during this time of discernment before taking the solemn permanent vows at a later time." I put on my brown habit, cincture at my waist, and Community necklace, a silver dove strung with a simple brown cord; I was an official temporary member. This began the next step of the journey into Community living.

CHAPTER 16

We Women Take the Baton

Since we have gifts that differ according to the
grace given to us, let us exercise them.
—Rom. 12:6

Following Evelyn's return from the Inner Healing
Conference, she announced a new vision for herself in her
role as the mother of the Community. "I no longer will be
in charge of the kitchen. You young women seem capable
enough to carry on the responsibility of the shopping,
planning, and preparing of the meals, so I think I will step
out and be the Mother with a capital M. I feel God wants me
to function as a religious-order mother. I will plan retreats,
offer counseling, give talks, and provide spiritual direction
to each of you."

As we sat at the kitchen table looking at one another, we
realized no one else needed, as Evelyn had, to be in charge.
We were a team. For the rest of my life in the Community,

none of the women was solely in charge of shopping or menus. We worked together, took turns shopping, and came up with a standard schedule. Either Evelyn taught us well, or we just never needed someone to be in charge. I do not know; all I do know is the kitchen had an element of freedom as we worked together. We were active in bringing our ideas to the menus. We found a system that worked for us, which became a reflection on the meals we prepared for family dinners and company.

We met together once a week, usually on Wednesdays, since Tuesdays was when the sale ads came out from the grocery stores. Each of us brought menu ideas, recipes, and coupons to the kitchen table for planning. We would pray, asking God to the planning, and then begin with the Community calendar and figure out what was planned for the week, what guests were coming, and what members might be gone for the week. When the menu planning was finished, we volunteered for jobs, and then the person grocery shopping for that week would spend the next hour or so filling out the shopping list from the menu and go through all three houses to see what staples needed to be purchased. To make the shopping list easier, I made up a master list of everyday items that we kept on hand all the time.

Grocery shopping was normally done on Thursdays, usually by one woman who might take along one of her kids.

Here's an example of a typical weekly menu:

> *Sunday: Breakfast: Crazy Pancakes, brown-and-serve sausage, juice*

Katherine Zyczynska

Lunch: Hot dogs, chips, and fruit

Monday: Dinner: Bunny's enchiladas, rice, refried beans

Lunch: leftovers

Tuesday: Dinner: Spaghetti with sausage sauce, lettuce salad, garlic bread

Lunch: Peanut butter and jelly, chips, and fruit

Wednesday: Dinner: Tuna potpie (Bisquick recipe), frozen vegetables, molded nippy salad

Lunch: leftovers

Thursday: Dinner: Barbara Bishop's mac and cheese, green beans, bread

Lunch: 1 guest, quesadillas, applesauce, chips, brownies

Friday: Dinner: Neptune's casserole (Pillsbury Bake-Off), egg noodles, mandarin orange salad, and bread

Lunch: leftovers

Saturday: Dinner: Zucchini Pizza, fruit salad, french bread

Lunch: Sloppy joes, tater tots, coleslaw

CHAPTER 17

The Lure of the Corrupting Influence of Power

Pride goes before disaster,
And a haughty spirit before a fall.
—Prov. 16:18

A subtle shift began after the Inner Healing Conference. It was not one I would ever recognize until decades later, but the deference Evelyn had always expected from all of us began to grow in ways that began to crowd out our own personhood. One example that repeated over and over again: "I cannot find my glasses! Kata, I need your help. I can't find my 'brains' [referring to her calendar]. Can you help me find them?" Evelyn called my name almost daily to "help" her find something she, in her own carelessness, had misplaced. I would then be expected to stop whatever I was doing and help her. Initially I felt proud of doing this. Since I was the one who found the glasses for her, receiving her praise meant I got not rejection, but Evelyn's goodwill.

There was an escalation in her "correction process." Evelyn was easy to read when she was unhappy or angry with any one of us. Her cheeks would get red. She would avoid eye contact and either avoid speaking to the person or yell at the person. Since my personality wants to be a people pleaser, any anger I felt toward her constant interruptions would build inside me till I exploded or pushed the anger down into self-pity.

Evelyn, noticing my sadness, would bring up my problem of self-pity at the dinner table in front of everyone else. The problem, therefore, wasn't hers but mine.

It was getting harder and harder to please her. When I worked in the kitchen with others, I cleaned up my area before leaving to do something else and believed it was clean. Another person working in the kitchen at the same time would leave her mess. Evelyn would enter the kitchen, see the mess, and reprimand me, even though it was left by someone else. If I defended myself by saying the other person left it, then I was "defensive." To avoid more conflict, I cleaned up her mess as well as mine. When I did this and got caught, that was wrong too, because "How is that person going to learn to clean up for herself?," and "You are just going to be resentful for having to clean up their mess."

Another controlling technique Evelyn used was the giving of assignments. One would find notes left on a corkboard designed by Evelyn and situated in a prominent place in the kitchen, close to the telephone for telephone messages, with a name prominently posted. The assignments were a list of questions for the person to answer, but first you had to decipher her difficult handwriting. When you thought you had the questions answered, the paper would be again left on the message board with highlighter to answer certain questions, which meant "do it over again."

Direct intervention in the moment also happened when necessary. One of my first experiences with Evelyn's wrath was in my room in the little house. This happened one time when L. T. and I sat talking one day when he came over to the little house to retrieve his clean laundry from me. Each woman did laundry for the men who were not married; I was responsible for L. T.'s laundry. Everyone loved L. T.; he was funny, talented, and likable. His relationship with Evelyn was very close. He would sit at her feet when we had a gathering in the living room. She was the only person he went to for problems. It was obvious that he worshiped her, and she soaked up his devotion with pride.

L. T. saw me reading on my bed and came in to thank me for doing his laundry for him. We were simply talking; he sat on Renée's bed, and I on mine. The door was open so everyone walking through the house could see us talking—nothing more. Someone spotted us and immediately told Evelyn.

She came in, furiously slammed the door, and yelled at L. T. that he "should know better." She glared at me and yelled, "How dare you tempt him?" L. T. left the house extremely angry with Evelyn for accusing us of doing something wrong; we never did engage in anything more than talking in public.

CHAPTER 18

Oh, the Weather outside Is Frightful

God thunders forth marvels with his voice;
He does great things beyond our knowing.
He says to the snow, "fall to the earth";
Likewise to his heavy, drenching rain.
—Job 37:5–6

When winter arrived the weather was very different from the year before. Instead of dry hot winds and brown trees, the season was cold and wet. Very wet. After one memorable night of downpour, the men living in the basement bedroom woke up in the morning and found themselves stepping out of bed into five inches of water.

"*No wonder* there was a large squeegee in the corner of the garage when we moved in!" exclaimed one of the men with soggy socks. At the time no one could figure out what the original owner ever used it for. Well, we finally found out.

As we lived in a still-remote area of the county, the local electric power lines hadn't been updated in decades. When it rained the electricity would predictably go out. We quickly learned of this pattern and kept candles and flashlights on hand all over our property.

Another surprise awaiting us this first rainy winter was the overflowing of our septic tank. Do the math: we had seventeen people using this one house with two bathrooms, plus a dishwasher that ran twice a day. All of the pipes for the main house were connected to one septic tank.

The wet rainy weather also brought mud, lots of it, tracked into the house all the time. To reduce some of the mud in the house, we spread newspapers in front of the doors for the piles of filthy shoes. Even the dog submitted to having his feet wiped before he came into the house. But he was usually disgusted with the towel-wiping process and figured out ways to escape the foot cleansing by running quickly through the kitchen onto the carpet into the bedroom, leaving a mess of paw prints to be cleaned.

We learned to be prepared to cook during these times. We adjusted our menu to be able to cook everything on our gas stove. We would quickly grab ingredients out of the freezer before we covered them with blankets to keep the cold in and then put together a big pot of soup or stew. Other times we cooked up Ramen noodle soup with peanut butter sandwiches. We always came up with some meal so no one ever went to bed hungry.

One winter when Gary's parents came for a Christmas visit, we had a powerful storm come through the county, and our entire town had no power. We figured the electricity would come back by dinner, but by six in the evening, there was still no power. Robert hooked up one line of power to our generator, enough to light one lamp in the kitchen. After seventeen hours and all of us huddled under blankets in the living room (since our electric heater was out), we all cheered wildly when the power came back on. Once again, the rule of life in our Community, lived out many times, was, "Flexibility is the rule."

Christmas this year was so delightful because of seven-month-old Michael celebrating his first Christmas. Often during the holidays, we had two or three extra visitors staying with us, and this year was no exception. The most memorable visitors of that year were two Australian women, Irene and Veronica, traveling around the United States. They purchased a small used truck to have the freedom to go all over the United States to see our country and meet the people in our beautiful country. They stayed with some friends who described our Community life and suggested they visit to experience Christmas in southern California with a unique family. The two women asked if we could be their last visit before they returned home to Australia.

Irene loved helping in the kitchen, learning how to make some of our American dishes, such as breakfast burritos, which were simply scrambled eggs in a flour tortilla. Irene and Veronica taught us all about Australian life, foods, and funny commercial jingles like Typhoon Tea. On their last night, they shared at the dinner table that they were thinking of a way to get rid of their truck.

Evelyn caught the eyes of the other members, trying to communicate an idea she had, which was, "we should buy their truck from them." When everyone gave a nod to the affirmative, Evelyn told the women that the family would like to buy their truck. The women were ecstatic.

God works in mysterious ways. Usually it took a long time for the Community to make a decision, but this time, God allowed us to make a decision in a minute.

Evelyn often came up with new ideas to add fun to our celebrations from articles in magazines she purchased or from how other friends celebrated holidays. One of her ideas was that we could have a secret Santa for one another, calling it Kris Kringle. To implement this idea, she wrote each of our names on a little slip of paper, put them in a plastic Christmas ball, and passed it around the table for the adults to choose a slip. After everyone received a name of someone who was not yourself or your spouse, we then set a start date and a date for the final gift exchange to reveal ourselves. During these two weeks or so, the idea was not to spend lots of money but to secretly do favors, leave little notes for the person, or do some other secret something.

Each of us had to be very sneaky to remain undiscovered, such as type up a message, contract one of the children to leave an item for your person, or perform a secret task after that person went to bed. One person shined shoes. Another emptied the bedroom trash or did their cleaning chores.

You might find candy dangling from the chandelier in the dining room with a note, or two or three puzzle pieces in a baggie for the person to put together as a teaser to guess who their Kris was.

We did this tradition for many years, and with each passing year, we improved at disguising our identities. At times, someone would not get a gift for a couple of days because the Kris had hidden it too well or the person was too preoccupied to look for a gift. In this case another person would hint or come right out and say, "Hey, so and so, did you see your note on the bathroom mirror?" One time a Kris chose a theme, and all year long, she bought candy after holiday sales. Then she saved them until Kris Kringle time, where the receiver got a gift for each holiday, starting at the beginning of the year clear through to Christmas.

One Christmas the person who drew my name thought of an ingenious gift; each day from the beginning of the two-week period of Kris Kringle, my person copied the pages of a lovely Christmas story written by one of my favorite authors. Kris left installments of the chapters at various locations, such as hanging from a lamp, in the refrigerator, or in the bathroom. Each discovery delighted my heart.

At the party, in place of revealing our secret identities, Evelyn played a guessing game, where each one of us had to try to see if we could guess who had our name as Kris Kringle. This game uncovered our very different personalities. Some people were able to disguise themselves so well no one guessed them. Others were obvious and were easily chosen; these same people were the ones who never guessed correctly who their Kris was. There were some Kris Kringle parties where several people were frustrated at being so transparent, whereas the secretive ones boasted about their great ability to achieve anonymity. Everyone, whether thrilled or disappointed, enjoyed cookies, hot toddies, and appetizers. One treat we looked forward to every year was Bobbie Jean's Kahlua Balls*.

Another annual event that developed during the Christmas season was neighborhood Christmas caroling. It was a very organized event. Each person had a small hymnal to carry. Every third person also held a flashlight. We all walked together to each neighbor's house, singing just one verse of the suggested carol, and then as we were leaving, we sang "We Wish You a Merry Christmas." We all looked forward to the hot cider and cookies, which we set up to enjoy when we returned.

I remember clearly one Christmas when we went out caroling to a family in our neighborhood that had recently moved in across the road from us. Their driveway was very long and dark, yet we sang a carol as we walked along. When we rang the doorbell, no one came to the door except their Doberman pinscher, barking ominously. As we turned to leave, singing "We Wish You a Merry Christmas," Evelyn looked back just in time to catch someone peering out through the window, pushing the curtain to the side.

A month or so later, a woman came to our house. She was the neighbor with the long driveway. It turned out she needed help with their phone system and asked to use our phone to make a call. She explained in her broken English that they had just moved into their house a couple of months before Christmas; since she and her husband did not speak English well, they kept to themselves.

"What language do you speak?" asked Evelyn.

"We are from Canada; we speak French," was the reply.

"Je parle français aussi!" (I speak French too!), responded Evelyn, who spoke French as a child.

The neighbor's face immediately relaxed into the warmest smile; she had a new group of friends from that day on.

Planning for Christmas meals became the focus for the kitchen beginning with Christmas Eve dinner, Christmas Eve party food, Christmas brunch, and Christmas dinner. I've shared about our special cookie and dessert baking. Now let me tell you about our holiday meals.

One way to include the whole family was to put up a paper on the refrigerator for people to have the opportunity to request favorite holiday foods for the special meals. We would consider these ideas when we made our final plans. We gathered the various ideas and recipes, both standard well-loved recipes to new recipes from magazine articles that someone may have found. Here is a small sampling of one of our Christmas menus.

Christmas Eve
Mushroom Soup
Pull-Apart Bread

Christmas Eve gift-exchange party
Tortilla Wraps
Cookie trays
Eggnog, Brandy on the side

Christmas Brunch
German Ometatta
German Butter Kuchen
Hot Fruit Compote

Christmas Dinner
Baked Ham with Dijon/Cranberry jelly sauce (equal
parts Dijon Mustard and cranberry jelly heated to a
sauce)

Twice-Baked Potatoes (Betty Crocker)
Fresh Steamed Broccoli
Cinnamon Apple Cups (Better Homes and Gardens)
Pillsbury quick and easy yeast rolls
Blitz Torte*
Persimmon Pudding with apple cream sauce

Besides all the food to prepare, we did a deep housecleaning
and made sure our yard had extra attention with seasonal
colors. Our dining room tables really consisted of
four individual six-foot-by-four-foot tables. In order to
accommodate guests by moving them around, we could
accommodate up to thirty to forty people, depending on
how the tables were rearranged. Evelyn managed the table
settings, place cards, candles, and floral arrangements to
decorate the tables, besides making the final approval of

our menus. One of her many gifts was transforming our common dining room into a magical experience, especially for the young children. The room twinkled happily of candlelight the moment someone turned off the lights.

Although the table may have been filled with lots of plates of food, if we kept to the "pass everything to the right" rule, the meal was a success. When everyone at the table appeared to be finished with his or her dinner, Evelyn and Poppa would lead all the guests to the living room to visit while the rest of us cleaned up the dirty dishes, put away the leftovers from the meal, and prepared the dessert. Sometimes everyone returned to the table to take a coffee count and dessert count; other times we gathered in the living room for dessert and coffee in a casual manner. What was funny was that no matter how loudly some complained about how full they were, they always had room for dessert.

It sounds like I am making Christmas all about the food, but our midnight Christmas service brought home the reality of Jesus's birth. We put candles all over the living room so that we could have our service in candlelight. Everyone dressed up, either in our religious habits or nice clothing to give reverence to our Lord for his special celebration. We sang several Christmas carols, read the familiar Scripture readings of Christmas, and then after each reading, there was a moment of silence for anyone who wanted to share a personal thought or feeling from verses they heard. Father Basil said a short sermon, and then we had our Christmas Communion.

Shortly after the service, we prepared the snacks and drinks for the gift-giving party, while the children went to bed to have their own gifts in the morning before brunch. Many of us put on our pajamas before our gathering. Evelyn separated the gifts under the tree in order to make passing them out more efficient. She always had the largest pile because since she was Mother, everyone wanted to get her a gift. As our family grew, Evelyn suggested we draw names, to reduce the number of gifts, but it still did not solve the problem of the bulk of gifts that Evelyn received.

When we cleaned up after our gift giving, we put out gifts for the children, at first just Michael. But each year the young married couples added more children to our Christmas morning gifts. One of my favorite memories was with Robert and Dee's daughter, Annie. She opened up her first gift, wrapped in a large rectangular box. She shook it and heard an unusual thump. She ripped off the paper quickly to get to her gift and shouted, "I have my very own toothpaste!" She went to each person in the room to show off her treasure. Annie had other gifts, but this one was the best. "Can I go brush my teeth now?" she pleaded. After brushing her teeth, she came back to the living room grinning with a bright smile and finished opening up her other presents.

After gifts came Christmas brunch, followed by preparations for dinner, each of us making our chosen item from the menu we had planned the week earlier. If we had to be accused of anything, it was that we loved to party around food, presents, and giving and sharing together. Although this marked so many occasions throughout the year, clearly Christmas was a time we truly celebrated on every level.

CHAPTER 19

New Perspective on an Old Life

Give the childless wife a home,
The joyful mother of children.
Hallelujah!
—Ps. 113:9

The year 1978 brought many changes to our Community. New people moved in. People moved out. Community vows and marriage vows, babies born and babies on the way were all part of that time. We would often say, "In Community one only has to go out to the mailbox, and on returning, something life-changing may occur."

I was able to take another trip to Michigan, again driving with my sister Susa and her family. Bonnie Jean wrote in an article, "The Community sent Kata back to Michigan to see if she was serious about her desire to become a member."

One of my first stops was to visit my brother, his wife, and their nine cats. They lived across town from my paternal grandparents. I decided it would a great surprise to walk over to my grandparents' house to see them. My mom agreed to meet me at my grandparents' house so I had time to visit with them alone for a while. When I rang the bell, I almost gave my grandmother a heart attack, for my mother had not told them I was coming for a visit. We had such a good laugh and time together.

I even got bold enough to ask if I could go to the second floor of their house. When I was a child, my brothers always told me that the upstairs was haunted. As an adult I still had some trepidation as I ascended the stairs, only to find a lovely apartment, with bedroom, bathroom, and kitchen. No ghosts at all. I went through all the rooms and found an old trunk. As I started to go through it, I heard a creaking from the stairway. I thought maybe there was a ghost after all, but it was my grandmother slowly coming up to see how I was doing.

"I haven't been up here for years. What did you find, Zdzislawa?" asked my grandmother.

"I found this fascinating trunk. What is the history of the things inside?"

There was a finely carved frame with a Polish translation of the "Our Father," written in old script, with delicate detailed pictures surrounding the words illustrating the significance of the message. Other items were an antique picture of a woman, blankets, and lace.

Grandma said, "This is a picture of my grandmother, who spun the wool for this blanket. She also made this lace for a tablecloth. I can't believe what good condition these things are in."

The memory of this moment will be one I shall never forget—the softness of the wool and the essence of mothballs to keep the fragile wool from holes.

I went back down the stairs to rediscover all the familiar places where I passed many happy moments playing alone, while my parents and older siblings sat in the living room talking, on our weekly visits with Grandpa and Grandma Zyczyaska. There was my grandparents' bed; their marriage certificate still hung over their bed. On the floor of their closet was a little box that held a teddy bear for me to play with while I sat in the big brown stuffed chair right under the giant moose head that watched me with his shiny glass eyes. I had to make sure they were glass every time we visited by climbing up to touch them. That afternoon I touched the eyes again just because I had to.

As I looked out the back door to the big red barn, which used to be part of my great-grandpa's farm, I saw up in the pine tree a beautiful red cardinal, looking redder because of the snow. What a gift to see him. I took a picture of my grandparents on their porch bidding me good-bye, not knowing whether it would be the last time we would see one another.

My mom and I covered a lot of territory visiting many relatives; my whole visit consisted of visiting family, including my dad's grave, which was in the cemetery next to the city park where my uncle Lester built a birding trail named after him. When we stopped by my uncle Gordon's house, I knew this visit would be difficult because he could have easily been my father's twin; their likeness was that similar. Even his laugh was the same as my dad's. We talked about funny times in the past. We cried together, remembering how painful it was for him to lose his brother and me to lose my father at such an early age.

The only teacher that influenced me in high school was my home economics instructor, so I decided I would call to see if I could stop by. She immediately invited me for an afternoon visit. We had a lovely time catching up over a glass of wine—it was a strange feeling to drink alcohol with my teacher. She seemed very intrigued to learn about the way I lived in Community. My chosen way of life was easy to explain to her since the Episcopal Church was very close to her Catholic faith.

Before I left I had to buy a bottle of apricot brandy, requested by Evelyn so that we could do a special ice cream topping recipe. Whenever anyone went on a trip, Evelyn always asked that the person bring her back something. I made sure I had that bottle, not knowing it would be a medicinal aid on the trip back to California.

When our family says good-bye, it takes quite a while; we hug, talk some more, hug again, cry, and finally leave. We packed the van with enough snacks, blankets, and pillows so that we could drive through the night. Our goal was to stop in Aspen, Colorado, so that Anton could ski. Then we would spend one night in Las Vegas, where we could stay cheaply on the nearby military base. Traveling at night, you never see the scenery, but you make good time on the freeways.

A few hours into our trip, little Sasha became cranky, increasingly by the hour. Susa felt his gums and realized he was in pain because he was teething. What could we do? We were in the middle of Nebraska, surrounded by rolling hills and no drugstores to buy teething gel.

Anton made a brilliant suggestion. "Open up that bottle of brandy, Kata, and rub that on his gums. Maybe let some of it trickle down his throat, too."

This solution worked. Sasha settled down, and the van was quiet again.

Around midnight it was my turn to drive. I would drive when it was dark and switch just before dawn in order to see the Rocky Mountains in the morning. The only traffic on the road was trucks, who, when passed them, they would flash their lights to let me know I had passed far enough to merge back into the lane.

As we drove into Aspen, Colorado, we could not find any parking, so we continued on. We found a place in Vale for Anton to ski. He enjoyed himself as the rest of us ate and then played in the snow. I enjoyed staying inside the restaurant watching people and had a great time speaking with a young single man.

It was early evening when we arrived at the top of the ridge overlooking the valley of Las Vegas. With its flashing lights, it looked just like I pictured the cities of Sodom and Gomorrah from the Bible. We found the base, where we planned to spend the night; we had a two-bedroom suite. Theresa and I slept in one room, Anton, Susa, and the boys in the other.

"Did you see all the cute men, Kata?" My sister was always the matchmaker.

Anton wanted to eat dinner at the casino called "Circus," a child-friendly casino. It had scantily clad women, but the show was like a circus.

I had a certain amount of nickels to gamble with, so decided when they were gone, I was finished, knowing I could easily go on and on without thought of how much I put in. After seventy-five cents worth of nickels, bells clanged, lights flashed, and nickels poured out of the machine. I had won! I stopped. True to my word, I have never gambled again, so I can honestly say, every time I have gambled, I have won.

We pulled into the Community late at night. I was living in the extra room up at Mabelle's house, so they left me off at the top of the driveway. I said good night to Susa and her family, thanking them for a wonderful trip. The walk down the driveway was unusually thick with mud. What was up? The note on the door said it all: "Because of heavy rain, there was a mudslide down the driveway that leaked into your bedroom. Please head down to the Big House to sleep tonight."

Once again our adage proved true: you never knew *what* might happen when you left the house!

CHAPTER 20

All We Need Is Love and a Firm Grip to Hold On to for Support

But Jesus said, "Let the children come to me,
and do not prevent them; for the kingdom
of heaven belongs to such as these."
—Matt. 19:14

As a Christian family ministry, we kept an open-door policy to help people in need. One such person was Tanya, who came from a broken home. In school she got herself mixed up with the wrong friends, who led her into a life of drinking and drugs. Her uncle was one of our associates, who suggested she move in to live with us. On the outside she was a tough tomboy teenager. But her eyes betrayed a sensitive soul who responded with eager openness to our kindness. As her roommate, I needed the sensitivity to be her friend, but as the adult, I also needed to be aware of keeping the rules intact, such as no smoking, drugs, or alcohol.

Evelyn's years of mothering seemed to have given her the gift of finding unusual ways to reach someone in trouble. She decided playing the game of jacks with Tanya would be an excellent way to reach out to her. It worked quite well. Together they held a jacks tournament that spread out several days, and to her great delight, Tanya won. It was a joy watching her grow in a home with stability, acceptance, and a solid dose of God's love.

Evelyn observed her changes and decided to enroll her in the local high school, where she entered as a junior, getting involved with sports and a Christian group of friends. Tanya grieved for her younger sister, who still lived with her mother in Las Vegas. Although Tanya longed for her sister to receive the same healing she felt, God knew Tanya had a lot more healing to be stable enough before her sister came to live with us. Tanya often had disturbing dreams that awakened her in the middle of the night, filling her with fear that someone was coming after her.

Evelyn suggested that we make a point of praying for her before we went to bed each night, using Ephesians chapter 6 as a prayer.

That night we opened the Bible, reading the verses aloud. We two got the same idea: "Let's make it a song as if we are getting dressed; a song will be easier to remember."

Here is the song we made up (based on Ephesians 6:14–17), adding a few extra lines to make a complete outfit of clothing.

Chorus: We put on the armor, the armor, the armor; we put on the armor, the armor of God

Verse 1: The helmet of salvation, the breastplate of righteousness,
The cloak of praise, and the belt of Truth.

Chorus: We put on the armor, the armor, the armor; we put on the armor, the armor of God.

Verse 2: The shield of Faith, and the shoes of the Gospel,
The sword of the Spirit and the jeans of JOY!

Repeat the chorus.

Every night in our little shared room, we sang this song, covering us with the protection of the Holy Spirit over Tanya's nightmares and falling asleep in God's peace.

We welcomed another person to the Community at this time. I had no idea the impact this man would have on my and all of our lives. In his forties, Darren had come the year before for counseling with his wife, trying to save their marriage. Unfortunately, his marriage ended, so friends of his encouraged him to inquire if there might be an opening for him to come and stay with us for a while until he recovered from the divorce. As a coincidence, he was the one Evelyn kissed on the top of the head when we performed our revue at an auditorium the previous year. We invited him to come to dinner and to spend the weekend. As a local attorney in private practice, his commute to work was easy. After that first weekend, we all agreed he could stay with us as he put his life back together.

Behind the house where Tony and Valerie lived was a small guest cottage. It had a bathroom, sink, and place to put a microwave, so it was just perfect for a single man. Plus, it was only a half-mile from the Community. He drove up to the main house for meals, counseling, and other family activities. Counseling usually meant meeting with Dee and Evelyn, or maybe just a walk around the block with Evelyn. Evelyn often shared that she did her best listening to someone's problems while walking. She found it was often easier for people to open up while walking rather than sitting in a closed-up room. One way to get Darren to loosen up was for Evelyn and Dee to hold a tickling session, one on one side of Darren and the other on his other side, just to get him to laugh. He loosened up quite a lot with this unusual attention.

Darren appreciated living a little farther down the road, rather than in the same house. It gave him needed distance from the goings-on at the main house. He confessed years later that he left after dinner still hungry that, instead of going straight to his house, he would go down to the frozen yogurt place for a large yogurt.

By now we had perfected serving meals for large groups. We began to frequently bake the many delicious casseroles we discovered, such as Trane's Casserole*. They were easy to prepare, since they could be prepared in the morning, sometimes in a double batch, two casserole dishes for dinner and two for the freezer for a later time. As a way to make sure there was enough casserole for everyone, we served up the casserole on each dinner plate in the kitchen. To make serving easier, we called, "Chain gang," and everyone lined up ready to take a plate and set it at a place setting on the table. (We ultimately changed to putting the casseroles directly on the table, which allowed many of us, now more calorie-conscious, to dish up our own portions.) Darren's mother made wooden casserole holders for our dishes, and they made a way to easily pass the pans around our table.

Our first Community child, Michael, was quite aware of the daily process, so one night while sitting in his high chair at his place at the table, he called, "Chain gang!" But in his eighteen-month lingo, we heard, "Chang ang." It took a few times of his repeating this before we realized what he was saying. Even though by then we had stopped the chain-gang process, he knew that this meant the beginning of dinner.

Another funny Michael story came during that Lent. We always made some sort of Community-wide sacrifice during this time, so we decided to give up desserts except for Sundays. In his little mind, Michael did not comprehend this decision, so when the first day of Lent arrived, we had soup for dinner, with a small sandwich and fruit for Michael. When the dishes were cleared, Evelyn asked who wanted coffee. At this point Michael knew what would come next: "'Who wants dessert?" He raised his hand up to be counted for dessert, but the question was not asked. When his mom and dad got their coffee, he anticipated getting his dessert, but none came. He looked up at his mom questioningly. "No dessert tonight, Michael; I am sorry." His reaction was a slow realization that he wasn't going to get something delicious. Tears filled his eyes as he realized the anticipated dessert would not appear. Poor Michael—he had always loved desert.

One day we took a call from Child Protective Services. "We have a young thirteen-year-old boy whose mother cannot control him, and his father is on death row. Can you take him in?"

Evelyn had taken the call and said, "He may come for the weekend, and we'll see after that."

Sam had the cutest curly hair, tanned skin, and nonstop energy. He had been living with his mother, and she could not find a way to control his attention-deficit problem. He had a hard time sitting still through board games or anything where he had to focus more than ten minutes, so finding things to interest him became a challenge. Evelyn enjoyed challenges, so she suggested he stay for the summer and see what God would do to help this child with some self-control.

At the same time, Tanya kept asking if her sister could come to live with us; her determination and confidence made refusing difficult.

Evelyn thought, *It can't hurt to have one more teenager in the house.* She shared this with the other Community members, and all were in consensus about Cindy moving in with us. Tanya was ecstatic.

With an increasing number of teenage girls, we needed more space. As a single twenty-year-old adult, I became the one to monitor the girls; we moved into the large bedroom in the main house, calling ourselves the "Back Room Girls," otherwise known as the BRGs. This move left the little house ready for Gary and Danielle to move in with Michael and prepare for their next child on the way.

A few days a week, L. T. went to the community college seeking a teaching degree. One day he brought home a young woman he had met at school. He had started a conversation with her since they both played the guitar, so he invited her to come for dinner. She was a shy young woman who played classical guitar. She was also an active 4-H member. When she saw our chickens, goats, and rabbits, she felt right at home. After dinner we asked her to play her guitar for us, but being shy, she declined. "Oh, Karen, you have to play, or I will have to sing—and believe me, you do not want me to sing a solo!" pleaded Evelyn. Danielle offered her guitar for Karen to play anything that came to her head. She sat on the edge of the sofa, tuned the guitar, and began to play.

At the very first notes, many of us gasped yet kept quiet until she finished. "That's the music from Michael's toy!" we all shouted.

Danielle explained that Michael's grandma gave him the toy as a newborn, but for the past eighteen months, no one recognized the tune. "Do you know the name of the melody, Karen?"

"Unfortunately, I know it only as the standard practice etude. I do not know the name either," Karen said apologetically.

Karen returned very often, at first to see L. T., but soon she grew to like all of us. We knew she never had any religious upbringing and felt that simply loving her and sharing our lives with her was the way she would be drawn to Jesus.

A few months later, she asked, "How do I get baptized?" She asked L. T. to be her godfather and me to be her godmother.

One Sunday morning Jesus cleansed her by the water of baptism. She joined the family of the faithful in Christ. She also became another member of the Back Room Girls, so she could experience living in Community.

As she grew in the Lord, she wondered whether God might call her to become a nun, not as part of our order but a nun in a convent. Her choice was to visit the nuns by the mission; knowing they were Catholic, not Episcopalian, did not deter her decision. I called asking for an appointment to visit, explaining Karen's request to see their order and the ministries they performed, plus information on how to become a nun.

One of the nuns took us around to visit the school they ran, explaining how they lived, but she did not go into detail of the sacrifices one makes to join an order. She invited us to have lunch with them and to answer any questions Karen might have to ask about becoming a nun.

As we left we drove in silence for a while until Karen said, "Thank you for bringing me here, but I do not think this is God's call for me. I will keep praying to find out what he wants me to do with my life."

"The important lesson God is saying is: 'Are you listening to me, Karen?" I replied. "God wants us to knock on doors. Trust him. He knows how to close a door if it is not right for us. So often we fill our prayer time with our requests or problems, but we do not stop to listen to his voice speak to us."

Karen lived in our Community for a short time, until she had grown enough in her relationship with the Lord to listen to his voice. She moved out a success story.

Our first impression of Tanya's sister, Cindy, was how opposite in personality and appearance they were from each other. Cindy was outgoing, with a positive attitude and trust toward people. Compared to Tanya's sandy-brown hair, muscular build, and tough personality, Cindy had blonde hair, an hourglass figure, and a feminine personality. Tanya knew, with Cindy's looks, she would be subject to many dangers awaiting her while living in Las Vegas. Witnessing the joy on the faces of these sisters, reunited at last, made us all the more determined to be a family for them both.

Not long after this, the local hospital called with a request on behalf of the mother of a teenage daughter in the mental ward. She was Maureen, heavily addicted to drugs, and needed a place to stay while awaiting a space to open in a drug rehabilitation facility. We felt once again the answer should be yes. Another addition to the Back Room Girls was Robert's niece, an active fourteen-year-old with attention-deficit disorder. She needed someone to teach her self-control, something that Robert's sister could not accomplish. Robert asked the Community if Cathy could move in for the summer. He knew that if anyone could reach Cathy, it would be Evelyn.

The Back Room Girls had to share a bathroom with L. T., Uncle Basil, and whatever guys lived down below in the basement bedroom. Somehow we made it all work. Tanya was a senior in high school; Cindy a sophomore. Karen was in college, Cathy in eighth grade, and Maureen was so spacey even without drugs, she had a difficult time focusing on any one project. She stayed only about six weeks—until she could not stand a life of regulations, which we enforced in Community.

There would be days when I needed a break. Taking a car somewhere was not acceptable without a good reason, so I walked out in the hills behind our house. There were days when work in the kitchen could be overwhelming, especially when fruits and vegetables came in from the garden needing to be frozen or canned. For me to be able to walk for an hour or two was just what I needed to be refreshed.

Living in one bedroom together, none of us had privacy. Often in the middle of the night, Cathy would sit up in bed yelling. She had no memory of it the next morning when we told her about it. Cathy was a large, muscular girl, needing an outlet for her physical energy and the powerful emotions pent up inside. Evelyn found a gymnastics team that seemed perfect for her. She practiced her gymnastics moves, especially cartwheels, anytime, anywhere. She had to be reminded to restrain herself when she wore a skirt. Her defense was, "But I have shorts on underneath!"

"You cannot do them in front of the bishop in the living room when he comes to dinner," reminded Evelyn.

Cathy was a challenge, especially when she was angry. One evening, we invited a priest to come to give a presentation on the Shroud of Turin. Just before the guests came, Cathy rebelled against Evelyn, refusing to get dressed for company.

"If you yell one more time, I will tell Robert and Darren to pick you up and put you outside wearing just what you have on. You may not come back in the house until you apologize," shouted Evelyn.

That is just what they did. It took both men to carry her out. Evelyn expected Cathy to beg at the door immediately, since she only wore light pajamas, but she did not. Our guests arrived for dinner, but still Cathy had not shown herself, and Evelyn got worried after three hours had passed. She explained to our guests the situation, asking for their prayers. Evelyn decided it was time to call the police to help in the search for her. When the sheriff arrived, he explained to the then-worried Evelyn that in these cases, Cathy most likely was hiding somewhere on the property. We emphasized that we did look everywhere we could think she might be. The guest priest gave his very interesting presentation on the Shroud of Turin, all while this drama went on.

Just as the evening ended and the guests went home, the sheriff brought in a very groggy Cathy. He found her sleeping inside the shell of the little truck we owned. It is funny how we put on two faces, one entertaining guests treated to an evening of theological learning and the other dealing with a missing teenager with police searching for her. Evelyn managed the whole event by way of begging for prayers for the missing Cathy and asking pertinent questions to our speaker. Clearly life with a batch of hormone-driven teenage girls was always eventful!

CHAPTER 21

Wedding Bells

That is why a man leaves his father and mother and clings
to his wife, and the two of them become one body
—**Gen. 2:24**

In the spring of 1978, Dee finished her commitment to the
military. She moved back to join the Community and to
make her permanent vows. Over the previous few years,
Dee and Robert had formed a friendship. Once she was back
with us, courtship and an engagement were announced.
They would be married in June.

First Dee had to make her permanent commitment to
the Community by taking her vows, as did the rest of the
members in March 1977. We had to have a service and
a celebration for her in April. This service was reverent,
with family and friends of the Community. Then came the
wedding preparations on the fast track.

Evelyn prided herself on being a great seamstress, so Dee asked if she could sew her wedding dress, and since Dee asked Evelyn to be her maid of honor, Evelyn also sewed her own dress. When Evelyn worked on a project, it became all-encompassing for all of us, with every conversation revolving around her. We all encouraged her to share because we knew it made her happy to show off what she had accomplished.

Dee's mother, a retired teacher from Chicago, came out to California a week or so before the wedding to see "what needed doing." Everything needed to be in order for her only child. She knew how to take charge; after all, she taught middle-school-age children!

The catered wedding reception, thanks to Dee's mom, saved us so much work. The caterers took over the kitchen. I loved having them in their black and white uniforms running around in the same kitchen I worked in every day.

Friends and relatives filled the living room to maximum capacity. Every sofa, chair, and floor space was taken. Although Dee is five foot two, several of her relatives were over six feet tall. Robert is six feet tall, as are almost all of his relatives. I recall sitting on the floor looking around the room at all the tall people at the largest gathering so far in my living in Community.

After we said our last good-byes to Robert and Dee, they left on their honeymoon to camp in Yosemite after a memorable trip to Catalina Island for their honeymoon night.

Katherine Zyczynska

Unfortunately, the following morning at prayers, Evelyn began the usual postmortem meeting to discuss what went well and what went wrong, so we would not make the same mistakes again. The difficult part of these meetings was that the joy of the event dissolved quickly by the exhortation of the negative aspects of how we mishandled the day. How I grew to despise these meetings, even though at the time I would not dare disagree with Evelyn.

CHAPTER 22

The Poustinia and Our Prayer Lives

Pray without ceasing.
—1 Thess. 5:17

Evelyn was an avid book reader, and when she found a book she thought we should all read, she would introduce it through one of her teachings. One book, by Catherine Doherty, was titled *Poustinia*, which is a Russian word meaning "desert." Small Russian villages often contained little one-room huts, where a "poustiniki" lived as a hermit. The villagers were thrilled to have a person of prayer interceding night and day, and they showed their gratitude by providing him food and care. These prayer warriors were available anytime there was a need, such as in times of personal crisis, serious illness, spiritual direction, or even as an extra hand in harvest season. The Poustiniki liked to serve the village physically and spiritually. "I think we need to build a poustinia here on our property!" exclaimed

Evelyn. "We have the space. Robert can build it. We do not need someone to live in it, but we could keep the reserved sacrament there, and people could spend the night in prayer before the consecrated host."

Evelyn's last sentence was, "Does anyone have a check?" This had become Community shorthand for, "Does anyone disagree with this as God's will?"

With all in consensus, Robert started researching how to build our own poustinia. When Robert had a project to do, he never procrastinated but got to the task at hand quickly and efficiently. We agreed that it should be out back behind the big house under the large eucalyptus tree where the tire swing hung. In a matter of weeks, we had a dedication of our eight-foot-by-twelve-foot building, our poustinia. It contained a small camp-size portable potty, a single bed, a kneeler in front of a tabernacle holding the consecrated hosts, and a jug of water on a small stand that also held a Bible and prayer book. A box of tissues sat to the side.

"I'll be the first one to spend the night!" volunteered Evelyn.

We sent her off with God's blessing to spend twenty-four hours in silence with God. In the morning one of us carried out a tray with a thermos of hot coffee, fruit, and a muffin. Leaving it on the step just below the door, we rang a small bell and left. The poustiniki opened the door at her convenience for the first of two meals. In the late afternoon, this process was repeated. When the twenty-four hours ended, Evelyn came into the kitchen. We greeted her joyfully, asking her to share what God had said in her time in the poustinia. She looked pale but rested and said she was very cold. If she had something to share, she would do so later.

Each of us in our turn took time out to spend our day and night in the poustinia. Over the years we had many people use the poustinia. One of the most memorable times was when Father Jim came to spend four days and three nights, bringing along his large collie, Hubert. He tied his dog around the large tree next to the poustinia, and Father Jim stayed inside. The weather was slightly warm, so Hubert enjoyed being outside under the shade. One afternoon when Father Jim opened the door to put his breakfast tray out, he noticed his dog was fast asleep. Right beside his beloved pet, a six-foot-long gopher snake slept contentedly. The Bible prophecy from Isaiah, "The lion and the lamb shall lie down together," was replaced in this scene with a dog and a snake. Father Jim quietly stepped out the opposite side of the poustinia and found Robert, who came to figure out how to remove the snake safely and without disturbance. Robert, an expert outdoorsman, moved around so quietly he did not wake either dog or snake. With one quick grab, he was able to pick up the snake. Only then did Hubert awake and look around, wondering what the fuss was all about.

We adapted our monthly day of prayer and fasting. We began the day before breakfast with a short communion service at the dining room table. Father Basil would consecrate an extra host to take to the tabernacle in the poustinia, where it remained all day, exposed, for us as we took turns to pray. We also placed on the kneeler a tablet of paper with prayer intentions. Each of us prayed the list and added to it as desired. Breakfast on these days consisted of a small glass of juice, coffee, or tea. Lunch was a bowl of Top Ramen soup or canned tomato soup. Dinner soup was either simple pea soup or canned soup. We also always added additional food for the children and Mabelle.

The poustinia also functioned for a while as a place where Evelyn and Father Basil met to say morning prayer together out of the *Episcopal Prayer Book*. This lasted for a couple of years—until Evelyn thought it would be better to include others in the morning prayer, and when we could, others began to join in this practice. Sadly, through the years, even this time of prayer was marred by Evelyn's constant correction of our tone of voice, our cadence, and our focus during the service. I started hating to have her there and was always relieved when she was gone.

CHAPTER 23

I Smell a Rat!

Then our mouths were filled with laughter.
—Ps. 126:2

One afternoon as I was standing at the stove preparing white sauce for Bunny Kaplafka's Enchiladas*, Danielle came in the dining room door. I looked up to greet her when she shrieked loudly, saying she saw a rat running in the kitchen. "You keep an eye on him; I'll go get Robert to kill him, Kata!" Danielle shouted as she ran out the door. "I think he went under the stove."

I turned off the stove so as not to burn the white sauce for the enchiladas. As Robert came in the door with an arrow in his hand, the rat ran out from under the stove to under one of the refrigerators. Danielle grabbed the nearest thing she could find in the cupboard: a can of roach spray.

I yelled, "He ran under the blue refrigerator!"

Robert pulled out the blue refrigerator. Danielle sprayed, trying to hit the rat, but suddenly the rat ran under the second refrigerator in the kitchen. In seconds Robert put his arrow under the refrigerator, but the rat ran out and under the kitchen table. Following the rat, we moved the chairs and table out of the way to get him. Danielle sprayed at anything but the rat, such as Robert's shoes. The chase continued into the living room. Robert moved each sofa and coffee table out of the way to get this energetic rat.

As the rat headed for the dining room, Danielle got one good hearty spray in the poor animal's face. Robert flew, pushing the tables away, knocking down several chairs at the dining room tables.

During all this process, I kept my vigilance of the location of the rat. "Robert, the rat is on the high chair; he's on Michael's high chair!" Spray! Whack! Spray! Whack! Whack!

Robert succeeded in the demise of Mr. Rat. For good measure (maybe to punish the silly rat for daring to get on her baby's high chair), Danielle gave one more conquering spray.

When we turned around and saw all the tables, chairs, sofas, coffee tables, refrigerators, and kitchen tables and chairs in complete disarray, it looked as if a tornado had blown through the house. The three of us laughed until our sides hurt, with tears running down our faces. Had there been a video taken in those days, without a doubt it would have made one of our modern television's funniest home movies.

CHAPTER 24

And the Babies Came

And God blessed them, saying: Be fertile, multiply.
—Gen. 1:22

Michael turned one year old that summer. As Danielle placed a large birthday cake in front of him with one big candle on top, his eyes grew wide as saucers at the sight of such a large cake just for him. As we started to sing "Happy Birthday" to Michael, suddenly Danielle called out, "Michael, wait!" Focused on taking a picture, she had not noticed that her young son did not understand that he had to wait until the end of the song. Before anyone could stop him, his tiny hands dug deeply into the cake, and he filled his mouth with fistfuls of gooey icing and delicious cake. All we could do was laugh. That was our Michael.

Another baby was going to join our family! Tony and Valerie were expecting in August. They had planned a home delivery. Those invited to witness the birth were her mom, Evelyn, the baby's godmother, Ann, Danielle, and of course Tony. All through the pregnancy, Tony displayed similar symptoms as Valerie, including the same cravings she had for olives, and upset stomach, fatigue, and even hot flashes. When the labor came, he could not quite bring himself to identify the intensity of pain she felt, so he tried to make jokes to lighten the atmosphere, which did not help. When her doctor arrived, Valerie was walking around in just her light nightgown, trying to relieve the pain of the contractions.

"I am so glad you're here, Doctor," Tony said, expressing his relief. "Could you look at my ingrown toenail? It has bothered me for weeks!"

Everyone reacted the same way. "Oh, Tony, we need to focus on Valerie!"

Nevertheless, the doctor looked at the toe, chuckling to himself.

I really wanted to be there but did not want to ask, knowing there were already enough people at the birth. It was difficult to sleep, so I decided I would stay up, ready to spread the word to the other family members when the call came to announce the new baby. I needed something to do rather than sit around reading. I knew just what would keep me busy for hours. A large kitchen task for the following day was preparing to make Zucchini Relish*. I got out all the necessary equipment to begin the process. I was using an old trusted recipe: you start with ten cups of ground zucchini, four cups of ground green and red peppers, and four cups of ground onions. I always begin with the peppers and then the onions. I had just finished the onions when the phone rang.

"Please, Kata, we need good strong coffee, now!" pleaded Evelyn, desperate.

It took no time at all to make the coffee, clean up my grinding mess, and drive down at four o'clock in the morning with fresh coffee for everyone except our laboring mother. Valerie was still pacing around the house in her negligee, trying to get the baby to drop.

"Now that you are here and the baby is about to come, why not stay and watch the birth?" asked Evelyn. Then a strange look came over her face, and she asked, "Why do you smell like onions?"

I was thrilled to be asked to stay and explained that when Evelyn called to say the doctor had arrived, I was so excited I couldn't sleep, so I started the first steps to make the zucchini relish. Everyone laughed and promised a jar of relish to the doctor when we canned it. I discovered that witnessing at-home labor is fascinating. Everyone is focused on assisting the mother through her contractions. You must wait along with her until the baby is ready to come. All your encouragement doesn't makes any difference to the baby or the mother. She is thinking, *Just get this baby born* now!

As labor was slow that night, the doctor suggested Valerie take a warm shower to relax a little. That did the trick. After her shower the doctor checked her one more time and announced, "It's time!"

Valerie lay down on her bed, Danielle to her right, Tony to her left. I stood in between Evelyn and Ann, both of them holding on to my arms. Tony knew ahead of time he would not make a good coach because, knowing his excitable Italian nature, he would forget all they had learned in the birthing class. They had asked Danielle to assist. That was the best choice, since she had a baby and was a capable take-charge person. I personally think she would make a perfect midwife. "Push! … Breathe! … You are doing great! Breathe; ten, nine, eight, seven, I see the head, one more push!" And out he came, no screaming, just a big smile and squinting eyes.

Noticing this, Danielle said, "Turn down the lights. He's squinting because it's too bright."

That insight allowed Tony Junior to stop squinting and begin to look around, as we stared back at him in wonder at this new birth. Suddenly we all spontaneously broke out in singing "Happy Birthday." Lost in this moment, I realized I had lost circulation in my arms because both Evelyn and Ann were holding each other so tightly, crying out of joy. Being that was one of the biggest highlights in my life, I cry even now as I write this, recalling that wonderful morning when T. J. came into the world.

T. J. was a very chunky happy baby, eager to imitate his father. Since Tony loved football even as an infant, you could find the two of them rolling together on the floor in sport tackles. One day T. J. was sitting in our living room while several adults were seated around the room on our sofas. T. J. looked around at everyone talking, and presumably he felt left out, so he rolled on the floor, sat up, and then realized everyone started laughing at his cuteness. He laughed too, looking around and realizing he had our attention. He figured that if it worked once, then twice would be better, so he repeated the same action, getting even heartier laughter. After T. J. tried his trick four times, his mom decided to stop it, or he would have lasted all afternoon.

When T. J. was nine months old, he was at the park with his mom and watching the other kids running around. He must have decided to try out this new trick himself. He pulled himself up from his sitting position and began running.

His mom called to him, shocked, to run back to her arms. He had missed that whole step of walking.

As the children came, one of the many roles I played was built-in babysitter. Danielle was pregnant again, and she craved ice cream. Not just any ice cream, but a chocolate dip cone. When Gary and she would head out in the evenings, I would bathe, read a story, and pray with Michael before putting him to bed. Many times we would sing, "Praise My Soul," the only hymn I had memorized from the installation of ROFM, mostly because I looked forward to becoming a full member with all my heart.

As Michael got a bit older, we would also play a game called "Name This Tune." I hummed a few notes from a hymn we sing, and he had to tell me the title or first words. If he guessed right, he hummed, and I guessed. Michael loved music. His mom played guitar, led worship music for the

Community, wrote many praise songs, and frequently sang as she worked around the home. When he ultimately chose a course of study and career, it was no surprise that it involved teaching music.

Shortly after T. J.'s birth, Gary and Danielle welcomed their second child, a little girl. Realizing they needed more space with a second child on the way, they had moved out of their room in Mabelle's house; the little family moved into the little house. Danielle spent the rest of her pregnancy scrubbing the walls, carpets, and windows, making the little house cleaner than it had ever been.

CHAPTER 25

Testing the Waters of Community

Then he said, "What is the kingdom of God like?
To what can I compare it? It is like a mustard
seed that a person took and planted in the garden.
When it was fully grown, it became a large bush
and 'the birds of the sky dwelt in its branches.'"
—Luke 13:18–19

During the summer, Bonnie Jean, a teacher in her thirties, contacted us. A native of central California, she had shared a personal dream with her Episcopal priest. She wanted to be a part of a Christian Community where a group of adults would live as described in the book of Acts. He suggested visiting our Community. "It already exists, and the Community is called the Olive Tree. This place is unique. I don't know how many are living there now, because the number of people who live there changes all the time. This place is just the place for you, Bonnie."

On the first day of her visit, I showed her where she would be sleeping: one more "girl" to add to our BRG collection. "I have never had a teacher as a roommate before," I said jokingly. "I hope I pass the test informing you of our rules and expectations."

Bonnie and I got along rather well since she was the same age as one of my older sisters. To make her feel part of the family, she received the opportunity to make dessert with me in the kitchen for dinner. She had never heard of Four-Layer Pistachio Dessert*, but since she loved to eat as well as bake, Bonnie was intrigued to learn a new recipe. On the other hand, I was more than happy to teach a teacher something new.

Bonnie spent the summer, participating in the usual kitchen duties: cooking, housecleaning chores, canning fruit, making jam—and completing all these tasks before lunch so that we could take the teenagers to the beach.

As the summer ended, Bonnie returned to teach at a school for troubled girls. But we kept in touch. She lived in an older part of Pasadena, in a lovely two-story home, divided into apartments. One time, five of us slept over when she invited us to the Hollywood Bowl to hear *The New World Symphony*, composed by Antonin Dvořák in 1893. During the stay at ROCF, Bonnie Jean only had a surface taste of Community life. When anyone visited with the intention of living with us or a desire to start a Community, as did Bonnie, that person never reached the depth of actually living the day-to-day workings of this lifestyle. Everyone who visited came with the glorious vision of a utopian Christian way of life.

Some would stay a month or two. Others moved out faster than they moved in. Bonnie Jean shared with me that when she left after the summer, she was certain that our lifestyle was too smothering for her.

We did not expect Bonnie Jean to return very soon.

CHAPTER 26

Permanent Vows

> I will pay my vows to the LORD
> In the presence of all his people.
> —Ps. 116:18

Six quick months had passed since I made my temporary vows, and I remained determined to take my permanent ones. Now it was up to the members to decide at their next meeting.

"Should we make a date?" asked Evelyn teasingly as the meeting ended.

It was the answer I was hoping for! My smile went from my face to my inmost being. We looked at the calendar for the next year to find a date. Like a wedding, it takes months of detailed preparation.

I called my mom and asked excitedly, "Mom! I have a date for my permanent vows. Do you think you will come?"

"I don't understand," Mom said, confused. "We thought you would straighten out and move on with your life."

I tried my best to explain to her why I wanted to stay. I was happy serving others in the Community. I cut most everyone's hair, cooked in the kitchen, cleaned house, helped with the troubled teens, and was like a nanny for the Community kids. It was an ideal life for me, someone who had no college degree, making a contribution to others. I had the feeling that living in the Community gave me the security of knowing I had a place to live and work for the rest of my life.

We set a date for my vows on June 10, 1979, at our Saint Raphael Episcopal Church. In the traditional Catholic orders, a woman wears a wedding gown to symbolize a virgin marrying Jesus as her spouse. I would have liked to wear a wedding gown, but the transformation I was looking forward to would be changing out of the brown habit into the blue habit of a permanent member of our order.

Two weeks before the ceremony, with invitations sent out to family and friends and programs printed, God had an unexpected surprise in store for our Community.

Darren had now lived with us for more than a year. As an attorney, he was able to aid the Community with many legal questions concerning its nonprofit status. To his own surprise, he grew close to the family through this process and began to deeply long to live our lifestyle. But he hadn't begun to verbalize this to even himself.

That evening Evelyn called an emergency meeting of the permanent members of the Community. "When Darren and I took a walk around the block after dinner, I asked him whether he had any thoughts or feelings about becoming a member of the Community. His response was an unspoken flood of tears, while nodding up and down profusely. I am going to ask Kata to make us a bowl of popcorn while you all think about this question."

Evelyn opened the door to the bedroom/meeting room. "Kata, would you please make us a bowl of popcorn with cups of water?"

"Right away," I called, knowing that with this request the members were in for a long night. The rest of us were watching a movie on television in the living room, eating popcorn. In about ten minutes I delivered a large bowl of popcorn, cups, and water to the meeting room. I only know what went on in the room because the story has been repeated hundreds of times, as are so many of the stories about the Community over the years.

After much silent prayer, there was much discussion over Darren's situation. He was a thirty-six-year-old established attorney. How would he handle taking vows of poverty (surrendering up all he owned to this Community), obedience (to the Community, rather than making his own decisions), and chastity (with several single women living with us)? Evelyn was insistent that it was the Lord's will for Darren to join the Community. There was a long pause in the room.

Then Gary came up with the best logical suggestion. "Well, I think if we can finish this giant bowl of popcorn within the next five minutes, we can determine that God wants Darren to become a temporary member."

Popcorn flew everywhere while hands dove furiously into the bowl to quickly empty it. From the living room we heard loud laughter.

Uncle Basil opened the door and called for Darren to enter the room.

Solemn-faced, he slowly got up and entered.

Thirty seconds later, the door opened, and Darren ran out of the meeting room, out the dining room door, and outside.

Evelyn and Danielle came rushing out and ran down the hall to the sewing room and back, carrying a man's brown habit.

Within less than two minutes, Darren knocked on the door and announced, "Don't think that the funny grin on my face signifies that my answer is yes."

We contacted the bishop the next day to add Darren's name to the list of those transferring into the Episcopal church and to the membership of the Community.

The warm June day of my vows was crazy, with preparations, transportation to and from the church, meals, reception, and much celebrating. Much of that day is a blur, except when the bishop laid his hands on my head, praying the blessing of the Holy Spirit; at that moment I once again felt God's *joy* fill me in a powerful way. I was now officially Episcopalian and a permanent member of the Community.

Evelyn and I decided beforehand that when I declared my desire to become a member of the Community and before I said my actual vows, she would take me into the sacristy to help change my habit from the brown temporary habit to the blue permanent habit, a practice of traditional orders. As soon as we came back out into the sanctuary, we sang in Spanish a lilting, beautiful song attributed to St. Francis:

> "My name is Francis.
> I used to run around the streets, wearing silks, expecting honor,
> But I have rejected all the riches for Lady Poverty,
> And my joy is in serving the Lord.
> I want to be a living example of the Gospel,
> Be completely abandoned in God's arms.
> I want to be like a child playing and sleeping
> While I am enveloped in the Father's love."

The only remembrance that I have of the reception was a photograph taken, probably by Danielle, of my mom and aunt sitting together in their long dresses, listening intently to Robert, who explaining something animatedly to them. Many of the older people who attended this service, including my mom and aunt, are now in heaven. I am so grateful for the photograph to remember them by.

CHAPTER 27

The Community Men
Work Together

Finally, brothers, rejoice. Mend your ways, encourage
one another, agree with one another, live in peace,
and the God of love and peace will be with you.
—2 Cor. 13:11

Once Darren became a member of the order, he became
an advocate for the men to pull together as a group. He felt
the women of the order had much more time to work and
serve together, while this was much more challenging for the
men, who had outside jobs and were gone all day long. He
organized a "First Annual Men's Breakfast." That Valentine's
Day the men got up on a Sunday morning to make breakfast
for the women. We all loved it so much it eventually turned
into an annual event every Valentine's Day dinner meal.

The men would meet in secret for weeks making
arrangements, keeping us ladies away from the kitchen.

The first dinner meal was most certainly saved by a moment during the day when Evelyn, forgetting the banishment, casually walked through the kitchen and noticed five *bulbs* of garlic on the cutting board.

Uncle Basil proudly shared that they were preparing Green Noodles Alfredo and the recipe called for five cloves of garlic.

Trying not to sound alarmed, she said calmly, "Basil, these are called bulbs, not cloves. Let me show you how much a clove is … This is one clove of garlic; just think how awful your dish would be if I had not walked through at this very moment to correct your mistake. Thank God I caught you before it was too late."

As things turned out, our dear men prepared enough Green Noodles Alfredo for a hundred people. Since we were only twenty, we ate the leftovers for several days. Every time the subject came up about the men cooking, this story was repeated—always.

Another year the men and boys chose to barbeque steaks for dinner. They had not expected the rain that came, but thanks to quick thinking, they assembled the grills under the open garage door, and dinner was a success. They always provided some sort of entertainment and decorated the dining room with flowers, hearts, streamers, and gift bags.

Another time they attempted some recipes from the television cooking show personalities by demonstrating a flaming shish kebab as entertainment. The problem was, the flames grew much higher than anticipated. It was a good thing we keep a fire extinguisher in the kitchen.

Through the many years of celebrations, our men enjoyed preparing and serving their annual Valentine's Dinner as much as we ladies appreciated the love and support *and* dinner show they would lovingly serve us.

CHAPTER 28

The Beginnings of a Spanish Ministry to Our Local Hispanic Population

He said to them, "Go into the whole world and
proclaim the gospel to every creature."
—Mark 16:15

Another idea Darren, a fluent Spanish speaker, brought to the Community was offering to teach a weekly Spanish class. There were about four or five of us with the desire to learn. I had often passed Mexican workers when I went on my daily walks and thought it would be nice to be able to carry on a conversation with them. We began the classes on Saturday mornings, when breakfast was a DYOT (Do Your Own Thing), so it did not interrupt anything.

As I began practicing my newly learned skills, I decided to try speaking to the Mexican gardener who worked for our neighbor. It was a cold and windy morning. I noticed he was only wearing a lightweight jacket, while I had a heavy-duty sweater keeping me warm. I walked over, introduced myself, and asked his name.

He said in slow, clear Spanish, "Mi nombre es Basilio."

I told him I was learning to speak Spanish, so asked if I might practice speaking with him.

He said he was happy to help.

Then I told him I had noticed his jacket, which was a very thin blazer. The weather was chilly that morning, so I offered him my thick sweater. Being a gentleman he told me he was all right, but when I told him I wanted to give my sweater to him, he took it, put it on, and was grateful to be warm.

Soon I began to put names to the faces of the Mexicans I met on my walks. Now, being a young, single woman, I did not see myself as attractive enough to garner any interest in anyone of the opposite gender, but I naively did not look at myself as the Mexicans saw me.

One day I left for my walk as usual. I saw Pedro, greeted him warmly, and asked him how his daughter, Aurelia, was. He handed me a folded-up piece of paper and waited for me to read it. I opened it up to see these words: "I look for wife, will you marri me?" I read it a second time to make sure this was not a joke. Then I replied in my best Spanish, "Yo soy una monja, no puedo casarme" (I am a nun, and cannot marry"). In truth I had no plans to marry, even though in our Community it might still be possible.

When I told Evelyn this story, I caught her anger. "I knew you would get in trouble. You just have to curb your flirting with anyone," she warned.

"I wasn't flirting; I just thought I was being friendly," I said, defending myself.

"It is all the same with Mexicans, or any man, as a matter of fact. Just stop!" Evelyn admonished.

This was another instance when my attempt to copy Evelyn, for she was always friendly with lots of men, did not work for me. Why was it all right for her to take walks around the block with Darren alone even though she was a married woman? I didn't understand it, but like many other things, I assumed if she said so, that made it all right.

When our Saturday Spanish classes ended, I wanted more, so I asked the Community if I could attend the classes offered at our nearby community college. I was already registered there, having taken music, voice, and other classes that interested me. My first instructor was from Spain. She made the class fun and easy to learn, and I realized I picked up her accent easily.

When that semester ended, I kept taking all the Spanish classes, and as an added practice, I stopped at a local taco shop to ask the owner if I could spend time practicing my Spanish with her. She was from Tijuana and had learned to speak English by watching American television. It was such fun speaking with her. In a short time, she had me waiting on customers. I took orders and made change, all in Spanish. In exchange for my work, I got a free lunch. In addition to this, instead of throwing out the chicken necks, wings, and giblets, they let me take them home to the Community for our soups. When no car was available for me to drive, I took the bus down to the taco shop, and Uncle Basil would pick me up with the free goodies from the taco shop, mainly chicken wings, necks, and innards that they never used in tacos.

When all the conversational classes finished, I started taking Spanish grammar classes to improve my Spanish. One of my instructors was a Caucasian woman this time, who spoke educated Spanish, which I was hoping to learn. The unique aspect about her was that she had five children of her own. After her husband passed away, she adopted twenty-seven Mexican children. I did not know all of the circumstances, but she shared that when she went down to Mexico for visits, there would be orphaned children begging in the streets. She felt so much compassion for the children, she wanted to give them a loving atmosphere in which to grow up. I would soon discover she lived around the block from me, and in the years to come, I'd get to know all her children by name.

CHAPTER 29

Adventures Thanks to a Priest Named Father Benedict

If there is any encouragement in Christ, any solace in love, any participation in the Spirit, any compassion and mercy, complete my joy by being of the same mind, with the same love, united in heart, thinking one thing.
—Phil. 2:1–2

In the beginning of 1980, we got a call from our bishop with this request: "We have a new priest working at the cathedral whose workload prevents him from visiting the elderly. Would you be able to come down once a week to help him?" The response to all requests Community members receive, even if it comes from the bishop, is always the same: "I will pray about it, check with the Community, and get back to you as soon as I can."

When Father Basil brought it up at our dinner table, Danielle spoke first. "I think it is a great opportunity for you."

Everyone agreed. But as always, Evelyn added, "I have a warning for you, Basil. When you get into situations where people compliment you on how wonderful you are, it boosts your ego so, and you become prideful of yourself."

Uncle Basil agreed that pride was a problem area in his life, but if anyone observed how well he communicated with the elderly, I would say he deserved the gratitude and praise for his sensitivity to their needs, not dire warnings of impending failure.

Then Evelyn came up with an idea to include herself with Father Basil. She knew a woman who had a psychiatry practice in San Poncho and offered to assist her with giving spiritual direction. She combined her visit with Father Basil's going down once a week to the cathedral and would have lunch with Father Basil and Father Benedict. Thus began a friendship that would last several years.

After Father Benedict worked at the cathedral for a few months, the bishop moved him to the Episcopal church in Buena Vista, our sister town. This meant Father Benedict would come to our house for his weekly lunchtime with Evelyn and Father Basil, and we could all get to know him.

One delightful memory I have with Father Benedict began when he mentioned he was going to attend a conference in San Francisco. A well-known Catholic priest, Henri Nouwen, would be the main speaker. The Community agreed to send some of us.

One foggy spring morning, Poppa, Evelyn, her longtime best friend, Betsy, Darren, Father Benedict, and I packed our large van. We planned to drive up the freeway that runs north through our state's Central Valley, which at this time of year contained fog so thick it was difficult just seeing the road in front of you. I was particularly frightened after hearing a traffic report that just north of us was a fifteen-car accident. I was so grateful that Poppa drove most of the way. He was an expert driver in difficult situations.

We arrived safely and settled in for the conference. The first evening the service began with evening prayer, but not like we have it in Community nor in the normal church setting. This was High Mass evening prayer, with the bishop wearing cope and mitre, plus incense, choir, and a myriad of several priests and servers. I loved every moment.

After evening prayer when most everyone left, the sacristan gave us a personal tour. He told us the history of the building and the significance of the side chapel and the stained glass rose window. He said the best time to see the magnificence of the window was in the early morning, when the sunlight started shining through each pane of glass. "It is as if it is coming alive," he told us with delight. "Sometimes we have had visitors spend the night just to see the window in the morning."

Evelyn got very excited about the aspect of spending the night in the cathedral and asked if we could.

"Absolutely, you may spend the night, but we will have to lock you in. You will not regret it."

Not all of us expressed interest in sleeping on a hard cement floor, but Father Benedict, Betsy, Evelyn, and I were more than ready to spend the night. What a strange feeling to hear the keys jingle as the sacristan locked the gate. It got very still. Only the small red light shone over the tabernacle, which assured us that Jesus was fully present with us.

I think I slept some but awoke around four o'clock, before anyone else. I found the restroom and the door to the main sanctuary, where I found the bishop's throne, so I figured that if I sat anywhere, I might as well sit in the best seat in the house. I recalled all the people, sounds, and smells that still lingered from several hours earlier. The window was dark, but I sat there wrapped in my sleeping bag, waiting for that moment when the first ray of light came through the glass.

Then to my right I heard a rustling. First Evelyn arrived, then Betsy, and finally Father Benedict. Evelyn went to the pulpit, Father Benedict to the altar, and Betsy sat in the pew, to represent the congregation.

Evelyn said, "Kata, you sing something to get started, I will preach, Benedict can consecrate, and Betsy can pray."

I sang the aria "Oh Thou That Tellest Good Tidings to Zion" from Handel's *Messiah*, a song I sang as my first piece of music for my voice class. I chose it because I loved the words and music—and afterward my instructor informed me that it was a very difficult piece to sing. Evelyn preached. "Jesus is Lord!" Father Benedict proceeded to consecrate a pretend chalice and hosts, while Betsy sat in devout prayer, and then the sun started to shine through the window, and we were all transfixed as the glass indeed shimmered with light and came alive. To this day it remains one of the most beautiful experiences of my life.

The next evening, before Henri Nouwen's talk, Father Benedict picked a Chinese restaurant for dinner. Much of the food was for me a delicious adventure. Shortly afterward, Evelyn said she did not feel too well. She became violently ill, and we realized she had an allergic reaction to the MSG that the restaurant added to the food. (We all forgot to ask about that since we knew of this allergy.) Fortunately, the sacristan found a separate room for her and would do whatever he could do to make her comfortable while the rest of us went to the conference.

Father Nouwen talked about his experiences living in a community. Father Basil and I caught each other's eyes in agreement at the similarities of our lives. After Father Nouwen's sharing, a line formed for people to greet him. I decided I *had* to go up. I was not sure what I would say, but I knew I needed to meet him.

When it was my turn, I shared a few sentences about our order (I was in my habit) and said I hoped he could meet the mother of our community, but that she was gravely ill due to something she ate. Dear reader, are you getting the picture now of my devotion to Evelyn? Several times in my life when I recalled my words to this world-famous author and speaker, it struck me that what was most important to me was talking about Evelyn. I held her in more esteem than this well-known, kind, humble priest.

"I would love to meet your mother; I will be praying she recovers quickly. What is her name?" Father Nouwen asked.

I went back to my group, feeling so privileged to have this connection with him. I became even more determined that Evelyn had to meet him. By the last talk of the conference, Evelyn felt well enough to attend, although she was still very weak and pale. I told her about the encounter with Father Nouwen, and when the line formed, I was as close to the front as possible. "Father Nouwen, this is the mother of our community," I said with obvious pride. In all sensitivity, he remembered from the night before, and asked how she was feeling. After a few words, we said thank you and went on our way.

I had arranged to have my uncle Ray, who lived with my aunt Norma (my mom's older sister) since 1945, pick me up on the steps of the cathedral after the conference so I could spend a couple of days with them. So happy to see me, my uncle drove as fast as a teenager and took me through all the sights in San Francisco in one hour. My aunt never got her driver's license, but she knew how to navigate San Francisco through the bus system perfectly. She took me to the Museum of Art.

I returned home by train the following day. I do believe my favorite means to travel is the train. You can get up when you want, eat in the dining car, or go to the upper-level lounge to see the coastline. I find it so much more comfortable and relaxing.

In June 1980 Gary and Danielle shared at the dinner table that they had a surprise announcement for the family. They were having another baby! They had not planned on getting pregnant so soon after their second child; the "normal" procedure in our Community was to plan ahead and ask permission to have a baby. God had a very special plan for this child though.

"Kata, Danielle and I would like to talk to you after dinner, if you are available," said Gary seriously yet with a very slight grin.

"Sure, as soon as I am done with cleanup," I responded.

About a half hour later, I knocked on their door, was welcomed in, and sat on the floor. I tried to think of anything I might have done wrong during the day, because usually when I was talked to privately, I was in trouble for something.

"We wanted to ask you to be the godmother of this baby!" Gary said.

I began to cry. I had no idea how to be a godmother but would be the best I could be. Immediately I went over to Danielle's belly and patted it, telling the baby that I would always love it. I did this every day of the pregnancy.

On December 20, 1980, Charity was born, healthy, happy, and my very own goddaughter. I was more fortunate than other godparents because I lived with my goddaughter, so I had contact with her every day.

A month after her birth, we had her baptism in our living room at the Community. We had a full house with Danielle's sister and brothers and her mom, besides all of us. The memorable moment for me was after Charity's baptism; while I held her in my arms admiring her, Danielle's mom came over and said, "Now, you take good care of our girl."

"I will; that's certain," I replied, smiling.

I tried to teach her Spanish by speaking only Spanish since I was studying it at the college. By the time she really started speaking, my Spanish was not fluent enough to keep up with her rapidly growing vocabulary in English, and so I gave up except for a few words. On Sundays, when we had church, at that time in the living room, I would be in charge of Charity while her mom played guitar and led the singing. Charity would begin to cry for her mom. I would get up to leave every time she started to cry until she got the picture that if she didn't cry, she could stay and see her mom from across the room.

CHAPTER 30

Jesus Has No Borders

Do not neglect hospitality, for through it some
have unknowingly entertained angels.
—Heb. 13:2

A new chapter in our Community was about to begin. Even
though not all of us were Spanish speakers, we sensed God
calling us to reach out to those around us in the Hispanic
community.

As it happened Bonnie Jean finished her contract with
the school where she taught. Her landlord wanted her
apartment, so while trying to seek God's will, she came
down for another visit. She said she was shocked to find
out that Darren and I had made our permanent vows to the
Community. While she stayed with us for a time, she found
a job teaching English as a second language at a high school
in the evenings. She has a gift for teaching and is smart;
she has a way of making learning fun and easy enough

so everyone can learn. For example, as a way to help the students learn new vocabulary, she brought props, such as a large bowl of different fruits. Dressing up in costumes to represent occupations, she took me along once to help teach the students new songs.

As Bonnie Jean flourished, Evelyn churned with ideas on how to incorporate a ministry using Bonnie Jean's students as a beginning for an outreach. How about using the play Evelyn and Danielle wrote several years previously, translate most of it into Spanish, and then invite the students to come to attend? During refreshments and visiting, we would ask them to come back the following week for Bible study.

Evelyn continued, "We would need a place. How about using that little house behind Father Benedict's church, which is available in the evenings?" Not everyone in the Community seemed ready to jump on this idea. It would take commitment on all our parts, Spanish speakers or not, but no one had a "check" as we went to prayer, so we continued to follow this new direction of our ministry.

When presented with the idea, Father Benedict liked it, but the vestry would have to approve the venture. He would do his best. Bonnie Jean would also have to get approval from the school board to move class that night from the school to the church.

Many of Bonnie Jean's Hispanic students showed up whispering that they did not know what to expect from all these *gabachos* (which was the kinder word for *gringos*). We brought homemade cookies and served coffee. Darren explained a little about the Community, such as who lived there, what our purpose was for living together, and how God met all our needs. He concluded by extending an invitation to all who were able to come the next week for a Bible-based talk, sharing, and of course refreshments. All were welcome.

We were elated with the response from all those who came and looked forward to the following week to see how many would show up.

The following Friday we brought plenty of cookies—after all, I made them! Yet after half an hour, no one had showed up. Forty-five minutes passed. For an hour we waited, prayed, and thanked God, knowing we were doing God's will. Undeterred, we drove home, praising and glorifying God all the way.

The next Friday, we gathered again as planned. Would anyone come? Then there was a soft knock at the door.

"Hola. Como se llama?" (Hi. What is your name?), Evelyn said, jumping up from the sofa. His name was Isidro, and he was one of Bonnie Jean's students. Poor man—he was the only one who showed up, so he got the full attention.

We must not have frightened him off because he returned the next Friday, bringing friends—a father and son. He explained that the father, Benito, had a miracle to share with us. He was working on a farm in Michigan when he fell and a tractor ran over him, crushing his back. He prayed, "Lord, if you want me to live, please, let me walk again." God answered his prayers, even allowing him to return to Mexico to be with his family.

Every Friday night for I do not recall how long, we continued this ministry, and every Friday night we stopped by the Doughnut Corner to buy doughnuts for Saturday morning, sponsored by Aunt Freda, Uncle Basil's great-aunt, who had moved to live closer to us.

Friday nights in the van on the way, my entertainment was listening in on Darren and Evelyn having a conversation in Spanish. They knew I listened. They thought it was cute the way I tried intently to pretend that I was not eavesdropping. Occasionally, if someone did not have a ride, we would go by his or her home to pick him or her up. Sometimes that "home" was no more than a part of a garage, or worse. It was heartrending to see their living conditions.

As word of our outreach grew, we met other Hispanics, particularly a woman who became everyone's mother, Doña Ema. She was from El Salvador and living with her son's family and her nephew Edwardo, who attended Bonnie Jean's class. Doña is a courtesy title given out of great respect. She carried herself with a sense of old royalty from Spain, coupled with an equal amount of humility. She came from a war-torn country, where Edwardo had to dodge bullets as he walked and ran to school each day. One time she came to the Community for a visit, and when waking up the path to her car, noticed our century plant in bloom. "May we please cut the blooms from some of your plants?"

We wondered what she would do with such large blossoms and asked her.

"We eat them, and they are particularly delicious cooked with scrambled eggs."

We were eager to learn some of Ema's cooking recipes and, with her, planned a surprise birthday dinner for Evelyn on the upcoming Friday night. Evelyn was leaving to attend a two-day church gathering, so it was a perfect time to bring Ema over to help us make tamales.

Under her able tutorage, we learned that El Salvador tamales are an all-day event. They are nothing like Mexican tamales. Hers had many more unique fillings and were wrapped in whatever was handy. Since we could not find banana leaves, Ema told us to use aluminum foil. I confess I loved these tamales because they were so moist.

Our plan to get them to the Friday group was to put them in the electric oven and hide it in the back of the van while we drove over to the church. Darren would distract Evelyn so we could bring in the stuff. But on the way over to the church, Darren hit a bump, and we heard the lid jump off the pan. There was no missing the smell. Fortunately, if Evelyn smelled the aroma, she gave no hint.

When we arrived Darren took Evelyn around to the back to show her something, as all the men inside ran out the front door to set up the "party." We finished just as Darren brought Evelyn back in.

The surprise worked perfectly, and we all thoroughly enjoyed ourselves. Our Hispanic ministry was alive and flourishing.

CHAPTER 31

Opening Our Arms and Home

"For I was hungry and you gave me food, I was thirsty and you gave me drink, a stranger and you welcomed me, naked and you clothed me, ill and you cared for me, in prison and you visited me." Then the righteous will answer him and say, "Lord, when did we see you hungry and feed you, or thirsty and give you drink? When did we see you a stranger and welcome you, or naked and clothe you? When did we see you ill or in prison, and visit you?" And the king will say to them in reply, "Amen, I say to you, whatever you did for one of these least brothers of mine, you did for me."
—Matt. 25:35–40

Several Hispanic men from Bonnie Jean's English as a second-language class began to attend our Sunday service, with Darren translating most of it into Spanish. Danielle only needed to hear a melody once to memorize it and pick up the melody to play. Thus, she learned several new songs and choruses in Spanish to add to her collection of worship music. We sang, danced, and praised the Lord each Sunday with our new friends.

We soon discovered our meals were, to be polite, very bland for them. We would usually serve an easy-to-plan menu following church, usually oven-baked burritos, fruit, and potato chips. Salsa for us was chopped tomatoes, onions, and one chopped chili pepper. To make our burritos spicier, we made sure we had Tabasco sauce alongside the ketchup at the table.

South Americans from El Salvador, Argentina, and Columbia, as well as people from different parts of Mexico attended our services, and we all learned from one another. One man from Columbia stands out in my memory because his way was always the correct way or manner of saying something. Jorge was a student in the ESL class and he learned English faster than the other students, so he felt it was his responsibility to correct the other students if they mispronounced an English word. This prevented him from making too many friends.

One day we got a call from the hospital with the sad news that he had been in an accident at work. The truck he had been driving collided with a crane, which hit an electric cable, causing a powerful current of electricity to flow through the crane to the truck. He was in the burn unit recovering slowly.

Bonnie Jean and I went down to see him—this man who only a week earlier was scolding me for saying a word in

Spanish with a double meaning and also advised me, "Never use this word; it means ####." (To this day I never use that expression when I speak Spanish.) When we found his room, we saw a changed man, quietly sitting reading the Bible we gave him. He believed God had saved his life that day in the truck. "Do you think God has a plan for me?" he asked.

Bonnie answered, "Absolutely God has some sort of plan for you; there is no other explanation for how you survived such a terrible accident."

His healing took many weeks, due to a severe infection he contracted in his foot. He had a relative living in the area who took him in so he could continue healing. When he was able to drive, he began to come on Sundays to our bilingual church services. He knew God loved him by the miracle of keeping him alive through such an almost impossible time. While he was hospitalized, the Lord provided him several Christian nurses who guided him both physically and spiritually in his new life. He went from a proud, arrogant man to a kind and thoughtful brother.

The director of social services from the hospital called about a Spanish-speaking patient who had cancer and needed a place to stay while he received treatment. Evelyn went to visit Alfredo in the hospital to meet him. At the same time, she met another young man, Lazaro, who lay in bed with both legs amputated. She asked the nurse about him and his story. The nurse explained that while running away from the immigration department, he tripped on the tracks and the train ran over his legs. She invited both men to come live with us for an undetermined amount of time. With their multiple medical needs for doctors, treatments, and therapy, I seemed to be the best person to go as a translator.

This time of my life was definitely challenging for me because of my limited Spanish in terms of translating medical terms and physical feelings. With Lazaro, I had to work with the prosthetic doctor, something I knew nothing about, so Lazaro lost his patience with me often. I did not understand how to communicate what he was feeling in the adjustments of his leg stumps. He had to take his pants off with me in the room while talking to the doctor. It was embarrassing for both of us, but it had to be done. The very same situation occurred when I took Alfredo to his doctor. With prostate cancer, the poor man had to be very vulnerable.

After a few months, Lazaro asked me one afternoon if I would have time to talk to him. We walked out to the garden—yes, walked. He had progressed so well with the prosthetics, he did not even need a cane. "You have helped me so much; I am so grateful to you. Would you marry me?"

This was all in Spanish, but I knew very well how to respond; I just needed God to give me the correct words to say. I thanked him for his kind offer but told him I was committed to the Community, just like a marriage; I could not have another life.

He was so embarrassed that within a week or so, he called friends of his to help him move out.

With Lazaro gone, Alfredo and I played games, took walks around the block every day, and discussed the Bible at the toadstool table that was outside the little house, a safe place to talk out in the open. We spent hours discussing, arguing, and pouring over scriptures for answers to his misunderstandings. Our conversations would get very heated at times, but in all, there grew a deep friendship. I had no suspicion whatsoever of his feelings for me other than those of a friend or father figure. He was an honorable married man with grown children down in Mexico.

One Alfredo story that touched all of us occurred on New Year's Eve. This was Alfredo's first time to celebrate New Year's Eve with us in the Community. Our celebrations were very different from any others; we adults gathered in the living room when the children were asleep. There were an abundance of savory and sweet snacks spread out on the table for people to serve themselves. Everyone sat around the living room eating and preparing to share how the Lord had worked in his or her life throughout the year. The New Year's before, we'd each gotten a Bible verse. Each December 31 some of us gathered in the kitchen with Bibles, packs of verses from daily devotionals, and the chosen method of hiding them in something. One time it might be hollow walnuts, glued back together with the verse inside, or balloons with the verse inside and blown up.

Alfredo was starting to believe that God was at work in his life. Because of the chemotherapy, his hair was falling out, so he said jokingly, "I want my verse to say that God will give me hair." We all laughed until he drew his walnut and cracked it open to read: "Turn your eyes away, for they overpower me. Your hair falls in waves, like a flock of goats winding down the slopes of Gilead" (Song of Solomon 6:2).

We sat with our mouths open and tears running down our cheeks, and as Darren translated, Alfredo's whole body shook from crying.

Tragically a few months later, he received a phone call from one of his sons, communicating that his wife was accidentally electrocuted in the house during a lightning storm. She had been ironing shirts, and the lightning hit the antenna and traveled through the lines through the house and her iron. Alfredo arranged to go down to Mexico to be with his family during the time of sorrow. He would find his own way back again to finish his treatments. We did not ask how or when he would return to our home, but we knew he would be able to face his family sorrow with his newfound deepening faith.

Through all this Hispanic outreach, I was getting increasingly exhausted. Sundays were especially taxing. I was getting up early to help set up for breakfast, help with cleanup, and set up for lunch, without knowing how many people we would be. Then came our church service, which became twice as long due to the need to translate everything. We made sure our guests were entertained while we set up for lunch by chatting in the living room. After eating there still was cleanup. Our guests, who in their culture were used to women doing the kitchen work, noticed that in our house the men and the women worked together in the kitchen. They began to follow the example of our men, joining in. After lunch the family members with young children disappeared into their rooms for naps, which left those of us who spoke Spanish to entertain our guests.

In Hispanic culture, Sundays were days off to relax all day, which meant talking, eating, and drinking beer. We played games, walked around the block, ate cookies, and talked into the afternoon. When they noticed we ran out of things to talk about, they eventually left our house to go somewhere else. These days were fulfilling but also physically and emotionally draining. Not only was this ministry tiring, but negative tension was building at home too.

CHAPTER 32

Dark Times

If we say, "We have fellowship with him,"
while we continue to walk in darkness,
we lie and do not act in truth.
—1 John 1:6

Behind closed doors Poppa's and Evelyn's shouting voices and slamming doors could be heard at all hours of the day and night. This had happened occasionally before, but now was occurring more and more frequently. Their disagreement went on for several days. Our breakfast table conversations were uncharacteristically silent. I could see Evelyn had been crying, as her eyes were puffy and her face red. Nobody dared ask any questions, afraid of what kind of response they would receive.

During one cleanup, Bonnie Jean asked me what was going on. After all, I was a Community member; I should have the inside information. I thought, *Even if I did know, which*

I do not, if the Community wanted it public, they would share it for everyone to hear. I asked Uncle Basil if he knew, but he told me he was not at liberty to share. Clearly something was going on with Poppa and Evelyn.

Meetings with a few of the Community members went on for several nights. Some of us were watching television in the living room when we heard muffled shouting. With Evelyn crying loudly, Poppa walked out the dining room door. Dee, Darren, and Uncle Basil walked into the living room to make the announcement. Uncle Basil said, "We have some sad news. Could you please turn off the television? Poppa has decided to leave the Community. We tried every way to help him with his anger issues, but he refuses to face his problems. He will move out soon." That was it … spoken directly as fact, with no other resolution.

It hit me like a ton of bricks. I was so sad. Poppa was like a dad to me, and we had such a good time taking the ballroom class at the college together. What had happened?

Then I switched to Evelyn, poor mother—must feel like the end of the world for her. My sympathies immediately stayed with her. *What did* he *do to her?* By this time I was so emotionally connected to Evelyn that whenever she went through a difficult time, I asked God to pass her pain to me. "After all," I reasoned, "I am not married, I have no children or grandchildren; let me instead of her have her pain."

On the third day after this announcement, with Evelyn having remained in her room alone, unreachable, we heard Danielle shouting outside. She sat on the step outside the door that was outside Evelyn's bedroom. "I do not care what you say; I am not leaving this step until you let me in. This is Community for you. I am here, and we have not let you down. If I have to stay out here all day and night, I will not leave." Eventually Evelyn let Danielle and Dee in her bedroom and back into her life; the healing process was beginning.

Poppa left the Community with his clothes, some money, and one of the Community cars. He was headed up to Central California, where our bishop had invited him to spend some time at the conference center. It was a somber day when he left. The order was only three years old, and already one of the founders was gone.

The weeks following were a blur. Thanksgiving, Advent, Christmas, and New Years were all overshadowed with the deep sadness of Poppa leaving. His leaving was so unexpected. What had really happened? There were so many unanswered questions that stayed unanswered for many years. I had hoped things could be worked out, but Evelyn convinced us he would never change. Sadly we took her word for that and never questioned this. Darren became a strong support for Evelyn while she endured the loss of her husband of twenty-three years. She told us several times the pain was like open-heart surgery.

The divorce was a blow to so many who knew them, including their three biological children, grandchildren, Community members, friends, and everyone associated with our Community. Several people did not understand why a Community whose vows to God were meant to be permanent, to live out the gospel as a Christian family, could choose such a drastic action as divorce. When people asked me, "How could this happen to such a wonderful family?" I could only repeat what we all said: "Poppa would not control his anger and did not want to change." How I hated to say this excuse.

It wasn't until years later that I realized how shallow this answer was. It takes two people to make a good marriage. It also takes both parties to ruin a marriage by divorce. But once again, my emotions were directed by Evelyn and her hold over me. Carrying on with a happy face while going through this hell was so difficult. My heart was broken with grief. Nevertheless, carry on we did.

Having our Friday night group gave us a purpose, but the divorce put a black cloud over our relationship with Father Benedict. Unfortunately our friendship became strained because not only did he disapprove of the divorce, but also at the same time, Bonnie Jean's ESL classes came to an end, which meant we no longer needed the room at his church.

What was happening? Why? These questions lingered in the air. I held on to the hope that things would get better. I took my Community vows seriously. They were vows for life, as in a marriage. Only death should separate us. Now there was this unexpected hole in the path. Even in practical things I wondered, *Who will do the house repairs? Who will do the bookkeeping? Who will be the poppa?*

Evelyn slowly recovered from her emotionally distraught state and joined back into our lives as mother. We all prayed for her recovery daily. Darren was able to coax her from her room for walks.

I was determined to do anything to make her happy. "Kata, would you bring me a cup of coffee? Kata, what happened to that batch of cookies you made? They tasted so good with my coffee." Anything, no matter how mundane or interrupting to my day, I did to please her. All I could think of was that it was my job to do everything to please her so she would mentally and physically come back to us.

In the midst of my sadness, there was one bright moment of joy for me. Praise the Lord. I became a godmother! Never in my wildest imaginings could I have known I would feel this bond with a little girl as precious as Charity Marie. I couldn't wait to go to the hospital to catch a glimpse of my goddaughter. The minute Gary showed me which bassinet she was in, I was so amazed. I fell in love.

When Danielle came home and put her in my arms for the first time, I thought I would burst. I had no idea what being a god-ma meant, but the feelings I had were so powerful they would overwhelm me with joy. From the first week she was born, I began to carry her around the yard, teaching her the names of all the animals and plants, but I used the Spanish words, such as, "Donde está la Luna?" "Where is the moon?"

"Now you take good care of our girl there—she is a precious gift," her grandmother Carol said to me as I held Charity in my arms after her baptism. I took my promise seriously when I said I would do my part to be in the child's life, in the spiritual upbringing of the newly baptized.

With all the emotional swings I was experiencing, I had no inkling as to what the New Year was to bring. Looking back, I saw God was giving me hints. I should have seen them, but I did not. Something was about to surprise and shock us all.

CHAPTER 33

New Leadership

Remember your leaders who spoke the word
of God to you. Consider the outcome of
their way of life and imitate their faith.
—Heb. 13:7

It was very late on a spring evening when all the Community members received a knock at their bedroom doors with a request to please come into the living room for a special announcement.

That was when Darren and Evelyn announced their engagement. I was shocked—as were the rest of the Community. I remember thinking, *I knew they had a special relationship. I could see they shared a common love of Spanish. They did seem to spend a lot of time together.* But the timing of this so soon after Poppa's leaving seemed very unseemly. Nevertheless, my emotional ties to Evelyn were so strong, and seeing her smile for the first time in weeks, I chose to accept this at face value.

I felt protective of Evelyn. I craved her love and acceptance so much I wanted to warn Darren that he had better treat her better than the way she was treated before. What a conflicted emotional tie I had to Evelyn! It really was a love /hate relationship. When she praised me, I felt loved. When she scolded me, I felt I deserved it. Whenever she yelled I shouted inside to myself, "You are so stupid, Kata! Won't you ever learn?" I dared not challenge this engagement announcement, even though I did not understand it.

How on earth we were going to explain the timing of this engagement to others became an issue we discussed that night. Darren and Evelyn told us that Poppa's anger issues were the problem. It was his decision to file for divorce and leave the Community. Therefore, Evelyn was free to marry.

It was difficult for our associates, family members outside the Community, fellow priests in the diocese, and other friends to understand how Evelyn could get married so quickly after her separation. Some did not believe that Poppa could be as angry as we described him. In public gatherings he was kind, friendly, funny, and soft-spoken. Their picture of who he was simply did not jibe with our story. We received letters with grievances, and several of our associates returned medals they'd received from our Community when they became associates, breaking all ties with us.

We believed we were doing God's will and that over time, things would settle down with everyone's concerns.

Clearly, we had rationalized our position. The timing of this upcoming marriage was simply too quick. In 1979 the turmoil in the marriage escalated into daily disagreements. By the end of 1980, Poppa was gone. Just a few months into 1981, Darren proposed, and by the end of summer, Darren and Evelyn were married.

After Darren and Evelyn returned from their short honeymoon, life in the Community continued. Visitors came to see how Community worked, and everyone went back to their usual chores. Tony and Valerie moved to Northern California following a job transfer. One tragic development from her divorce and subsequent marriage was that Evelyn's other two grown children cut off any communications between them. They could not condone her kicking out their father and marrying so soon after to someone almost their same age (Darren was eleven years younger than Evelyn). This meant she would have no relationship with her grandchildren, with whom she had spent so much time and energy securing a relationship. This must have been difficult, but Evelyn had a new life and new family in marrying Darren.

In the worldview, Evelyn married up. Darren came from a well-to-do family and was the son of a judge. His mother was a respected retired educator, his brother a dentist. Poppa, a navy veteran, never progressed beyond a high school diploma. By contrast, Darren earned his Juris Doctor and was a Vietnam vet who worked as a judge advocate. With credit to Jane Austin, she was "very fortunate in her catch."

I remained confused, with feelings I couldn't resolve but dared not verbalize. Some people when they lose a spouse in death or divorce never recover from the loss. I know my mom did not. Yet here was Evelyn, clearly overjoyed with her new upscale lifestyle, family, and status that marriage to an attorney brings. I could not understand how she so quickly moved from Poppa to Darren in her allegiance. Only years later did I learn so many others in the Community were experiencing the exact same thoughts.

During this time our Hispanic outreach continued. Several men became regulars at our Sunday service. One young man who visited us from Cuernavaca, Mexico, was named Mario. He was a man of many talents, with a trade-school education in Mexico, and he caught on quickly to the English language. Eventually he asked to be baptized. Darren and Evelyn were thrilled when he asked them to be his godparents. He and his mom lived with his aunt in Buena Vista, in a small trailer in the back of the yard. About fifteen relatives lived on that one acreage, but like many people living here illegally, they were glad to have a roof over their head. This Mario was to have major implications for my life and that of the Community, but I had no idea of that at this point in time.

CHAPTER 34

An International Food Journey

So whether you eat or drink, or whatever you
do, do everything for the glory of God.
—1 Cor. 10:31

Over the years we had visitors from not only Hispanic countries but from many other continents as well. Each time a visitor from another country spent time with us, Evelyn would ask, "We shared our meal with you tonight. We hope you will cook a meal from your country before you leave. Talk to the kitchen girls to plan a menu so they can buy the ingredients you need. Or perhaps, you could go shopping with them." Her ideas for us were typically this spontaneous. She would volunteer one of us in our presence. Thus, we felt obligated to agree to her plans even if we had to change our own family activities.

One time we had a missionary visiting from India. He was happy to cook a meal for us. He said when we got to the store he would buy what was needed. Danielle and I went with him to the local Indian market. He walked in, greeted the proprietor in his own language, and asked where he could find the ingredients he needed for certain dishes. I learned more about India that day than at any time in my life. He passed on so much interesting information to Danielle and me that we were on overload with facts about Indian languages, food, and even knowing what part of India someone was from by the color of his or her skin. To this day I recall this lesson and am able to distinguish between someone from Kashmir and Bangalore. "The store owner is from Bangalore. I could tell by his dark skin, his accent, and he smelled like fish; the district is a fishing district." The next day I began helping him in the kitchen right after morning prayer; we worked until lunchtime. We cooked together for six hours until Danielle gave me a break for about an hour, and then I returned to work until dinner, when we served all eight dishes. A few of the dishes were too spicy for some family members, but everyone ate the bread called Naan. All the hard work was a delicious success.

Once, a South African bishop visited. He had a long, tiring week traveling from city to city, meeting many people, and raising funds for his home diocese. Evelyn could tell he was tired, so she caught my eye. Motioning in our own private communication, her gestures said, "How about offering the bishop to take a nap on your bed?" I motioned in the affirmative.

"Bishop, we have a small room at the end of the hallway. Would you like to take a nap there before you have to leave?" asked Evelyn.

"That would be very kind if I am not causing any trouble for anyone," the bishop replied.

"Kata, show him where he can sleep," said Evelyn.

"Just come this way, Bishop, but I must let you know, this is a water bed. Have you ever slept on one?"

"To be honest, I have not. There is always a first time for everything," responded the bishop.

"I hope you feel comfortable. Here is a blanket, so enjoy."

After I closed the door and walked down the hall to the living room where a few of the family still sat, I said, "Well, now I can tell people I had a bishop sleep in my bed!"

"Leave it to Kata to think of that!" commented Evelyn.

Another time Evelyn suggested that Mabelle's friend Rose, who was Chinese, come and cook one of her favorite native meals. The day was set, and we offered to buy what she needed. But she declined the offer, saying she could take care of that for us. Normally when we prepare a meal for everyone, we may spend a couple of hours from start to finish in preparing a casserole for dinner. In the morning we do all the preparations and put the casserole in the refrigerator so that the afternoon is free for naps, reading, or housecleaning. This was our expectation when we came into the kitchen to help Rose with the meal.

We began working in the kitchen right after 9:00 a.m. prayers and continued until it was time to set the dinner table. It took so long because each dish had to be chopped, sliced, or grated evenly, and we also had to learn the story behind each dish. We began with great enthusiasm, but after three hours, we started to get tired. We soldiered on until dinner, however, and were all glad when it was time to sit down to eat.

"My mother makes the best enchiladas I have ever eaten," boasted Mario one Sunday at the lunch table after eating our oven-baked store-bought burritos.

"I do not believe you. How can I know they are the best unless I taste them for myself?" exclaimed Evelyn. This was her open door for another project for the kitchen crew.

Fortunately for us, Mario brought his mom the next Sunday, with enchiladas premade the day before; all we had to do was heat them up. We had to agree they were a delicious treat for everyone.

CHAPTER 35

Dirty Secret

Oh what a tangled web we weave,
When first we practice to deceive!
—Sir Walter Scott, *Marmion*, Canto VI. Stanza 17.
Scottish author and novelist (1771–832)
(c) 1994–2015 QuotationsPage.com and
Michael Moncur. All rights reserved.

Each person is tempted when he or she turns away
By his or her own evil desire and enticed.
—James 1:14

You might expect a marriage proposal would bring me great joy. But not when the engagement is stained with sin.

More and more often, Mario would come to Sunday church and linger for the rest of the day. Although he was invited to join his friends when they left, he often declined, stating, "I want to stay and play a game with Bonnie Jean and Kata."

When Evelyn found out that Mario's mother was moving back down to Mexico, she wondered whether she might become his American mother, asking him, "Why not move in here, so you have family?"

Mario's current living situation was far from ideal. Moving into the Community would be a palace in comparison to the minimal arrangement he lived in with his aunt. Evelyn asked the Community at the dinner table if anyone had a "check" on inviting Mario to come live with us. No one had a check, but questions did come up about whether it was legal. He was, after all, an undocumented Mexican worker. We had felt a moral compunction at times in the past to assist Hispanics with major medical needs. But Mario was a capable, functional adult, albeit an illegal alien. Were we breaking any laws by having Mario live with us? Darren checked into the immigration laws and discovered that as long as there was no exchange of money, no law was broken. If he got picked up by immigration, we could not provide means for him to return back into our country.

We were safe from any lawbreaking, or so I thought. I had no idea nor do I believe anyone else realized Mario had something else in mind when he moved in, and it would involve much more serious lawbreaking—breaking God's laws.

On August 3, 1983, Evelyn called me from the bedroom to come in to talk. I had no clue what the subject of her request was until I saw Mario in the room with both Darren and Evelyn. I shivered inside for fear we had said or done something inappropriate. "Mario wants to ask you something," stated Evelyn calmly.

Haltingly he asked me, "Would you marry me?"

I said yes before asking myself deep down whether I was in love with him. I so wanted to be married, and Mario was my best offer. When we walked out of the room, we shared the news, and everyone seemed happy for us. The next journey in my life began as a woman engaged to an illegal Hispanic. I never would have thought my life would take this turn. But by being married, Mario could become a legal resident. About every other month, Mario would be picked up by the immigration officers and transported back to Mexico. We would get short phone calls saying where he was, and he would make a guess as to the time he would be home. We went on dates, walked around the block, played board games, doing all the right things, enjoying my engagement. I was very content.

My engagement ring came from Mabelle, whose husband mined the rock himself in Julian (in Mexico) several decades earlier. It was a lilac amethyst set in a silver ring.

Evelyn asked if I had thought of what kind of gown I would like to wear.

I replied, "I had always wanted to wear my mother's wedding dress if she had one, but during World War II, that was impossible."

"Why don't you wear mine? I am certain we can make the alterations," offered Evelyn. It was settled; I would wear not only Evelyn's gown but her tiara and veil as well.

I have to confess I am embarrassed at this recollection. I lied to her. I was trying to figure out what would please Evelyn the most. That was my whole motive for the answer I gave her.

The holidays that year were more of a delight to me, for I had a man now to shop for just like the married women in the Community. Bonnie Jean, our other single adult woman, had recently left for Panama City, having accepted an offer from her missionary friends to assist the manager of an orphanage there.

Then came my journey down a very dark path. My bedroom was in Mabelle's spare room, where the newly married lived for privacy; it had a separate entrance and its own bathroom, with a door between the room and the rest of the house. Often Mario walked me home. We would kiss for a while, with Mario getting a little more earnest each time.

Etched in my memory is Monday, January 9, 1984, three o'clock in the afternoon. We had finished lunch cleanup. It was nap time for most everyone, so I decided to walk up to my room for one also.

"I'll go with you," offered Mario. He must have planned very carefully what he said and did, because when he kissed me, he did it with more fervor than ever before. He pushed his hard penis against my groin. I am sorry for the details,

195

but you must know that when we left the main house, this was not my plan. Mabelle was gone all day to a convention connected to one of her clubs. No one was around. Mario guided me into the bedroom, all the while pushing and pulsating against me.

"No, this is not right. We can't do this. It isn't right," I cried.

He whispered, "We are going to get married anyway. Why not a little sex? It won't hurt anyone, and no one needs to know. You won't tell anyone."

I became like rubber as he removed my clothing. We had sex on the carpeted floor. I had succumbed to the enticement of Mario and the moment. The sex was not special like the way it is portrayed in the movies. I experienced no great orgasm, no panting or screaming.

I know that I had already lost my virginity, but the reason I came to this Community was to let Jesus change me into a new being. I convinced myself that I was not the same slutty woman I had been. I really believed that I lived out "If anyone is in Christ, he is a new creation, the old things are passed, all has become new" (2 Cor. 5:17). Worst of all, I had failed God, failed the trust of the Community, and failed myself. I broke the vow of chastity I had made before God, the bishop, and the Community. I felt violated, and at that moment, I hated Mario.

"This is wrong; we need to go confess to the Community what we did!" I said, weeping.

"You had better not confess. If you say anything to anyone, I will leave," Mario threatened, his face red with anger at me.

I realized he was blackmailing me. I did not want to lose him; convinced that there would never be another man who would love me, I agreed.

"Good. This will never happen again, I promise," assured Mario.

I believed him, convinced he was sincere in his promise, but it happened repeatedly, always ending with the same threat and promise. I should have said to him, "Go fuck yourself! Get out of my life!" but I whimpered under his seductive manner.

My inner torment manifested itself in arguments with Mario over stupid little issues. The family had a difficult time watching us bicker like two old enemies.

One evening Darren and Evelyn called Mario and me into their room. "We can see that maybe getting engaged might not be the best thing," they explained.

In my mind, it was, *Say something. Confess the sexual sins. You know the cause of this darkness, so just say it!* However, I said nothing.

"We think you two should take a break from being engaged, just for a while, and see if this engagement is God's will for you," announced Darren, with Evelyn nodding in agreement.

Mario said nothing, not one word.

I said something like, "Okay, I will agree to this."

For the next couple of months, Mario hardly spoke a word to me—until he got a letter from his mother stating she wanted to come for a visit and stay with us in the Community. We had another meeting with Darren and Evelyn to decide what to say to his mom; being that the extra bed in my room was unoccupied, she would sleep there as my roommate.

"We believe the best solution to your not being engaged is to live as if you were engaged just for the time while Dora is here. We can see how it goes and relook at the issue after she leaves. Is this all right with you two?" they asked.

"Yes, we have no problem with this plan," was all we could say.

Every evening Mario would walk his mother and me up to the room. I stayed outside for a while with Mario to feign being in love with him. Then his sexual desires kicked in again. I should have kicked him in the balls to squelch his longings, but I was putty in his Latin lover ways. We went into the shed; he pushed my head down and made me have oral sex with him to appease him. I hated every second; really, I know no worse way to demean a woman than by making her do sexual acts against her will. He finished himself off in the bushes, making some joke about the bush growing overnight.

When I went inside to get ready for bed, Dora wanted to talk to me. She had me promise that I loved Mario and that I would never get divorced as she did.

I gave her the answers she wanted. I hated myself, disgusted for the lies and the inner torment of my sin.

Dora left after two weeks, convinced Mario and I would have a glorious wedding and wonderful life, granting her plenty of grandchildren. What a farce! I had no idea I was such a good liar.

We had another meeting with Darren and Evelyn. "After this time period, were you two able to find a way to get along better?"

"Oh, yes," Mario assured. "I believe Kata and I were meant for each other."

"Good. Then we can get on with the plans and make a date," Evelyn gleefully responded.

I can't remember saying much, but I was in such a confused, disgusted state. Mario and I reestablished our engagement, with Darren and Evelyn maintaining a close watch on how we handled difficulties, of which there were many, mostly when we were away from their close watch. But they also invited us to go out with them more often so that we could see how to act like a married couple. We began to dress in matching outfits, as Darren and Evelyn did. We ate at the same restaurants, joined them in their bird-watching hobby, and "enjoyed" (for I did not enjoy wine) wine in the garden with them. They suggested we have a Mexican-themed ceremony in this same location. It was a beautiful spot on the corner of our property, with benches, a carved wooden cross, and a running fountain.

We spent many summer evenings over cocktails planning a beautiful, simple wedding. Danielle wrote a special song just for us. Charity was my flower girl. Darren was best man, and Evelyn, of course, was matron of honor.

My mom came out a week early so that she would be part of the preparations. Darren, Evelyn, and I took her with us on a trip down to Tijuana to buy dresses, decorations, and any other items that might make the day memorable. As we walked across the bridge that crossed into the city, down in the bottom of the cement riverbed, we watched a police car chasing another car. Then a man ran away from the car as the Mexican police drew their guns and fired at him.

"We had better get out of here quickly," said Darren. He did not have to repeat himself.

Fortunately, the rest of the day was uneventful. We found dresses for my mom and Evelyn and Charity's flower-girl dress. We also bought several bunches of the colorful paper flowers to decorate the garden. When we finished purchasing all we needed, we walked back across the bridge, thankfully this time without incident.

On my wedding day, we had brisk March weather, but the sun shone brightly on everyone seated outside for our garden wedding. Darren walked me out the door, down the steps, and up the flower-strewn path as Charity walked in front of us. Evelyn's wedding dress with alterations fit me perfectly. Uncle Basil heard our vows, Danielle sang for us, and we exchanged vows. Then came our reception, with food, cake, and gifts from the Community, our families, and our friends.

We had packed the car for our weeklong camping honeymoon the day before, so that we would be ready to leave right after the reception. We planned to spend the first night of the honeymoon at the hotel in Julian, and then the rest of the week, camp in a park in the desert. When we unpacked a few things for our hotel room, I uncovered an addiction Mario had kept hidden from the Community and me. I found a mini portable television tucked in the backseat. I accidentally broke an antenna. Mario was angry with me but worked hard to hold in his emotions. He brought the television to the room when he discovered the hotel did not provide a television for their guests.

I had hoped our first night together as husband and wife would be wonderful, but honestly, it was a complete letdown. I felt little joy in our sexual encounter. In addition, on the floor above us, a child cried almost all night long, making sleep impossible. Mario turned on his little television to pass the time.

The next day we headed off to the desert for camping, hiking, and a peaceful week. We should have known better than to plan a desert camping trip in March. Cold winds blew off the snowcapped mountains, over the desert, and out to the ocean.

Now, more than twenty-eight years later, I recall only the negatives of our honeymoon. Every night we watched programs on the mini television, except for the night the wind blew so hard it lifted the stakes of our tent right up out of the ground. That moment was the only time I remember laughing.

We returned to Community and our new bedroom, complete with a water bed, the same kind as Darren and Evelyn had. Our bedroom was located in the lower level of the big house, a nice large room, but to go to the bathroom, we had to go up the stairs down the hall, sharing the bathroom with Robert, Dee, and their little daughter, Annie. I was very accustomed to sharing this bathroom—it had a door between the bathtub side and the toilet side—but Mario had a more difficult time.

A few months into our marriage, I began to have a strange symptom in my right wrist. The wrist felt numb sometimes; other times I did not have enough strength to grasp anything with it. I did not want to say anything, but when I started to drop kitchen items while working on meals, I had to say something.

"I need prayers, please, for my wrists. I am feeling pain and numbness in my wrist, and at times the pain shoots up my arm." Asking for prayer for a physical problem was always the first step in the healing process before jumping to the doctor.

A couple of people laid hands on my wrists, asking for God's healing.

"I think you should also get that checked out by the doctor. Do not take any chances," suggested Evelyn.

The next day began the first day of my new journey in life that I am still dealing with on a daily basis.

CHAPTER 36

More Room Needed

Unless the Lord build the house,
They labor in vain who build.
Unless the Lord guard the city,
In vain does the guard keep watch?
—Ps. 127:1

Because of our growing families, we needed to add more room for our Community members. Fortunately, we had the ability to add another home on the corner of our property where our garden stood. After many nights of prayer, we realized the first step was to go to the Planning Commission for the approval we needed.

Evelyn and I had the adventure of going together. The Community asked for God's blessing and wisdom. On the way down, Evelyn explained to me that this was not her first time talking to a planning commission. That was why she was prepared to show them our plans in a way to get permission to build. My job was to be praying silently while she did the talking.

We made our way through the maze of buildings and met with a young man, explaining our plans to build our six-bedroom, two-bathroom house. He nodded as Evelyn smoothly explained how we were going to build the house. The civil engineer looked at the plan and was very intrigued. We also explained that we owned two adjacent properties. While the land was connected now, they were easily separated for a possible later sale. Our plan was approved!

We praised the Lord all the way home. Our elation overflowed to the family, and we eagerly began the next steps for our new home.

Evelyn suggested we each choose a construction company from any source and get estimates, initial plans for the house, and timing for getting it done. A few weeks later, we each came with our paperwork. Robert and Dee came with their presentation, which was nice, and then Uncle Basil came up with his ideas.

When Gary started his presentation, he had a large paper with little cutouts of prospective bedrooms and two bathrooms. Each bathroom had dividers between the toilet section and shower/tub section for multiple people to use the same area at the same time. He pulled out the footstool, placing his ideas on top so several of us could see. Everyone knelt down to look at his ideas. His engineer mind had made these little models to illustrate his ideas.

Evelyn asked, "Gary, what is the name of this construction company, and how did you come up with it?"

"Well—" He paused and, with his characteristic dry sense of humor, replied, "The name is Chris Acker Construction. And they were the first name on the list in the telephone book."

It was clear to all of us that Acker Construction was God's selection. When several of our men approached the business to explain our vision of building in stages as finances became available (an unusual approach), much to our delight they were more than accommodating to meet our needs.

Once the slab and house framing was complete, the next step was the installation of the "innards," such as electricity, plumbing, heating, and finished walls. This was where the group we mentioned to the planning commissioner came in. The Mappers, as they called themselves (Mobile Missionary Assistance Partners), were a group of retired contractors, plumbers, electricians, and builders who traveled around the United States in their RVs, helping nonprofit organizations build churches, homes, and retreat centers at no cost. In several batches, for about a month at a time, groups of three or four couples arrived. Using the building supplies we provided, they would do whatever we needed to help us construct our new home.

Each day it was exciting to watch the progress of the Mappers and our own sweat and blood work together sanding, cutting, hanging doors, painting, and so on. Working with the Mappers was a lot of fun. Most of the time, they ate in their own vehicles or visited with each other, but occasionally we had the groups in for dinner with our group. As the home drew closer to completion, we had a meeting to work out the housing assignments.

Darren and Evelyn had recently started adoption proceedings for two Hispanic teenagers, Desiree and Ludo. They were in the foster home system and desperately needed to be adopted before they became too old to be incorporated into a new family. Our new home would offer the opportunity for them to live with their new parents in the main house.

In addition, Darren's sister, Adele, had come from Michigan to spend time with her brother. Over the months she announced in a loud voice, "I am staying here forever! You are not getting rid of me!"

Then we all rejoiced as we watched a budding romance develop between our bachelor uncle Basil and Adele. Adele went through her temporary, then permanent vows, and she and Uncle Basil, now a married couple, also needed a bedroom.

Mario and I were to move in to the front bedroom of the new home. Robert and Dee, with their two children, Annie and Zachary, took two rooms. Gary and Danielle, with their two daughters and two sons, Michael, Michele, Charity, and Marcos, shared the rest of the bedrooms.

Then, near-tragedy occurred. Danielle had begun moving a few things into the new bedrooms, and while she was busy with this, her younger children were playing in the empty front room that Mario and I would inhabit. The lunch bell rang, so she gathered up the children and headed to the table. Mario had driven our large stick-shift truck to run an errand. He was late for lunch so quickly parked the truck in the upper parking lot just up the hill from the house. The driveway had a noticeable slope.

After lunch Robert went outside, and we heard, "Oh *no!*" very loudly. Mario had not set the brake tightly enough, so the truck rolled forward down the hill into our bedroom, breaking the window and the wall. A mere five minutes before the accident, children were playing right where the car was pushing through the wall. No one was mad at Mario for this mishap. We were grateful for God's protection and added the repair work toward the completion of the home. After the repairs were finished, no one could see where it was damaged.

Finally, more than a year since we had first broken ground, our new home was finished! God had been faithful! We not only had a new home, but since we only paid as we built, we had no mortgage! We invited our bishop and his wife to join us for dinner, a blessing on our new home, and to celebrate the burning of the mortgage in the new fireplace. It was one of the most joyful celebrations ever of our Community family.

CHAPTER 37

From This Moment On, I Am Never Going to Be the Same

Make friends with the doctor, for he is essential to you;
God has also established him in his profession.
—Ben Sira 38:1

"Let me see your wrist. Now squeeze my hand—harder. Is that all you can squeeze?" Dr. John said, examining me. He had the most intriguing bedside manner. His eyes hardly ever looked open. His best guess was that I might have carpal tunnel syndrome. He gave me a wrist brace to relieve the pain and stress. He also sent me to an orthopedic doctor to take x-rays and for a confirmed diagnosis.

The following week I went to the specialist, who told me I did not have carpal tunnel syndrome but rather rheumatoid arthritis. He advised me to use the brace and take aspirin to relieve the pain.

I do not recall why everyone was sitting around in the living room when I came home from the doctor, but I was grateful. It saved me from having to repeat the diagnosis several times. Evelyn was in her rocker, and all the rest of the family members sat around the room.

"So, Kata, what did the doctor say?" she asked.

"I do not have carpal tunnel syndrome. I only have rheumatoid arthritis (RA)," I lightly replied.

"Only! This is not something you need to joke about. You have a serious condition. What did the doctor tell you to do?" Evelyn was sincerely shocked at my casualness.

"He said I may wear the wrist brace for support when needed and to take aspirin for pain," I replied. As far as I knew, arthritis was not a life-threatening illness. I could deal with this. After all, I was only twenty-seven years old and looking forward someday to bearing children. It was not as if I had cancer.

This was how my next journey began. I do not know whether the pain increased because of my learning more about RA or the pain increased as a result of the inner turmoil I felt over the sinful transgressions with Mario before we got married, but the pain increased dramatically. Stress plays a major role in the intensity of RA. If one can reduce the amount of stress, then the disease is much more manageable. But stress always leads to flare-ups.

My marriage continually fluctuated between fun and stressful, based on our moods. When we had an argument, Mario dealt with our disagreements by giving me the silent treatment. No one in the Community ever noticed because he talked to everyone else. This would last for up to three days, until he determined I had suffered enough. He refused to get help to work out our problems and told me to not tell anyone.

To be fair, we had some fun times too—cookouts in the parks and visits with his Buena Vista family. He loved going to the movies, so we went often to the inexpensive theater. However, there were so many areas where we were so vastly different. As I shared before, I learned about his addiction to television on our honeymoon. That never stopped being an issue between us. I could walk into our bedroom, and there he would be, standing in front of his television as if in a trance, watching cartoons, completely unaware of my presence.

Our bedroom was still in the basement at this time, with a small electric heater for warmth. The room was very cold and damp during the fall and winter. In addition, when it rained, our room would flood. This aggravated the increasing pain in my joints.

I did not know why this disease was progressing so rapidly other than the fact that I held inside the distress I felt over the marriage with Mario. Every time we argued, he threatened divorce. Yet I always held that we would get through these difficulties as the other couples did. Living in Community as a married couple is difficult because in one sense there is no privacy. You have to leave the property to feel alone together. It was an ironic, sad situation. I was surrounded by people, yet due to the isolation I felt in my marriage, I was in many ways totally alone.

CHAPTER 38

Aquatic Exercise

My God will fully supply whatever you need, in
accord with his glorious riches in Christ Jesus.
—Phil. 4:19

That spring the Community received an invitation to
vacation at a desert retreat house. We could relax for a three-
day weekend, and there were sufficient sleeping facilities for
all of us. Many of us were free to attend, while some stayed
home to care for the children and property.

When we arrived we were treated to a lovely potluck dinner,
followed by a Spirit-filled service and a tour of the grounds,
and then we were shown where we could sleep. Mario and I
slept in a bedroom with a view of the San Jacinto Mountains.
A friend shared that if you arose before the sunrise, there
would appear on the side of the mountain a shadow image of
an angel. I made sure to wake early to see this phenomenon.
Sure enough, the angel was there in all its glory!

The next morning our friends took us to a spa center, which had five indoor pools fed by the underground hot springs, each a different temperature and depth to accommodate every desire or need. When I entered the warm water, my body, wracked with pain and stiffness, soon relaxed. I was able to move around freely without pain. I recalled seeing an advertisement about water classes at a pool in town offered by the adult education organization, but I had paid no attention to it because I believed it cost too much. I am the kind of person who will always look at the price first to determine whether I say yes or no to paying the price. The paradox is if I am buying something for someone else, if it fills his or her need or desire and I can afford it, I will buy it for him or her.

Evelyn, seeing my face free from pain in this wonderful warm spa water, asked me, "Wouldn't it be nice if we had a pool like this for you?"

I replied, "Just this month I saw an advertisement for classes at the indoor pool where Mabelle taught school. The handicapped children use it in the mornings, and the adult school offers classes in the afternoon."

"Why didn't you say something? That sounds like a good idea. How much does it cost?" asked Evelyn.

"If I remember correctly, the cost was thirty-five dollars for six weeks, a class three times a week. I didn't say anything because I thought it was too expensive, and it would mean being gone three nights a week from dinner preparations, meaning I would be late for dinner," I explained.

"Well, I think you should bring it up to the Community," encouraged Evelyn. "You do not have to go all three days. Perhaps you could go just two days."

I thought it was a waste of money to go only twice weekly, but I said I would bring it up at our next meeting. As it turned out, the Community thought it was a good idea.

I began classes the beginning of the next month, choosing the arthritis class over the aerobic ones, not knowing at what level I would be able to exercise. I drove myself to the school but found it difficult to find a parking place. That made me wonder how crowded the class would be. When I walked in, I almost turned around and walked out. The pool area was crowded with wheelchairs, chairs that wheeled people clear down into the pool, and a whole lot of bodies. The main pool area, though, was spacious compared to the restroom/shower room, which must have been no more than eight feet by ten feet; the toilet and shower were in the same location, and there was a door, but no privacy.

I had carried my swimsuit separately to put on when I got there, but as I looked at the other women, they wore their suits to the pool covered by bathrobes. After exercise they removed their suits and left covered only with their bathrobes. My initial thought was, *What if they get in a car accident on the way home?*

I will never forget the first time entering that pool. I was in so much pain, it took a great amount of effort just to use the steps. The moment my foot touched the water, my body felt the same sudden pain relief I experienced in the desert spa water. This pool water was kept at a constant ninety-two degrees water temperature. So comfortable for my body! That class was the only place I felt truly at peace in my body and with God.

For sixteen years, I continued attending classes at this pool, not only for the exercise but I also established several deep friendships with several people from those classes. I would depend on those relationships in the years ahead when crises assailed me.

On March 16, 1987, I was on my way out the door for my aquatic exercise class when I noticed that I had red dots all over my body. I didn't feel any different than on any other day, so I figured I would ask someone when I got back from class to look at my rash.

As I walked through the kitchen, Danielle looked at my face and asked, "What is wrong with you? Your face is covered with a red rash."

Evelyn looked at my arms, all spotted with red dots, and then she took my hands, examining my fingernails, which were almost pure white. "You need to see the doctor; you are extremely anemic."

Danielle took me to see Dr. John. He took one look at me and knew it was serious. "I will get some blood work done and refer you to a specialist to take a look at you. Don't be surprised if he says you have lupus."

According to Wikipedia, lupus is the name given to a collection of autoimmune diseases in which the human immune system becomes hyperactive and attacks normal, healthy tissues. Symptoms of these diseases can affect many different body systems, including joints, skin, kidneys, blood cells, heart, and lungs. This described perfectly the ongoing symptoms I had been dealing with.

The next day, March 17, 1987, Danielle took me to see the specialist. The office was brightly decorated with St. Patrick's Day decorations, and when Dr. Frank introduced himself, I noted his kelly-green sweater under his lab coat.

Dr. Frank looked at me gravely and said, "I am looking at the lab results; your blood work shows you are severely anemic. I want to admit you into the hospital for treatment. Will that work for you, Mrs. Lopez?"

Danielle volunteered, "I'll get her there," and then went on to explain how she was related to me and somewhat about the Community we lived in.

Dr. Frank came in as soon as I was admitted and set up in my room. Once the nurse gave me prednisone, I felt relief from pain, like someone had poured warm oil over me.

It took a weeklong stay in the hospital to get back on my feet. Mario was faithful to come every night to visit.

Living with lupus became a daily struggle. I walked every day, not just to keep my body fit but to burn off the frustrations from pent-up emotions. I was always fatigued, but I knew I needed to keep my body moving, and so I walked on. My medication regimen was elaborate. I had to keep track of when to take each pill—which ones to take on an empty stomach and which to take with a full stomach. I had to keep records of the changes in meds, which Dr. Frank adjusted frequently to manage my varied symptoms. He also needed me to log all my reactions to my pills, weighing the side effects with the benefits.

One example was prednisone. Prednisone is a great medicine to reduce inflammation, yet side effects of this medication include significant bone loss and weight gain, increasing the risk of osteoporosis. I had to be extra careful to avoid falling so that my brittle bones wouldn't break. There are mental side effects as well, such as an inability to focus, mood changes, and depression. I read the side effects casually, trying to avoid the temptation to believe I had contracted all these symptoms. The problem was that I experienced some of the emotional problems before my diagnosis of lupus. According to my blood tests, I already had lupus in my system as part of my DNA. After the diagnosis, I questioned my sanity several times in situations where I did not think all the way through any given situation, such as during a kitchen project, taking phone messages, asking all the questions possible when I went to my doctor, and in general, daily dealings with others in the Community.

Chapter 39

Freedom from Secrets

Take no part in the fruitless works of
darkness; rather expose them.
—Eph. 5:11

In April 1988, a group of us were in the living room for nine o'clock prayers when Evelyn asked, "Where is Mario?"

I didn't know. Maybe he went on a walk. I had not seen him since breakfast.

About fifteen minutes later, Mario walked in and announced he was leaving.

I asked, "Where are you going?" thinking he meant he was going out to town.

"I am leaving. I have a friend outside, and I am leaving for good," he said, turning to walk out the door.

I sat on the sofa in shock, not knowing whether to run after him or cry. I knew him well enough to know that when he decided on something, nothing could change his mind. I learned that lesson from day one. Everyone was shocked, not knowing what to say. When I couldn't hold my pain in any longer, I began to weep.

"Did you know he planned on leaving, Kata?" asked Evelyn.

"No, I had no idea he had plans. He never shares anything with me," I said. I could not believe she thought I would have been part of his leaving.

Evelyn replied, "I will call Darren and let him know what's going on. Maybe he can find out from Mario what he is thinking."

That night we were all called to the living room by Evelyn to find out what role each of us played to cause Mario to leave.

Darren had spoken with Mario at his aunt's house, where Mario stated he was sick of Community life and wanted out. Darren went around the room as Evelyn peered at us like a prosecutor. We all had to share one situation where we'd missed the mark in our relationship with Mario. What a folly. Why was it our fault?

Evelyn told me to examine carefully those areas in our marriage where I failed and to look at those times when I said things to him that were demeaning to his manhood.

When Desiree spoke up, I was not surprised but ashamed. "When Mario and I worked together on my school lessons, we went to the poustinia and were making out a lot. I am so sorry." Evelyn sent Desiree to bed, accepting her apology.

I continued to sob. I could hardly speak, but I confessed the sin that Mario and I had sex before we were married.

"Oh, we knew already; we could see the signs," Evelyn remarked casually.

Even now, it makes me sick at heart that if they saw the signs, why did they still encourage us to get married? If only I had been strong enough the very first time to stand up for myself and expose the wrong we had done in darkness. Mario would have left long before we entangled ourselves in our deception … ("Oh, what a tangled web we weave when first we practice to deceive" was one of Evelyn's favorite Walter Scott quotes, which she repeated often.)

Mario called Darren at his office, asking that someone pack his belongings and put them on the front porch so he could pick them up at a specific time.

Evelyn asked Darren to arrange a time for them to meet him for lunch to talk.

It took very little time for me to pack up all of the items Mario wanted, especially his beloved television set. I would have rather thrown the television out the window to watch it break into little pieces, just as Mario did to our marriage.

Darren and Evelyn had their lunch meeting with Mario, returning to share with me, "We had a civil lunch with

Mario, asking him what his plans were, and he never asked about you at all!"

That proved to me that our marriage was a farce. I thought, *What a waste. Yet at the same time, what a relief to have all my sins confessed and out in the open.* What I lacked, however, was the ability to forgive myself and go on with the next phase of my life. I thanked God that the vows I made to the Community were the firm foundation I relied on.

When a tragedy like this happens, most people don't know what to say. Don't say, "Oh, I am sorry for your loss," because no one died. Don't sympathize with, "I know how you feel." No, they do not know how I feel, only how they feel. Or, "I know what you are going through." Do they really know? Only one person really did know and said the right thing. "Come here; let me give you a big hug. You are my other daughter; I am your mama." She was Dee's mom, Ethel, recently moved out here to be near her only grandchildren as they grew up. A couple of times when she went on a trip, she let Mario and me "play house" in her apartment; we both enjoyed those times, pretending we were just an ordinary couple. I realized during these times, if it were not for the Community, our paths would have never met, nor would we have chosen each other to marry. It was a miracle we lasted three years.

I was taking a voice class at the nearby college when Mario left. Mabelle had told me she used to work with my instructor, Dr. Sherman. She recounted to me that he had been through a terrible divorce, so she encouraged me to go to the class and share with him what had happened. He would understand. It helped to know that Dr. Sherman met Mario when we went to his house for a class party, yet I dreaded going to class to sing the song I was working on in front of the other students. I did not want to break down crying right there for everyone to see.

I went to him before class. "Dr. Sherman, I am not really feeling ready to sing today. I had a terrible thing happen to me yesterday. Do you remember my husband, Mario? Well, yesterday he left me, without any hope of reconciliation."

"I understand. I am glad you came to class. This shows me how committed you are to your voice. You will get through this difficult time."

I appreciated his encouragement. He gave me a hug and then began class as usual.

In my case, the divorce legal proceeding was rather smooth; we hired a Spanish-speaking paralegal to arrange the documentation. We had no children to worry about and no debts. All he owned fit into his car, so the transition from married to single again was easy on paper, but emotionally, it tore me apart.

I wanted to lay blame on Evelyn for letting Desiree tempt Mario into breaking his vow of chastity in our marriage. But I rationalized I could not blame her because I broke my vow of chastity before we were married. Mario not only threatened to leave when we had an argument between us, but when he felt dominated by the Community, he would ask me if he left, would I go with him. "No, I made vows to the Community," I would respond.

I experienced two different sides of Mario. One was in our room, where he complained constantly about being told what to do, whether working for Robert in his woodworking business or working next door for our neighbor in his factory, making avocado bags in the building in the back. The other face of Mario was when we were with Darren and Evelyn. Then he acted like a perfect gentleman. He was congenial, soft-spoken, and kind, copying Darren's treatment as a husband. I hated the hypocrisy but never said a word.

Right after Mario left, Uncle Basil came to the dinner table to announce that he balanced the money in the cash box down to the penny. It was not a coincidence at all that after Mario left, the ten-dollar shortage that was a consistent mystery miraculously stopped. Again, my embarrassment arose, knowing he always had money. I always believed him when he said, "I saved up my allowance."

After my divorce I went back to my own last name, Zyczyaska.

To aid in leaving the memory of my past, I asked Evelyn if I could change bedrooms and get rid of the waterbed.

She offered the tiny bedroom at the rear of the main house where she and Darren lived, next to where the now-adopted Ludo and Desi had their bedrooms. "You can be our nanny, so that when Darren and I go out, you can 'babysit'!" suggested Evelyn.

Did I really say, "Yes, that would be fun"?

CHAPTER 40

If I Only Used My Brain

He gives power to the faint,
Abundant strength to the weak.
—Isa. 40:29

"You have a brain, and I don't understand why you don't use it!" Evelyn would become very disgusted with me, raising her voice when I did not think something through. During these reprimands, I came to believe that she treated me this way to get through my stubbornness so I would think on my own. This abusive relationship continued through the rest of my days in the Community. I lived in fear of her all the time, like a rabbit's fear of the lion; the lion can sense the fear and lingers to attack just to build up the fear in its prey, so the prey will be so fearful it will not move. Evelyn most likely saw me as a fearful weak person to prey upon every negative detail of my character as she knew I would not fight back. The other people in the Community had their own means of responding to the wrath of Evelyn, but whenever I sat in the hot seat, no one said anything; if they had, it would have been like putting gasoline on an already burning charcoal fire. We all knew our places.

Evelyn was becoming more and more critical. Issues that needed her correction were over things as small as, "Why did you make coffee cake to serve twelve people? You know we are only seven for breakfast. Plus it is too sweet; we need to cut back on the amount of sugar." Or, "I don't know why the mothers in the other house should not have breakfast over here. Everyone has to go to school at the same time!"

No one wanted to tell Evelyn that sometimes they needed a break from examining every little misdeed, or even misspoken words, while eating. We were used to it at dinnertime, but first thing in the morning was too early to start in on a discussion about what was wrong in a person's morning tone of voice. The dichotomy was that when Evelyn woke up from a nap, everyone knew better than to confront her with a request or problem. "Can't you see I just got up from a nap, and you expect me to answer questions without having my coffee?" was her excuse.

Living in my little room got me out of my old bedroom and those memories, but I was right back in the situation of having no privacy. My room was also an exit, with a sliding glass door leading to an outside porch.

Then I lost what little privacy I had in my small space even more when the Community purchased a computer. The available space to put the computer for bookkeeping was the other half of my room. Often someone would be on the computer late at night. They exited out the sliding door on the porch to avoid disturbing me. But I still had to get up and lock the sliding door when they finally left.

I mentioned this situation to Evelyn, who told me, "You always find a reason, no matter where you are; you will never be satisfied." I believed her, so even though someone was on the computer until midnight, I had to say nothing. Somehow it was selfish of me to ask him or her to stop earlier so I could sleep, no matter how sick I felt. I was tired, so very tired, every day. I told myself that Evelyn was right. It was bad enough to be a nanny to Desi (a constant reminder of my past failures with Mario).

To be in the same house where Evelyn lived meant she could keep watch over my every move. She considered me her personal assistant. She would call out from the other end of the house asking me to find something for her. She made me her in-house beautician. She chose which books I should read.

I have to say there were fun times being a nanny. I really did not need to be a babysitter since they were teenagers, but Evelyn insisted the relationship would be advantageous for all parties, so I played the part. They included me on many outings with the family. They even introduced me as the nanny, which, I now realize, made it appear that Darren was a well-to-do attorney who could afford one. I was expected to adjust my life around what I needed to do for Evelyn and Darren, to be accepted by them and included in their life.

I was in great internal emotional pain. I was in great physical pain. Would there ever be a way for me to be free from this combination? I prayed for an answer.

Chapter 41

Listen to the Signals

Do you not know that your body is a temple
of the Holy Spirit within you, whom you have
from God, and that you are not your own?
—1 Cor. 6:19

"I read a magazine article about the overuse of salt, and I think we should change our diet habits by not putting so much or even any salt in our food."

This was Evelyn's latest dinner pronouncement. By now we had come to expect the constant ideas she brought to the table. I looked down at my plate of low-salt turkey with carrot sticks, while everyone else ate hot dogs and chips.

This idea of everyone cutting back on salt came about when I was hospitalized for severe swelling in my legs. My tongue was swollen, and it felt like I had swallowed a golf ball that was stuck in my throat. My ankles looked like an elephant's legs, one fat stump from the knee down to the foot.

When I explained my symptoms to Evelyn, she told me to call the doctor. "Robert can take you to the doctor or hospital; let me know what the doctor says." This response was a standard every time I had to go to the doctor or hospital—someone else could do it; I cannot recall a single time Evelyn took me to the doctor or hospital. I assumed this reluctance to take me had something to do with her biological daughter, who, since she was sixteen, was in and out of the hospital almost on a monthly basis.

The doctor admitted me immediately to the hospital. I had felt stupid for coming in for something I thought was minor, but clearly I was mistaken. Blood tests revealed a dangerously low platelet count. A liver test showed a lupus form of hepatitis. I was very sick indeed.

I missed the Community Fourth of July festivities, something I always looked forward to. As the children were growing up, Evelyn thought it might be fun to form a parade around the block, singing Americana songs, decorating the bicycles, wearing red, white, and blue costumes, and inviting the neighbors to follow us home for more singing, led by Danielle with her guitar, cookies, and punch. After this a few of us would go to the beach in the evening for fireworks over the ocean. Other years we went to watch the fireworks at the city park, but it always took us more than an hour to arrive home from what was normally a ten-minute drive home because of traffic. Many times we brought the television out onto the deck, plugged in the television, and watched the Fourth of July concert from the White House while we sat in the lawn chairs down below the deck as if we were at an outdoor movie, without the crowds or traffic problems.

That hospital day I missed the hamburgers, potato salad, and strawberry shortcake. I felt very lonely.

Then Danielle arrived. "I have a surprise for you," she said, with a frozen yogurt in hand. "You have to come out and eat it in the waiting room."

That seemed strange to me, but then I saw my very own goddaughter, Charity, who ran to me and hugged me tightly. Many times during difficult times of my life, she alone gave me enough reason to live.

I must include here the kind of nursing I received at this hospital. There were times I felt I was not in a hospital but a hotel. The food service catered to the desires of the patient. If I wanted a tortilla with eggs and salsa, they found a way to make sure I had that. The nurses showed me a list of movies I could watch in my room in addition to television. Once they borrowed the video recorder from the conference room, put in a movie, and there I was in all luxury, watching *Cyrano De Bergerac* starring Mario Ferrer. When the movie ended, I was in tears, so the nurse came in, worried something was terribly wrong. I explained it was just the movie.

Another time Uncle Basil and Adele were visiting with me, and I had to use the bedpan. I called the nurse, and she called back, "Put a cork in it!" We laughed until our sides hurt. She was definitely my kind of nurse.

After two units of blood, three sessions of IV immunoglobulin, and large doses of Benadryl, my body returned to a tolerable normal, and I was discharged eleven days after I was admitted, with an order to remain on the low-salt diet.

Mealtimes at home were uncomfortable for me, since almost daily one of the children would ask, "Why do you have something special?" I would try to explain graciously why I had to eat something different from what they were eating. I hated to call attention to the low-salt diet—so much so that I would eat a couple of spoonsful of low-salt peanut butter before the meal and then only eat the vegetables or salad, same as everyone else.

That stopped working when Evelyn called attention to how little I ate at the meal. No matter what, she made sure I could never win. "If you need to eat something different, you can bring it to the table and eat it with us too!" Evelyn explained.

CHAPTER 42

Breathe, Just Breathe

For the spirit of God made me,
The breath of the Almighty keeps me alive.
—Job 33:4

It was time for me to change bedrooms again, this time back up the road to Mabelle's private-entrance bedroom. Evelyn's biological daughter, Valerie, the only one of her children still in contact with her, was ill both physically and mentally. She and Tony, with their now-four children, had relocated back down to a job closer to us. The family of six was in serious financial trouble. The household was a disaster. Valerie was unable to even cook or keep her home clean. The marriage was falling apart. Evelyn suggested Valerie coming down by herself for a break might help. I did not mind this move. I loved it.

The nightly starlit walks, the rainy mud-soaked road, and the cool breeze from the ocean pushed me up the street every evening. Anyone living up at the house had a freedom to simply be. Mabelle created this atmosphere. That was how she lived. Having taught handicapped children, nothing fazed her. "Everything will be just fine, honey heart" or "Now, lambie-pie, you shouldn't try to work so hard; the trash can wait until later." I always worried about who emptied the trash. Even when I went to the hospital, I asked Uncle Basil, "Who is going to take out the kitchen trash or wash the kitchen towels?"

Wherever I slept, my bed had to be under a window, so I could feel the breeze on my face at night. Even as a child, with storm windows attached, I would open the inside window to let the freezing air in through the little holes in the bottom of the storm windows so I could hear the sounds of the howling wind. My bed at Mabelle's house was under a window with the view of her backyard. It had rosebushes, persimmon trees, a purple jacaranda tree hanging over the covering to her patio, and every kind of crawling creature scampering around the marguerite daisy bushes. Here in this little room, I felt peace, mostly from the essence of peace from Mabelle that resonated throughout with the love that she and her husband, Benedict, put into the care in creating this house and the furnishings. He died here in his thirties after battling brain cancer. She recovered here from tuberculosis.

In this house she and I spent many hours over several days restringing her beloved piano because, "It is so much cheaper to do it ourselves," she said. I maintained a position on the floor ready to attach the string that she passed to me from above behind the keyboard. Several nights we were up past midnight because, "We can't stop now—only one more string!" we proclaimed.

I slowly regained strength and a regular routine. I believed I was getting back to normal until my next lupus event, which put my body and the Community to a larger test than the one a month before.

It was a Tuesday, housecleaning day, and it was my turn to clean bathrooms. Usually this was no big deal, but it took every bit of effort to simply bend down to clean the bathtub. I thought to myself, *Why is it taking so much effort for me to breathe?* But I said nothing. I figured that I was tired, so I waited through lunchtime to be able to go to my room to rest.

By dinner I had to say something. I really was having difficulty breathing. I was in my bedroom up at Mabelle's house and asked Mabelle to call Evelyn at the main house to see if I could stay and rest instead of coming down for dinner.

"Maybe we should call the doctor," suggested Evelyn, concerned about my medical history.

I answered, "I think if I rest, I will be all right."

All night long I sat up trying to breathe. I walked quietly around the house. I even went outside to get some fresh air, but nothing helped me to breathe better. I remember sitting on the sofa waiting for morning to come, clutching a firm sofa pillow, wishing for the first light of dawn. I prayed the Twenty-Third Psalm repeatedly: "Yea though I walk through the shadow of death …" I felt like I would die right there in the living room and they would find me stiffly holding on to that pillow. "I will fear no Evil, for Thou art with me …" I knew God was with me, sitting right next to me on that couch while I waited for morning. He gave me strength to hold on. He wiped the sweat from my brow as I waited to get help.

Uncle Basil came out of his room for his daily ritual of coffee and prayer, and he saw me crouching on the sofa. I explained as well as I could in between breaths what my problem was. He immediately picked up the phone and called my doctor. Then he called the main house to share that he was taking me to the emergency room.

Since it was midweek in early morning, we had no problem getting in or seen quickly by the cardiologist, who immediately noted I was in congestive heart failure and getting inadequate oxygen to my blood. The emergency department at our hospital is the best-run ER around, but that is just my opinion; everyone knows his or her job and does it efficiently, while at the same time making the patient as comfortable as humanly possible.

When they held up an oxygen mask, I remember clearly saying, "Wait. Please don't put that over my face. I can't breathe!" In my irrational state, I thought the mask would keep me from breathing; if I had been clearheaded, I would have realized oxygen would fill the mask, helping me to breathe. After the nurse explained about the mask, my rational mind knew what it was.

Suddenly, what felt like hundreds of people were poking, prodding, hooking up tubing, x-raying, and wheeling me off for more tests. I finally got a room in the coronary care unit. All this time I did not see Uncle Basil. I worried about whether he got breakfast. He hadn't had time to get his morning coffee.

I continued working hard to breathe, but I got to the point when I thought that it might be easier just to stop breathing rather than try anymore. I simply could not find any position that would help me breathe. It was plainly too difficult. According to my medical records, each time they tried a new medication, I would get an "angry rash" on my bottom, indicating an allergic reaction. Not only was I experiencing breathlessness, but I was also, even after megadoses of diuretics, as swollen as I was when I was admitted to the hospital the last time.

Hours passed, and during the middle of that night, I think I actually slept somehow, but I heard someone's voice either reading to me or softly humming, most likely both. When I opened my eyes, it was Dee, quietly sitting with me all night long. I got enough strength to thank her and then continued to try to find a position where I could breathe. She wrote out this verse:

> Whom else have I in the heavens?
> None beside you delights me on earth.
> Though my flesh and my heart fail,
> God is the rock of my heart, my portion forever.
> But those who are far from you perish;
> You destroy those unfaithful to you.

As for me, to be near God is my good,
To make the Lord GOD my refuge.
—Ps. 73:25–28

The following morning Danielle visited while I was still having a hard time breathing. I was so tired. I told her I felt like giving up.

That was when Danielle, in her sternest "mommy voice" (having raised five children, she had that voice down), got into my face and said, "*Kata*! See this picture, Kata? This is Charity, your goddaughter. I am taping it to the foot of your bed so that every time you open your eyes, you will see her. She needs you to stay alive for her. You need to stay alive to watch her grow up. Do you hear me? You have to want to stay alive for her!"

Her words connected me back to reality. Danielle was right. I *had* to keep fighting.

That night at exactly 11:30, I saw my doctor's face. "What are you doing here, Dr. Frank? Why aren't you in bed?" I managed to say.

"We have an important decision to make," he replied soberly. "We want to try one last-ditch effort to stop the progression of your congestive heart failure, but you have to make a decision. This Cytoxan treatment we want to give you may help, or you might die from it. But we hope this will help."

Never had I seen him so serious before. "I think you should ask the Community about this," was my automatic response. I noticed the surprised look on his face, but he agreed he would call them to get their decision. Dr. Frank called the Community even though it was after midnight; the lupus symptoms were out of control and needed immediate measures. Evelyn and Darren responded with immediate consent to commence with any therapy needed. They needed no time to agree to the treatment in spite of the risk.

Cytoxan therapy began with an attempt to control this lupus flare-up and reduce the corticosteroids in my system. They based the amount on my weight, 145 pounds, and my height of five feet two inches. Unfortunately after two separate infusions, I still could not breathe, and when the pulmonary doctor inserted tubing in my back to remove a two-liter bottle of fluid from one lung, I felt only minimum relief. They did the same procedure to the other lung, and I finally experienced some relief.

But other complications arose, which sent me to the intensive care unit. The picture of Charity followed me to ICU, where my room had two doors, one that opened directly to the nurses' station and one that led to the hall. If I had a problem, I had my own nurse assigned just to me for help. I could breathe fine, but several severe internal complications needed constant monitoring. I appreciated it when they left the door open so I could hear their conversations, but one in particular caught my attention.

"I am here to see the patient in room 102; her name is Zdzislawa."

"I am sorry, madam, but only family are allowed here. You will have to wait until she is on the general floor," replied my nurse.

"I am her mother! I want to see her right now!" countered the woman, whose voice I recognized as that of my other mother, Ethel. Clearly she had Negro features, while my skin is a very Polish white. But no one *ever* disagreed with Ethel—ever. She had the right personality for the job she had for forty years as a middle-school teacher in southeast Chicago, handling all the tough kids. So these nurses were no challenge at all for her. Within ten seconds her loving arms were around me, warming my heart and my soul with her love.

Finally, after entering the hospital unable to breathe, several intravenous injections of this and that medication, two severe adverse allergic reactions, both lungs drained of liters of fluid, a couple of blood transfusions, and hundreds of pills, I was discharged ten days later. It felt like I had been there for six months. My weight on admission was 145 pounds; on discharge I weighed 124 pounds. I do not recommend losing weight in this manner.

I believed that with this difficult lupus flare-up behind me, my life would finally get back to normal. I could go to my aquatic exercise class at the pool, work in the kitchen, do fun projects with the Community children (such as Halloween Pumpkin Cookies* and St. Nicolaus Speculatius (Kris Kringle) Cookies (German Spice Cookies)*), and bake and decorate their birthday cakes.

It is said, "Do you want to make God laugh? Tell him your plans." God laughed at me. He had other plans in store, which carried me where I did not want to go.

CHAPTER 43

"I Saw Everyone I Ever Knew!"

The LORD is my shepherd;
There is nothing I lack.
In green pastures he makes me lie down;
To still waters he leads me;
He restores my soul.
He guides me along right paths
For the sake of his name.
Even though I walk through the
valley of the shadow of death,
I will fear no evil, for you are with me;
Your rod and your staff comfort me.
You set a table before me
In front of my enemies;
You anoint my head with oil;
My cup overflows.
Indeed, goodness and mercy will pursue me
All the days of my life;
I will dwell in the house of the LORD

For endless days.
—Ps. 23:1–6

My dad made a poster for me of this psalm, written in old-style German script, and posted it in my bedroom. I prayed this nightly with him all the eleven and a half years I knew him.

On November 25, 1968, he came into my room as he did every night to hear me recite his favorite psalm, give me a kiss on my forehead, and say good night. That night, instead of my purposely making a mistake (as I always did as our little joke) on the next-to-last line, I recited the whole psalm correctly, and then said, "Good-bye, Daddy!" Why did I say good-bye and not good night? God knew that this would be the last time I would see my father alive. Only thirteen hours later, the sheriff knocked on our door to take my mom to the hospital. "Your husband has been in a serious car accident."

My dad was driving on an ice-laden road, when to his horror, a truck was driving uncontrollably toward him in his lane. To avoid a head-on collision killing both drivers, my dad swerved to the right, crashing into a large tree. The other driver drove right on past, leaving my dad in his car. At the same moment, a man waiting at the end of his driveway for his car pool witnessed the entire incident and ran over to help my dad, who was calling out for help. The man recognized him. My dad was his Boy Scout leader. He called the ambulance, which took my dad to the hospital.

My mom arrived in time to make the decision whether to keep him alive as a vegetable or let him die naturally. The doctors told her he suffered a fractured skull, and even if he survived his injuries, he would be severely brain-damaged. Knowing her husband and his fierce independence, she made the painful decision to let his life take its natural course. The day was November 26, 1968.

This may sound crazy, but our family believes that our father somehow knew he was going to die. One month before his death, he was driving his favorite VW Bug on the freeway, and it accidentally swerved out of control, rolling over several times. He arrived home in a tow truck with a mere scratch on top of his head, laughing as he described his brush with death. Was it a miracle or a warning? The next day he took out a large life insurance policy for his family in case of a sudden death. He started reading his Bible daily, underlining scriptures that spoke to his heart.

The night my father died, my distraught mom went home and sought the privacy of her bedroom. It was all so unexpected, so sudden. Here she was a forty-four-year-old widow with six children—three who were already out of the house, one adult daughter still at home, a five-year-old son, and eleven-year-old me.

In the morning my mom shared with me an extraordinary experience. In the middle of the night, my mom said something or someone told her to open the Bible next to her bed, the Bible my dad read. She opened it up randomly, and her eyes landed to where my dad had underlined this verse from 1 Thessalonians 4:13: "We do not want you to be uninformed about those who sleep in death, so that you do not grieve like the rest of mankind, who have no hope." Coincidence or God-incident? She went on to read the next verse: "For we believe that Jesus died and rose again, and so we believe that God will bring with Jesus those who have fallen asleep in him." This memory of how God was present at the death of my father and the comfort my mother experienced helped me in my next journey with lupus, which led me to an even deeper transformation.

I do not remember the headache, vomiting, diarrhea, or collapsing in the driveway on the way to my appointment with Dr. Frank, but this is what I do remember. Valerie's voice was soft and uncharacteristically comforting. I saw nothing but heard her telling me what to do, as if we were in a tunnel. The next thing I recall is hearing my voice asking, "Where am I?"

A man responded, "You are in an ambulance on the way to Tri-City Medical Center."

The only other voice was Father Basil softly singing to me. I saw nothing, but I was not scared or worried. Instead, I felt carried along gently by loving arms.

When I became conscious on the way to the hospital, I was aware of a severe headache. The paramedics' notations indicated a dangerously low blood pressure. No wonder I was lethargic and disoriented. In the emergency room, they began with several series of tests and determined my kidneys were not functioning normally.

Once again I was placed in ICU, and there I had a grand-mal seizure, with several other lupus-related complications affecting my brain and eyes. Over the following seventy-two hours, I received many tests to find out what was going wrong, and new, dangerous medications were tried to stop the progression of my lupus flare-up. What I experienced during the poking, prodding, and scanning was amazing. I was happily without pain and having dreams of a beautiful place. Clearly, God spared me the trauma I was experiencing. When I did "awaken," I felt shocked and depressed as I became aware of tubes coming out of almost every orifice in my body and the many sounds of monitoring machines. I had no recollection of anything that had happened.

Dee, who was waiting at the hospital, called home to report to the family: "Dr. Frank says that Kata's kidneys need prayer."

The nurses were also concerned by my despondency.

The next day, Dee, Robert, Uncle Basil, Darren, and Evelyn stopped by for a time of prayer, talk, and decisions.

"Have you thought about death, Kata?" asked Darren.

I felt like he had just turned on a light in my head. In all the turmoil, I had almost forgotten. "Yes!" I replied. "Let me tell you about the dream I had." I shared that I had found myself standing in an in-between world, where below me were all the people I had ever known. Above me hovered beautiful angels, not the little cherubs you see on Christmas cards, but strong, mighty angels, more glorious than the pictures

I have seen of the Sistine Chapel. They were all singing with wonderful voices. I felt no pain, only joy, until I heard Jesus speak.

I knew his voice, and he said, "I love you, Zdzislawa Katarzyna, but they need you down there more than I need you right now."

I did not know how long I stood there before he spoke, but after he called me by my name, I woke up.

Everyone was silent for a moment. I wondered why until Evelyn said, "That was not just a dream, Kata. We thought we had lost you!"

I immediately understood why I had been so depressed. No wonder I longed to return to that beautiful visit with Jesus! All of us rejoiced around my bed as the story of this vision revealed the hand of God over my life. He was not done with me yet!

CHAPTER 44

Happiness Happens

> Then he had a dream: a stairway rested on the
> ground, with its top reaching to the heavens; and
> God's angels were going up and down on it.
> —Gen. 28:12

From that time forward, I have believed I had a near-death experience. Although I didn't "really die," as Jacob's dream encouraged him, God gave me my experience to be an encouragement for others. In the ICU I had a stroke. The MRI showed mild brain damage but no outward signs. Happily, the medications also seemed to be working to relieve my symptoms.

As I improved, to pass the time, Dee offered to bring me books on tape. Around midnight one night, not able to sleep, I decided to put in a cassette. As I reached over to retrieve the cassette from the bedside table, it dropped. Not wanting to disturb the nurse just to pick up the tape, I thought I could reach down and pick it up off the floor. I forgot how weak I was and how high the bed was. I made it almost all the way down to the cassette but not quite far enough. *I'll just have to get back up and wait until a nurse comes in*, I thought. I could not get back up, so there I was—stuck dangling between the bedrails as I quietly called for help. No one heard me. Then I saw a shadow walk by, so I called out a little louder. When the nurse saw me, she was horrified, thinking I must have had another collapse. "I am all right," I assured her. "I just tried to pick up my cassette and got stuck reaching for it."

Finally it was time to remove all my tubes and monitors, and two doctors came in to see how I was doing. All they saw were my feet where my head should be. I had been very bored and uncomfortable, so I tried a different position to lie in bed. Once I repositioned myself, they decided to play a joke on me, speaking medical talk on each side of my bed. They carried this "doctor speak" on for several minutes, until I asked, "All right, now, please say all this in English."

"We think you are ready to go home." They laughed.

When I was finally discharged, I went home eager to get back to normal, but that was not what happened. A few weeks later, I returned to the hospital with similar symptoms, necessitating another round in the ICU with tests and medications. Even as bad as I felt, I later read my medical record, in which the emergency room doctor stated, "Miss Zyczyaska is a delightful thirty-four-year-old woman with severe systemic lupus." And "Thank you for the courtesy of this complicated referral. I will be pleased to follow her course as appropriate." What a sweet doctor! This time I had hoped to go home and stay there, with instructions to spend a good deal of my day resting.

Once again Dee found a book on tape from the library that she thought I would enjoy. I kept my mind active with the variety of wonderful books she introduced me to. One of my favorites was the biography about the Italian opera singer Luciano Pavarotti. After reading his book, I decided I wanted to find a way to write to him, but would have to research his address at the library after I recovered. When I found the address for Mr. Pavarotti's manager, I sent him a birthday card that had a picture of a happy Italian family having dinner on an outdoor patio. Not only did Mr. Pavarotti send me a thank-you note for remembering him on his birthday, but a week later he sent another thank-you note, stating he wanted to make sure I had gotten a thank-you. I believe it was God's way of showing me that a little kindness can touch a great heart.

Little did I know that all my away-from-home outings alone were about to end, all because of a hot pad.

CHAPTER 45

"I Am So Stupid!"

God set forth as an expiation, through faith, by
his blood, to prove his righteousness because of
the forgiveness of sins previously committed.
—Rom. 3:23–25

While I was recovering, an incident arose with Mabelle that put me in the doghouse with Evelyn. One day Mabelle asked me to call the family, telling them she felt a little stomachache and would not make it to dinner. She said she just needed to rest but told me to stay away from her in case she had the flu. Mabelle did not want to risk my catching a germ with my poor immune system.

By morning Mabelle was in a lot of pain, and when I told the family, Evelyn challenged me. "Did you take her temperature?"

"No," I replied, on my guard. "She told me to not get near her." By now I knew by the tone of Evelyn's voice that she was upset with me for my neglect.

Bonnie Jean hurried up to care for Mabelle. She had a fever of 101 and was in terrible pain.

"We need to take you to the emergency room right away," ordered Evelyn over the phone through Bonnie Jean.

"May I go in my nightgown?" asked Mabelle, who was raised a proper southern lady and was embarrassed at going out of the house without being properly dressed. (She looked proper even when she wore blue jeans and a sweatshirt, because no matter what she wore, it was always ironed.) As it turned out, she had appendicitis.

Evelyn sternly reprimanded me for being neglectful of my duty to Mabelle. "She could have died!"

In situations such as these, I yelled at myself for being so stupid, hating myself to the core, wishing I were the one that had appendicitis and died. I repeated these kinds of thoughts every time Evelyn yelled at me for being stupid.

"I don't understand why you can't use the good brain God gave you!" I had heard this statement so many times from Evelyn's mouth, I knew it was coming. I learned the only response she would accept was to agree with her by groveling for forgiveness and expressing remorse.

What a contrast this was to Mabelle. Over and over I apologized directly to Mabelle for my poor judgment. She was never upset. "You did not know, honey heart. I have gone through so many painful experiences, I truly thought it was just flu. God took care of all of us."

It was Evelyn who would not let go of my neglect in caring for Mabelle. From that time forward, whenever I made what Evelyn determined was a nonthinking choice, I would be reminded of the time with Mabelle and her appendicitis attack, when she almost died because of my neglect.

As soon as I felt strong enough, I got back into the daily routine of working in the kitchen, doing housework, driving myself to my aquatic exercise, and grocery shopping.

Then disaster struck.

I was baking a casserole one day and accidentally dropped a hot pad in the oven when I opened the door to check on the dish. I didn't notice this—that is, until the oven started to smoke and the smoke detector started blaring.

Evelyn watched in disgust as I made mistakes like this, convinced that the mild stroke I had, prevented me from thinking as well or as quickly as I used to. She questioned my ability to drive a car. She convinced me that I had to give up my driver's license until I showed improvement in thinking and reacting. She assured me that the whole Community thought the same thing. It was the safer choice. After all, I had to admit my reaction time was slower. I did not want to kill someone while driving by not having a rapid reaction time.

Instead of asking Dr. Frank whether he thought the brain damage was severe enough to discontinue my driving, I merely reported to him what the Community had decided. During the remainder of my Community life, someone else had to drive me. This change in my driving meant I lost any adult independence. Gone were college classes, grocery shopping, library visits, and the times when I did errands on the way home from aquatics class. I had to rethink my entire lifestyle, adjusting to so much less freedom.

I knew from the other women who went shopping that getting out to shop meant time away to be by themselves, eat out, go to bookstores, thrift-store shop for "new clothes," and even pray in the Blessed Sacrament Chapel at the Catholic church. God forbid that Evelyn, who often spoke disapprovingly of the Roman Catholic church, insisting we were already "Catholic," should find out. I was dependent on others to take me to doctors' appointments and to my aquatic exercise classes. If I wanted to go to the library, it had to be when someone else went out and only if it was convenient for him or her.

To find some way to be alone, as I regained strength, I began walking again in the very early morning hours, always being sure to get back before my responsibilities had to be fulfilled. It was getting harder and harder to even pray at home. Our morning-prayer times had degenerated to Evelyn's constant criticisms of us. Under the guise of walking in the light, these prayer times could take hours, not ending until the person agreed totally with Evelyn's rebuke and accepted her appropriate corrective changes. It was terrible.

It sounds crazy as I write this, but there *was* one reason why I went along with the decision to give up driving.

CHAPTER 46

Obey

Remember your leaders who spoke the word
of God to you. Consider the outcome of
their way of life and imitate their faith.
—Heb. 13:7

I took seriously my vow of obedience to the Community. As my "mother," Evelyn was my spiritual elder. I never saw myself on an equal plane with her. She made sure I could never live up to her expectations. She was louder than I. She always told us she was more intelligent than the rest of us. She was "the *mother*," just as in any traditional religious order. My job was to agree and obey. I made myself believe that serving her was my ministry. I colored her hair; I gave her coupons to clean her bathroom or her bedroom. When she misplaced something, I found it for her. I helped her when she entertained, serving, but staying in the kitchen. She allowed her "rich" friends to believe I was her personal nanny, with the benefits that came by being included in special outings with them.

I forced myself into believing I was happy being part of her personal circle. This is the reason I went along with the decision to give up driving; it was part of my obedient submission to her authority in every aspect of my life. When she decided that women in general had stopped dressing like women, not wearing skirts or dresses but only pants, she declared, "I would like to make a ban on pants. Let us promise to wear skirts or dresses whenever possible. We women can all wear jean skirts with Community T-shirts and call them our work habits; we could wear them every day."

She often ended her pronouncements with, "What do you think?" Of course, she really did not care what we thought. She would do what she wanted anyway. I would agree with her 98 percent of the time; the other 2 percent I kept my opinion to myself. I did not want to counter Evelyn in anything because I would always lose. Like a wife who stands by an abusive husband, I received positive attention from Evelyn when she called me to do something for her. But she remained determined to control my life and "fix" my problems.

I got so tired of the assignments she gave me to help me see how I was destroying myself. One example: I came into my bedroom, and on my bed was a poster of various shapes of medicine bottles, with labels such as anger, pity party, judgmental, low self-esteem, critical, pride, and negative. A note read, "Bring this poster to the next Friday Girls' meeting to discuss what this poster represents." My reaction to this poster fueled the hatred I felt toward myself so much I seriously considered suicide. I felt I could not take any more disapproval from Evelyn. I knew no way to escape her constant scrutinizing my every thought.

Girls' meeting only made my already-burning hatred rise to the next level of almost exploding, but I held it in. "Do you know why you have lupus?" she asked me at the meeting, not waiting for an answer. "It's because you keep taking the wrong medicines; the names on these bottles are what you are feeding yourself. They are psycho-toxins that you keep telling yourself, and your body responds to them by making you sick." I started to understand the picture she was trying to get across, but the last comment stung deeply. "It is your fault you are sick; you made yourself sick!" I did not respond; I was torn between the truth of what the doctor told me and the lies Evelyn was trying to make me believe. The safest way out was silence, to simply comply by saying nothing. In this way she would think she succeeded in convincing me that she was correct in her assessment.

That night in the kitchen before dinner, at the stove she asked, "Well, what are you going to do?"

My irrational response was, "I think I should just go take the whole bottle of prednisone and end it all."

Her reaction was typical Evelyn. "Why don't you just go behind the poustinia and hang yourself? It's quicker!" she said with a smirk on her face.

It was supposed to get me out of depression and make me laugh. I faked that laugh, knowing deep down I could not commit suicide. That would be an unforgivable sin.

When I related this conversation to Dr. Frank at my next appointment, he was horrified. "How in the world could anyone make a joke in this way, especially since your emotions are not the cause of your illness? The tests proved you had lupus in your DNA. It only manifested itself now."

I assured him that her saying what she said made me look at how ridiculously I was acting. He was not convinced.

Shortly after this I wrote an article for a lupus publication describing, "How I Live with Lupus," stating in this article my near-death dream and Evelyn's suggestion to hang myself behind the poustinia to startle me out of my depression. Out of two hundred or more stories, the publishers picked only ten. Mine was one of them.

When I read my article aloud at the table, Evelyn grinned when I added the statement "why don't you go hang yourself?" I put the sentence in my article simply to please Evelyn. What truly pulled me out of depression was Dr. Frank giving me a prescription for an antidepressant medication that I was secretly taking. I dared not let Evelyn find out. I imagined her saying to me, "If you take that medicine, you might as well tell Jesus, 'I don't believe in you anymore.'" I know this because I have heard her make that accusation to others in the Community when they tried to follow their doctors' prescribed medications.

Then I found out that the Lupus Foundation had a fundraiser walk to raise money for a cure. I figured a great way to use the article I wrote, as a means to raise money was by sending the article to family and friends with a request for people to support the fundraiser. I brought the idea to the Community. Everyone agreed this was a good idea except Evelyn. She suggested I not walk. "You have extreme sun sensitivity, so you need to ask the doctor first. I know I am right."

I did not bother to ask Dr. Frank. I simply chose not to fight this battle with her and did not walk. The reason it became a battle for me is that anytime I wanted to do something on my own, Evelyn would always say, "Are you sure Dr. Frank would approve?" I asked if I could still raise money without walking, and the Lupus Foundation was happy for any money. I told everyone I knew to help raise money for lupus research, and the response was phenomenal. By the deadline I had raised more than $2,400 for lupus research. Because of this, the Lupus Foundation sent me an invitation to an award ceremony. I offered to make a cake to serve at the reception, with the Lupus Foundation logo on top.

Adele and Uncle Basil took me to the ceremony. I felt proud of my accomplishments, but was on my guard when it was my turn to share at the next dinner meal. I expected Evelyn to find some reason to downplay my accomplishments. Sadly I was correct. Before I even finished my story of the plaque, Evelyn interrupted. "That's nice, but I need to share what happened at the office yesterday." I did not look at her; I looked at Danielle. The frustrated look on her face spoke volumes. How could one woman be so impossibly unkind and at the same time profess her love for all of us? How could she continue to treat us like slaves—extensions of her personal world?

Unfortunately, this would be demonstrated yet again as any mental space and freedom I had living up at Mabelle's house was about to disappear.

CHAPTER 47

Peace Takes Hard Work

With firm purpose you maintain peace;
In peace, because of our trust in you.
—Isa. 26:3

Valerie and Tony were in trouble again. After spending several months recovering, Valerie had returned to her mother … but things never improved. They were about to be evicted from their home. Valerie remained emotionally unstable. Evelyn decided the entire family should move in with us. She announced Valerie would be moving back into my room at Mabelle's. I was told my new bedroom was back in the main house, the same awful, little, no-privacy room. I would share the bathroom with her two grandsons.

Desi and Lupo had become adults and moved on with their lives, so those bedrooms were available for this arrangement.

I prayed multiple times to have God's peace as I lived with the boys in the same house as Darren and Evelyn. They were noisy, with no proper discipline from their grandmother. They knew exactly what to say to get what they wanted from her. I always felt strange when I took a bath. The main bathroom had two sinks, so we decided to separate the bathroom, putting in a sliding door between the bathtub side with sink and the toilet side with sink. I always had the feeling like someone was on the other side of the sliding door peering at me. The grandsons would go down to the basement and watch television at all hours of the night. They also roughhoused, as boys do, making a lot of noise while I was sleeping.

I tried to share my concerns with Evelyn, but she told me to mind my own business; she was working on it. I asked myself many times, "I know I trust God, but why is it I do not trust the Community, or rather, Evelyn?"

One uncomfortable request came when she asked me to be her spy—although she didn't call it that—on Bonnie Jean.

"I want you to keep an eye on her," she whispered conspiratorially. "She puts on this 'little girl voice' around Darren. You need to tell me when this happens; she won't do it when I am around, so let me know when you hear it."

Even though I didn't want to do this, I complied. Until now I never saw it as being a spy, but now I see that Evelyn's request stemmed from her jealousy and insecurity.

There was one night, however, that I was grateful my bedroom was next door to the boys. I went to bed not feeling well. I spent the night with great pain in my thigh, waiting until morning. I knew something was bad when I could not put any weight on my legs, so I crawled from my bedroom to Tony Junior's room, where he was asleep on his mattress on the floor. "Tony, I need help. I can't walk," I whispered.

He jumped up, shocked at seeing me at his head. I did not know what was going on with me, only that I was in excruciating pain in my leg and groin. He went to his grandma, Evelyn, to get help.

Robert and Gary picked me up gently and carried me out to the station wagon; Danielle drove me to the hospital. It was six o'clock on a Saturday morning. When we got there, Danielle got a wheelchair to get me into the emergency room.

That was when she heard a voice behind her ask, "What are you doing here, Danielle?" It was Dr. Steve, who knew Danielle from both their sons attending the same high school.

When she explained the situation, he was able to expedite my care. I went through the usual routine, medical history, my current symptoms. They gave me an IV of morphine and let me rest on the gurney in a small room next to the check-in room with no nurse, no call bell. This was a significant oversight because I needed to go to the bathroom. I waited for quite a while for someone to come in and check on me, but no one came. I tried to think what to do. "I will figure this out," I said to myself. There was a restroom right around the corner. I carefully lifted the IV bag off the pole, and somehow I hopped on my better side to the toilet, did my business, and made it back to the gurney before anyone knew I had left.

The next step was getting an MRI on the groin to see what was going on. The technician asked me to stay still during the exam—impossible! I prayed hard to relax. If anyone has had an MRI, they know the noise this test makes is far from relaxing. I was not a Catholic, but all I could do was pray: "Hail Mary, full of Grace, the Lord is with thee, blessed art thou among women and blessed is the fruit of thy womb, Jesus." I used my fingers as my rosary; that helped me to find peace in the midst of pain. The diagnosis was a peritoneal bleed.

"Now you know the pain of having a baby," reassured Dr. Frank.

"Then I am glad I won't have to go through it," I joked back. "So what's next?"

The doctor told me the bleed was caused by the Coumadin I was taking to keep my blood thin (to prevent another stroke). One more time medication intended for good caused me damage.

I tried to lighten my attitude by telling Dr. Frank, "Well, here's one more medication to add to my list of complications!"

Again the wonderful medical professionals treated me, and when I returned home this time, it seemed my lupus was finally stabilized.

CHAPTER 48

Home Can Be Anywhere

Then they set out and went from village
to village proclaiming the good news
and curing diseases everywhere.
—Luke 9:6

In the midst of all my medical crises and our children moving through grade school and beyond, as a Christian ministry we still actively tried to serve our neighbors, especially the Hispanic community. Here is that story.

Over the years, the more we got to know the neighborhood Mexican workers who walked past our home early every morning and at dusk in the evenings, the more curious we became. Basilio, who continued to return seasonally, knew where these men lived. He asked if Bonnie, with her Spanish teaching expertise, could come up to their little village to teach English. We felt this was our opening to see how we could assist these men. What we found was humbling. Past the road, past the brush, in the corner of the hill above us out of sight, there was one little section of flattened dirt in an orange orchard where a few dirt-floor shacks stood. Each housed three or four single men or a small family with young children. One "lucky" family resided in a broken-down trailer.

Basilio met us as we drove Bonnie's green VW Bug up the dirt road. He introduced us, then took us in behind one shack that had been transformed into a kitchen/dining area. Elena was a soft-spoken proud woman with jet-black hair neatly groomed, who welcomed us in her "home." The table was neatly covered with a tablecloth. Clean coffee mugs hung on the walls. Plates were set on shelves, and she was kneading dough into balls for flour tortillas. We drank coffee and ate the best-tasting tortillas while we visited with Elena and her twelve-year-old son, Gonzalio. Her husband, Gonzalo, was out working. Her stove was an old oil drum that Gonzalo had cut out a hole in the side and filled with dirt and cement to form a shelf inside. Elena filled the drum with wood, which heated up the top of the drum to boil water for coffee, make soup, and fry tortillas. I also noticed rabbit meat drying over the smoke that rose from the fire.

One time when we arrived, Gonzalo was waiting for us, carrying what looked like a large cat, but when we got closer, it was actually a dead bobcat he found in the dumpster. That was to be their next meal.

As a child I would visit my cousin who lived on a farm. Her dad made her a small playhouse with pretend stove, table, and chairs. This shack reminded me of that little playhouse, only this was real life. They got water from the hose outside, connected to the same one that watered the orchard. There were no toilet facilities or trash recycling.

Those of us who spoke Spanish took turns heading up to "the camp" once a week to visit with Elena and whoever else was there, to read a Bible story to Gonzalio, and to see how we might make their meager living situation a bit more tolerable. We held church services up at the camp, helped the families paint the shacks, and worked with the property owner to pay for portable toilet and trash pickup.

That winter Evelyn and I were looking for a special meal during the holidays that we could cook for them. We found this in one of our magazines: "Every New Year, Menudo, a special soup is always made." We couldn't wait to try this out and surprise our friends. The recipe called for tripe (something we had no idea what was), but the rest of the ingredients looked "normal" to our American palates. I cut the tripe (cow stomach, it turned out) into bite-size pieces and put it in the pot, making a huge amount. We did not realize tripe had so much fat; there was a thick layer of melted fat on top of our broth.

Excitedly several of us drove up to the camp in the dark and knocked on the doors to invite our guests to a surprise meal. Silly Americanos, we did not figure in that when you do not have electricity but only candles and the weather is cold, you go to bed early. We shyly asked if they wanted to join us for a special dinner. Everyone graciously got dressed and came down to our house. I bet they wished they had stayed in bed. We learned the reason Mexicans eat menudo on New Year's was to cure a hangover, not because it is a delicacy. Needless to say, the joke was on us, and we all had a good laugh. By the way, no one ate the tripe—it was like rubber.

One time when we went up to the camp, a chain blocked the road, so we found another way to get in. I had to lift a chain up, stretching it to the limit, just barely making it over the roof of the small VW Bug. We found a group of men standing around nervously when we arrived. There had been a fight. Gonzalo was drunk and had a gash in his ear profusely bleeding. My immediate reaction was to take off my new white sweatshirt and put it up to his ear to stop the bleeding.

"We need to take him to the hospital. Is there anyone who can go?" I asked. His cousin took him, with someone putting pressure on his ear (not with my sweatshirt).

Soon after this the owner sold the orchard. The inhabitants moved on from what they had called home for many months.

We missed the people we had gotten to know and love, but we looked ahead, knowing that our God, who closes one door, opens another.

CHAPTER 49

Olive Tree Thrift Store

> Do nothing out of selfishness or out of vainglory;
> rather, humbly regard others as more important
> than yourselves, each looking out not for his own
> interests, but [also] everyone for those of others.
> —Phil. 2:3–4

The idea came, naturally, from Evelyn: "Darren and I just returned from a trip to Tijuana, where we went to a thrift store. In the middle was a small chapel where anyone could pray. I thought, wouldn't it be a fun venture to try that for ourselves?" After discussion and prayer, we decided to look for rental spaces to see if anything might be available. Evelyn volunteered to start the search. Robert assisted her on one trip; another time I joined her.

We found space in a downtown building located between a barbershop and a deli/liquor store. Robert built all the racks, shelves, hangers, and tables to use in the thrift store. He also constructed temporary walls to build a chapel in the corner. We wondered about whether we would get donations to fill the store, but with our many contacts, we discovered there was nothing to worry about. Our first place to advertise was the local Episcopal church. That was enough, and by the time we opened, we filled not only the store but also a whole garage!

We had many interesting experiences working at the store. I will share just a few of the more memorable times at the store.

One of my favorite customers was Socorro, a homeless woman who came to our store with people she met on the street who needed clothes or shoes. She often smelled of whiskey but never acted drunk. Her generosity to others was a joy to watch, especially with the prostitutes who came with her to get warm clothes. One day a well-dressed woman with a Hispanic accent and perfect English asked if we had seen a woman with Socorro's description. She was her sister. I explained that we never knew when she would come in but that she did so often. Her sister had offered her a place to live in her home, but Socorro preferred to live on the streets. I told her sister how blessed we were every time she came in to buy something for someone else in greater need.

Adele and Uncle Basil were working the store on a cold, rainy Friday night. I arrived an hour before the store closed, walking there from my aquatic exercise class.

"Only two customers came in all day long, but we provided a warm dry place for one homeless man to spend an hour out of the rain. We gave him a nice hot cup o' noodles, a peanut butter sandwich, and prayer, which made being here worthwhile," shared Adele.

Two men became regulars, who supported themselves by buying merchandise at our store and then reselling it at the swap meet. I watched them intently as they looked over our jewelry, paying specific attention to what they purchased. I learned from them to recognize good jewelry from costume imitations.

One day a woman dropped off her large bag of donations, and when I went through the bag, I found a ring box with a green jewel in it. "Adele, I am going to set this aside. I think it may be an emerald."

When I took it to the jeweler, it felt nice when he offered $250 for the jewel. We had no way of knowing the woman who dropped off the bag to return it, so we earned a lot that day. On the other hand, we lost money frequently when we received counterfeit twenty-dollar bills.

There are times I am simply a klutz or accident-prone. I offered to go next door to get us deli sandwiches. On the way back, I noticed some change on the ground underneath the newspaper stand. As I bent down to pick up the change, I bumped my head on the corner of the stand. I then noticed blood on the ground. I thought, *I don't remember seeing blood on the ground; I wonder who is hurt.* I literally looked around to find someone bleeding and, seeing no one, went back to the store.

"Oh my God, what happened to you?" asked Adele.

"Why? Am I bleeding?" I went to the bathroom and was shocked to see blood running down my face from my head. I grabbed a towel, but that was soon soaked with blood. Then I grabbed ice, but the blood still flowed. "Adele, would you please call Robert. I can't get the blood to stop flowing."

Robert came down quickly to assess the situation. He did his best to put antibacterial medicine on the wound and bandage it. None of us ever thought about going to the emergency room.

However, when I saw Dr. Frank the following week, he said, "You should have gotten stitches; this is a pretty bad wound."

I may have dodged that hospital visit, but I did end up in the emergency room after a day's work at the store.

I was walking our dog, Abraham, right after breakfast. Halfway around the block, a dog behind a fence startled him enough to make him dart in front of me; I tripped and landed on top of him. I protected my heart by putting my left hand on my chest. My hand hurt, but I did not think it was serious. After prayers I left to work with Adele all day at the store.

I should have put ice on my hand all day, but I was focused on a task to do for Evelyn. I had a little craft project where I made cute little boxes from used greeting/Christmas cards. She had asked me to make twenty boxes for her for people in the office, so I spent all day making boxes. By the time we got home, my hand had swollen up to three times its size.

"What did you do to your hand?" asked Evelyn.

I explained I had fallen over Abraham on my walk after breakfast and hurt my hand.

"You need to call Dr. Frank and see what he says."

Always when I had any little problem, the answer was to call Dr. Frank. I figured, "I will—but he will just tell me to ice it." I was wrong.

Five minutes after I talked to Dr. Frank, Uncle Basil was driving me to the emergency room. When we got there, I presented my medical card, explaining that my doctor wanted to have my hand looked at. When they took me to my cubicle, I felt like I was the sideshow of the evening. Every five minutes someone came in to see my hand, from nurses and emergency medical techs to doctors, all of them asking whether it hurt. I knew the peace of God was on me.

Typically all I worried about was whether Uncle Basil had gotten dinner. I asked a nurse to send a message to him in the waiting room to go to the cafeteria to get dinner. We were there from six o' clock to midnight. I was shocked to learn my hand was broken in five places!

Our thrift-store ministry lasted for a few years until the city rezoned the area for upgraded development, meaning our owner had to sell the building. The outreach had allowed us to help with more than just providing physical needs such as clothing. It had given us an opportunity to work closely together in a completely different environment—right in the heart of our town.

CHAPTER 50

New Feet

He leaped up, stood, and walked around,
and went into the temple with them, walking
and jumping and praising God.
—Acts 3:8

The aquatic pool classes closed for summer vacation. Evelyn suggested I ask her mother-in-law if I might exercise in the pool at the complex where she lived. That meant she had to accompany me as I used it. I felt uncomfortable asking since I never like to inconvenience anyone, but it turned out "Gram," as we all called her, was delighted. Uncle Basil would transport me on the days he did errands.

One summer day, before the birthday party planned for Uncle Basil and Valerie at the same pool, as I began to jog in the pool, I felt a pain in my foot. I didn't want to say anything because Gram was doing me a kindness in letting me be there. When I finished as best I could, I had to walk on the outside of my foot to relieve the pain.

The next day for the party, I was responsible for several food-related items and setup. It is funny now, but I limped the whole day because of the great pain in my foot. Only Danielle asked me why I was limping, and she worried about my walking on it. "I can't call the doctor; it is Saturday, and there is so much that has to be done. I'll rest when this is all over," I assured her.

On Sunday, the pain was worse, so at church I asked for prayers, promising to call the doctor on Monday. I called on Monday, explaining to the doctor what happened with my foot and how bad was the pain I was having. He gave me a referral to a foot doctor.

Adele took me to the appointment, where they took an x-ray that showed a hairline fracture in my right foot. No wonder I was in such pain, but how was it possible to break the foot in water? The reason was obvious: I do not have strong bones—because of two factors, first, rheumatoid arthritis, and second, I take prednisone, one of the side effects of which is osteoporosis. Dr. Eric, the foot doctor, gave me a boot to wear on that foot to help it heal. I had to wear it anytime I walked.

This began my relationship with this tall, curly-haired Norwegian doctor, whose wife had lupus and was a patient of Dr. Frank. He told me it would be a good idea because of lupus to see him on a regular basis too, and like a diabetic, get my toenails cut by him. If I cut myself clipping the toenails, I could easily get an infection due to my impaired immune system.

After seeing him for several months, he asked if I might consider having surgery to get the bunions on my feet removed. I had read about the surgery years back, but the expense was costly. Ill-fitting shoes sometimes cause a bunion, and it becomes painful to walk on. Another medical thought is that bunions are a genetic defect. In my case both theories are true. I recall looking at my paternal grandmother's feet. She wore the typical "grandma shoes" but had cut out the leather of the shoe to relieve the bunion pain. It was obvious she was in constant pain just by watching her walk, but she never complained.

I asked the Community if anyone had a check on Dr. Eric submitting a request to my health insurance, Medi-Cal, for permission to do the surgery. "How long will you be incapacitated?" asked Evelyn. "Who will color my hair?" She meant it as a joke, but I felt guilty that I would not be able to stand long enough to color her hair.

When I got the go-ahead for the surgery, Dr. Eric explained the plan in great detail. He would remove the bunion, as well as do a complete reconstruction of all the bones in my toes. He would cut the bones in two places in each toe, putting a long six-inch pin down the center of each toe that would need to stay in for at least eight weeks.

"May I be awake to watch the surgery?" I asked seriously. One thing he and I had in common was fascination with the body and surgery. We both watched the Learning

Channel when they broadcast surgeries. I have watched a heart transplant, liver transplant, hip and knee replacement surgery, and brain surgery. I have also read many books written by doctors about their experiences.

"Believe me, you do not want to see or smell the surgery," he responded.

"Smell? What do you mean?"

He asked me if I knew the smell of burning hair, which is the same smell as cutting bone. I ended up being under anesthesia.

When I opened my eyes after the surgery, I felt wonderful. I wanted to get up and out of bed right away. There was no pain at all. What Dr. Eric did not tell me was that he had injected a strong pain medicine in my foot; when that wore off, I felt the full intensity of the pain. The physical therapist came in with crutches to help me learn to walk again. I needed to get moving, and the crutches were a necessity.

Hanging in the window of my room when I got home was a lovely welcome-home poster. It felt good to be back home, but being confined to my room was difficult. Something I will never understand about Evelyn is when I was physically capable to do things for her, we were close, but when I became disabled, she avoided any contact with me. We lived in the same house, but it was always the other women who brought the meals and books on tape or sat to visit with me.

A year later, I had surgery on the left foot and was in recuperation, staying in my little room in the big house. Evelyn had asked the men to construct an art room for her. The art-room space removed my small closet and enclosed a part of the outside porch. There were two entrances to her art room, through my room or the outdoors; but 98 percent of the time she walked through my room. When she wanted into the art room, she would knock once if the door was closed and then enter, not waiting for an answer from me. With a brief hello and no eye contact, she walked through, closing the door behind her. It takes effort to ignore someone when he or she lives in the same house, and I never understood this strange behavior from her. Not once did she come to my room with a dinner tray, or even just to visit. Everyone else in the family would bring books on tape or snacks from the kitchen—or just come to chat and share their day with me. The trials I bore after my foot surgeries were a lot easier than the emotional roller coaster I lived in my relationship with Evelyn.

Then a routine mammogram revealed a cancerous lump in Evelyn's breast. Everyone was supportive through her treatment, praying for her through repeated rounds of chemotherapy and radiation. God answered all the prayers by making her cancer-free. I am not making light of the seriousness of her trial, but every conversation at all mealtimes should not have centered on her breasts and treatments, but it did. Evelyn always had a habit of repeating herself, but after the cancer scare, the repetition increased dramatically. She had gotten so ingrown she showed no interest in others but only cared about herself. Still, my habits were automatic.

I was dedicated to serving her no matter how inconvenient it might be for me.

My therapy at the aquatics pool continued, although I switched to another indoor pool in a gym across town. I met my best friend, Klara, at these classes. I had never clicked with someone as quickly as I did with Klara. During the rest of the time attending these classes, she became my best support.

Klara was my only friend outside Community, and she and her husband, Kent, are still my best friends. She is outgoing and very observant. After her first visit to the Community, she commented, "Is Evelyn always so frenetic? She talks nonstop, quickly, and kept interrupting Darren anytime he tried to share."

My response was very typical of how we as a Community defended Evelyn. "She is this way because she is a New Yorker."

Like so many people who have come and gone, Klara and Kent were able to see the real dominant, controlling Evelyn when the rest of us had blind eyes.

CHAPTER 51

From Mother to Prophet

Beloved, do not trust every spirit but test the spirits
to see whether they belong to God, because many
false prophets have gone out into the world.
—1 John 4:1

Darren and Evelyn came to the dinner table and asked to
attend a four-day weekend seminar titled "Prophet School."
They had read the book written by the seminar leaders and
were eager to confirm what they kept telling us: that Evelyn
was a prophet. Upon their return they were ecstatic. They
were convinced that, indeed, Evelyn had the prophetic gift.
Darren even prepared a document for the Community to
sign declaring her as a prophet sent by God, not just to our
Community but also the world.

It is difficult to look back now and recall any good that
came out of the times she attempted to use her prophetic
skills outside the Community. For example, we held several

luncheons with a guest speaker to talk on a specific theme of our choosing. After their speeches, there was a question and answer time. Evelyn chose the speaker. On one occasion she invited Bishop H. in order to drill him with specific questions revealing inconsistencies in his preaching and life. She had her questions planned well ahead of time, even sharing them at the dinner table weeks before. After his speech, with other questions first, Evelyn then came in for the kill with her prepared questions. He was deeply humiliated in front of priests and friends from his diocese.

I felt so embarrassed at Evelyn's calculated attack on the man. He couldn't leave quickly enough but graciously did take the time to thank those of us working the kitchen for the lunch. I knew something was wrong in how the whole day was planned. Is a prophet of a living, loving God supposed to be mean and nasty? Is it really her job to embarrass a bishop?

Evelyn kept telling us that she was another Jeremiah from the Old Testament, the weeping prophet to whom no one listened. "A prophet is happy only when everyone is crying in repentance, and crying when people are rejoicing in sin," she repeated often. She often played a song about Jeremiah titled "I Am a Prophet." She would parade around the living room, dancing in a strange and psychotic manner, pointing her finger at us accusingly. Her purpose was for us to feel guilt for wallowing in the same sins repeatedly.

Then she pronounced that for our Friday days of prayer and fasting, she would now provide spiritual direction. Based on a form of guidance used in Catholic orders, she instructed:

"You go to the poustinia.

"I knock and say, 'Benedicite.'

"You answer, 'Deo gratias,' and I enter.

"Then you share in this manner: Physically I feel … My thoughts are … Emotionally I … Spiritually I … Where I intend to get or what I hope to attain spiritually is … What I would like from you is … I will listen prayerfully, saying little. Then I will pray and share what the Lord gives me: dialogue, advice, suggestions, or whatever."

By now many of us knew that Evelyn's suggestions were really mandates, and even though no one was eager to be subjected to yet another form of private correction from her, to keep the peace I signed up. It was a disaster.

After several months of spiritual direction, she told me, "This is not working for you. You are not growing, and you say the same things every month. I believe we should discontinue this direction until you prove you have made a change."

She left me in the poustinia to ponder her decision. I was devastated. Again, I felt the only escape from her reign was to kill myself but knew God would not forgive me for committing that sin. I imagined many ways I could die, actually wishing for my death. I kept trying to figure out from my dream in the hospital Jesus saying, "They need you down there more than I need you up here right now." I questioned God: "Are you finished with me, Jesus? Why don't you take me back now? They don't need me anymore. I am just a slave to whatever Evelyn wants."

When I got back in the house, Evelyn called, "Are you ready to color my hair, Kata?" She asked this in the normal way, acting as if nothing dramatic had happened, or maybe she was just trying to make me feel better. I was never sure.

After her cancer treatments, she also had two major knee operations. That was when her already frenetic irrational behaviors escalated even more. One dinner she announced that for her seventy-fifth birthday, she wanted a Queen Esther party—which coincided with the Jewish feast of Purim. She and Darren would be costumed as king and queen. There would be a huge dinner, and we would invite all her friends, especially her Jewish ones. Danielle was the best organizer, so she received the job of completely planning the event. Evelyn said she wanted the party to be a surprise from her, but every time we gathered to plan, she found ways to interrupt to provide suggestions. We tried to plan on the days she was gone, to keep some of it a surprise. But as soon as she got home, she insisted on knowing the progress we had made.

One of my tasks was to construct crowns for Darren and Evelyn and headdresses for the women guests. I spent a month day and night stringing beads into headdresses and meticulously sewing sequins on for the crowns so they would sparkle. I also made fifty-some headdresses for the women and girls for the party. Danielle filled a notebook on what to serve, how to serve it, table settings, tables and chairs, the invitations, the speakers, the gifts. It was a monumental affair. Robert constructed a dais so that Evelyn, Darren, and particular friends could sit up higher than everyone else.

Watching Evelyn so thoroughly enjoying herself up on the stage, I saw how she wanted us to treat her on a daily basis: as unchallenged mother superior and prophet. I watched in wonderment, thinking of all the times she had boasted about how humble she was. It made me sick to my stomach that I continued, out of fear of rejection, to do what she asked. I had a wonderful relationship with my own mom, who was nothing like Evelyn. My own mom, Katarzyna, was gentle and loving, so why did I feel I had a need for a mother such as Evelyn? I had sacrificed myself to be the person Evelyn wanted me to be.

Later in the year, Evelyn and I were changing the sheets in the guest room for the bishop's visit. She asked me, "Have you thought about asking Dr. Frank whether you could start driving again?"

"Yes, I have!" I immediately replied. "I have thought about it for so long. Thank you." I was ecstatic over the idea of driving again.

She told me to bring the idea up at the table for Community agreement, and everyone was thrilled with the thought of me driving again.

At my next appointment with Dr. Frank, I asked him if he thought it would be all right for me to start driving again.

His response puzzled me. "I never told you that you couldn't drive. You were the one to say that the Community didn't want you to drive, and you agreed with them."

I learned that since I hadn't driven for years, I needed to attend a driving school. I shared with Evelyn what I had learned. The cost turned out to be more than I expected, $300, but I knew the Community was happy for me to get my driver's license. Then, unfortunately, when I presented the amount at the table, before anyone else spoke, Evelyn interrupted me, saying, "Three hundred dollars is a lot. Much more than I thought. I don't think you should go at this price. You do not have to drive that much."

I held back my tears, burning inside with disappointment. I had felt so happy to know that I would be able to start driving again, having the freedom I'd missed for seventeen years. Then on a whim, Evelyn changed her mind in front of us all. Later, Danielle shared how angry she was that Evelyn built up my expectations, just to smash them to pieces. Things were coming to the breaking point under Evelyn's tyrannical leadership.

CHAPTER 52

Taking Steps Forward

Therefore I tell you, do not worry about your life, what
you will eat [or drink], or about your body, what you
will wear. Is not life more than food and the body more
than clothing? ... But seek first the kingdom [of God]
and his righteousness, and all these things will be given
you besides. Do not worry about tomorrow; tomorrow
will take care of itself. Sufficient for a day is its own evil.
—Matt. 6:25, 33–34

The grandsons had grown and moved out of the house, so
Evelyn suggested I move back into the house Mario and I
had shared, but in a different room. I didn't recognize at the
time that this was yet one more way she and Darren could act
like they were special, with their own private home. I shared
a bathroom with Danielle and Gary, who welcomed me
warmly. That was much easier than sharing a bathroom with
Tony and Valerie, whose marriage difficulties and passive/
aggressive anger spilled over into all their relationships.

Evelyn's mental state was becoming more unstable. She remained manic in her actions, spoke incessantly, and commented multiple times a day how she was God's prophet and the one in charge. For a time we viewed Evelyn with guarded caution. After all, with her multiple surgeries, cancer treatments, and medications—coupled with her age—all this might be a response to that. We hoped things would begin to settle down soon.

Only later did I learn that Danielle and Dee had gone to Darren expressing concern about Evelyn and wanted to ask for permission to contact the bishop so he would be aware of her difficulties and the effect it was having within the Community. Danielle and Dee had made the unfortunate assumption that since Darren was their spiritual leader and an attorney, their conversation was confidential. Fifteen minutes after that private discussion, Darren brought them both before Evelyn with the words, "You know I never keep anything from my wife. Now you tell her to her face what you just told me." They were forbidden to make any contact with the bishop—even though that was their right as members of a religious order.

Danielle shared with me later that, "This was when I realized we had moved into dangerous, cult-like leadership and something needed to be done soon." No longer in the same home as Darren and Evelyn, I was just starting to become aware of the growing tension among the Community members. With the last of the children gone off to college or to apartments, the subject of what the adults would do, now that raising children was finished, came up quite a few times. I did not realize that several of us were determined to never let any other person move into the Community. They did not want anyone else to deal with the untenable situation that Darren and Evelyn's leadership had fostered.

Finally, in the fall of 2008, it was Valerie who reached her limit. One weekday morning Evelyn called a meeting immediately for all who were home. It was clear she was furious. She learned that Valerie had privately invited Danielle to join her to visit Poppa's home nearby. Valerie had kept a close relationship with her father and his new wife. Danielle was happy to share in the fun of a TV ball game and picnic meal. Darren sat beside Evelyn, fuming quietly, while she queried everyone in the room about how they felt about this betrayal, as she termed it. When everyone indicated no problem with what Valerie and Danielle did, Evelyn stood up, pointed her finger at everyone in the room one by one, and said, "Well, you *should* feel the same way I do!"

That day was the beginning of the end. Valerie exploded privately with Danielle. "I've had it." No matter what Valerie did, what she wore, how much she weighed, how she kept her room, her every move was scrutinized and commented upon repeatedly. She continued, "Evelyn has always tried to manage my life. I have never had freedom from her almost dictatorship over my life. Now I have to 'feel' what she tells me I am to feel? *Enough*! I am sick of it. Something has to be done."

Valerie secretly penned a letter to our bishop, informing him of our dangerous leadership situation.

CHAPTER 53

The Intervention

If your brother sins [against you], go and tell him his
fault between you and him alone. If he listens to you,
you have won over your brother. If he does not listen,
take one or two others along with you, so that every
fact may be established on the testimony of two or
three witnesses. If he refuses to listen to them, tell the
church. If he refuses to listen even to the church, then
treat him as you would a Gentile or a tax collector.
—Matt. 18:15–17

But if we walk in the light as he is in the light,
then we have fellowship with one another, and the
blood of his Son Jesus cleanses us from all sin.
—1 John 1:7

Verses quoted from
The Rule and Constitution of the Community of ROCF 1977

November 3, 2008

All the adult Community members except two were sitting around the dinner table. Danielle shared in a somber tone that Gary would be a little late this evening. The other member, Bonnie Jean, was away visiting family in Hawaii. Uncle Basil and his wife, Adele, Robert and his wife, Dee, Tony with his wife, Valerie, and I started eating.

As always Evelyn controlled everything, still treating us as school-age children and prompting her husband to begin the conversation with, "So, what did you do today?" No one volunteered to speak, so Darren and Evelyn started to talk about their day: clients that came to his office and Evelyn's trip to town to get some new shoes she needed for an outfit she had bought to wear at a Christmas party at the office.

Evelyn asked if anyone had heard from Bonnie but remarked she would not be surprised if she decided to stay a longer time with her family or not return at all. The day before Bonnie left for her visit to her brother's, we were all present at the lunch table, including a divorced older man, Eli, who had been living with us with the intention of staying. Evelyn accused Bonnie of flirting with this man—and not just being a flirt, but acting like a whore with any single man who came through our door. Evelyn made Eli say directly to Bonnie his intention not to get married again and that he was not interested. This was humiliating, and I watched Bonnie's face turn hard and ashen.

Evelyn not only voiced openly that she hoped Bonnie would not return; she was trying to recruit us to agree with her.

Obviously Evelyn's jealousy of Bonnie's long-ago and long-past attraction to her husband was still motivating her feelings.

After about thirty minutes of forced conversation, Gary walked in with a guest he had brought, Dr. El-Amin. A few moments of silence passed.

Darren started to ask Dr. El-Amin a question, but before he got his words out, Danielle interrupted him.

She announced, "Evelyn, this is an intervention. Concerning you."

In shock, Darren and Evelyn demanded, "What is this all about?"

Danielle continued to explain that Dr. El-Amin was the Christian therapist recommended by our family doctor to be present as some of the members presented to Evelyn and Darren letters of grievances concerning their leadership of the Community.

I was taken completely by surprise! I thought, *This can't be happening*. Frankly, I was terrified, not knowing what was going to happen next.

Dr. El-Amin started very calmly to explain what the intervention entailed. You could see hidden rage on Evelyn's face. Whenever she was upset, her cheeks would turn red, and boy, were they burning red that night!

It was obvious this intervention was well planned. Basil, his wife, Adele, and I were not informed beforehand. The other members had assessed, correctly, that if we had learned of this action, we would have immediately told Darren and Evelyn.

Dr. El-Amin encouraged everyone to speak directly to Darren and Evelyn and instructed that they could not respond so that the person sharing could speak without interruption. First one and then another of the members who were involved with the plan read aloud letters of deep pain they had held in over many years. All of them involved how Evelyn had managed, manipulated, and controlled their lives. The stories shared the same dynamics: belittling, constantly admonishing them in front of everyone, insisting they have the same interests she did, demanding they feel the way she felt, and interfering with the couples on how to raise their children. No matter what they had tried within our rule of life to settle their problems with Evelyn and Darren's leadership, they were always rebuffed and then punished with even more restrictive assignments for their behaviors. Hence their extraordinary action necessitating this intervention.

When it came to my turn, the words came out before I could stop them. "You have broken the Community in half!"

"You sure got that right, Kata," shouted Evelyn. She immediately saw me as an ally.

Three long, painful hours passed as the three married couples poured out decades of deep emotional wounds.

Evelyn, ignoring instruction, kept trying to defend herself, but Dr. El-Amin would regain control, demanding Evelyn sit quietly.

Darren spoke in her defense most of the evening. Yet there was one point when he started to see the picture everyone was painting about Evelyn. I remember watching his face, seeing the truth dawn on him that his wife had severely hurt the lives of ten other people by her need to be in control all the time. It only lasted a brief moment before he reverted back to a defense mode of his beloved wife. His blindness to the verbal abuse Evelyn spewed out, in the name of God, prevented him from seeing how much emotional damage she caused to those around her.

Dr. El-Amin realized that the meeting had hit a block. She had asked Evelyn to go around the room asking forgiveness from each person. But it was insincere. It was simply an attempt to end the evening—not to acknowledge any self-awareness of responsibility.

When Evelyn got to me, she said there was nothing she did to merit forgiveness. I actually believed her! The only thing I remember feeling was fear and confusion. I kept thinking, *What will happen to the Community? Why are they treating Mother in this way, as if she were a criminal?* My heart felt broken and raw.

In closing, Dr. El-Amin made two demands: first, each of us was to go to our respective rooms. We were not to speak about what went on that evening. Second, after forty-eight hours, we should meet as a group, bringing letters stating what we believed to be the next step to bring healing and wholeness back to the Community.

"After you have met together, call me, and I will help you work out a strategy to help heal this family," her soothing voice reassured us. "I believe this is a fixable situation. I will be willing to meet with each of you individually and collectively in a minimum of twelve sessions. I will walk this journey with you all."

We agreed to these demands; Darren and Evelyn went to their room in silence. The rest of us cleaned up the dishes, with almost no conversation except for the immediate task in front of us.

Gary walked Dr. El-Amin out to her car, and then each of us went to our rooms.

My room was directly across from Danielle and Gary's. Danielle perceived my pent-up rage. She knew if she did not talk to me, I might go to my room and commit suicide.

"Please," Danielle pleaded," I know Dr. El-Amin told us not to talk about the intervention, but I need to tell you the reason why we didn't tell you before."

I really did not want to talk, but I dutifully waited to see what she had to say before I retreated to the darkness of my room. I was not informed because the others knew I would leak the plan to Darren and Evelyn. They were right. I would have voided the purpose of the intervention. Frankly, this whole experience was terrifying. I was afraid of what the future would be for me if the Community broke up. I could not see how I could move to any of my sisters' or brothers' houses. I did not have a driver's license, money, or job to help pay my way. As I went into my room and plopped onto my bed, I was not considering suicide as I had done at other low points of my life. Instead, I felt a terrible heaviness inside. I finally fell asleep, wondering what the next day would bring. Maybe I would wake up and find out it was all a bad dream.

But the next morning, I knew it was not a bad dream, because I heard knocking at my door. Robert came into my room to assure me that he and his wife would take care of me. Although Robert meant it in kindness, it was *not* the message I wanted to hear, and I was not encouraged by his sentimentality.

I needed to get some space, so I put on my hat, took my purse with my medications in it, and started to walk. After walking for a couple of hours, I bought a cold drink at the fast-food store and just sat next to the street sign, crying. I am sure I looked pathetic—an old woman in a straw hat wearing overalls.

I was about five miles from home when a neighbor saw me and, realizing she had never seen me this far from home, offered me a ride home. As I sat there, she was so kind as not to ask any explanations as to why I had walked so far from home. Instead, we talked about her work as a horse-riding instructor. I am so grateful for the kindness she showed me that day.

Danielle visibly relaxed when she saw me come in the door. Once again she apologized for the necessary step of leaving me out. She then shared her love and concern for me. "You are family, Kata," she reminded me. "You are a godmother to one of my children. Please, please, can you read the information Valerie and the rest of us sent to the bishop, our doctor, and Dr. El-Amin?"

I was simply too exhausted to focus on reading the many pages I saw in her hand. "Would you please read them to me?" I sighed. I saw relief on her face. First, she needed to call Gary, her husband, to let him know I was safe. Then slowly, she read all the letters aloud. It went on for a good forty-five minutes. She carefully explained that the point of the intervention was to bring out in the open the emotional abuse caused by Evelyn's need to have control of our lives. It took months of planning with letters, visits, and phone calls pleading for help, from both our bishop and the family doctor. Only after all those efforts did our doctor recommend Dr. El-Amin.

Later I asked Danielle what she was thinking at that moment, and I share it here as another aspect of my journey:

"As I was reading, I literally saw the scales fall from your eyes. In a voice I will never forget … with a cry from your heart that to this day I can recall with great clarity … and with the relief that you truly did *see* with God's grace that our act of desperation the night before was out of love … you said the following. Kata, these were your exact words, as I could never, ever forget them … 'You mean I don't have to do puzzles the way Evelyn says anymore?' (This was *new* information to me.) At that I burst into tears, stood up, went over to hug you, and as I wrapped my arms around you, I said, 'Oh, I had *no* idea it was even down to that with you!' And what followed were the ongoing insights that you had about E's real domination of your life."

The yoke of bondage I had put myself in under the guise of being a beloved daughter of Evelyn's was now broken. I knew it would be a tough road ahead. But at last I was set free.

After this, I walked over to the main house. A note had been attached to the door of the main house; it stated no one was to enter unless he or she needed to get to the cash box.

We didn't know the purpose of that note until our meeting Wednesday night with the psychiatrist. Still trying to remain in control, Darren and Evelyn insisted they would go first. They announced that within two days, they were packing their belongings and moving out. Then they simply stood up and walked out of the room—leaving the rest of us to read our letters without them. "*What?*" was the collective reaction? That was not following the agreement we all made together just two nights earlier. Once again I was frightened and confused.

Dr. El-Amin came the following day to discuss the next steps and whether we would try to stay together living as a Community or go our separate ways. Due to our vows of poverty, we personally owned nothing. All the money and property, according to the rules and constitution of the nonprofit corporation and as a religious order, belonged to the church. In our case this was the Anglican Church. Father Basil did some research and shared that in no way could we individually divide the money or the property. Our bishop would need to navigate the needs of each family unit separately.

In times of stress, what did I do? I cleaned! The next morning, with my head in the refrigerator as I scrubbed furiously, someone knocked on the front door.

Jan, a longtime Christian friend of Danielle's, was at the door. She had come down from Orange County to check on the house that she and her husband, Bob, owned, which was up around the corner next door to Mabelle's home.

Danielle invited her in for a cup of coffee. They talked about their children, who grew up together and were now all college-age. The conversation was quite normal, and Jan left. Danielle immediately felt bad because she did not share about what had just transpired within the Community. So, after calling Gary at work and explaining how she felt for not being honest with Jan, they both agreed that she needed to call and tell her about the Community breakup.

When Danielle called, explaining the whole situation, Jan's response was, "The granny flat behind the house is empty if anyone needs a place to get away! Just let me know." Danielle's first thought was, *Maybe this would be a perfect situation for Kata!* When she asked me what I thought, I jumped at the thought of my own place. "May I rent it?" I asked aloud. I had no plan or idea as to how I would get

Katherine Zyczynska

around without a driver's license, car, or a way to support myself.

Was it even possible to live as an adult for the first time in my life?

With the love and support of the remaining family members, I stepped out in faith, trusting God's provision.

.

CHAPTER 54

Out of Community

We know that all things work for good for those who
love God, who are called according to his purpose.
—Rom. 8:28

With the intervention and dissolution of our order behind
me, I began attending a nearby Roman Catholic church
with Robert and Dee. Robert and Dee had visited this
church before and found it very welcoming, so there was
no question of where to go but the Catholic church, rather
than the Episcopal or Anglican church.

I felt welcomed and secure, knowing the firm foundation of
the church that traces its roots back to St. Peter.

I had a deep confirmation in my heart that I was right where
I needed to be when we got a tour of the church. One of the
staff members, after finding out that I worked in the kitchen
at the Community, offered, "You need to see our kitchen!"

She was very right; the kitchen at this church sparkled with cleanliness and order.

Another woman from the staff, Sr. O'Malley, rushed in with an urgent request. "Zdzislawa, I heard that you speak Spanish fluently; we need your help. A couple of our parishioners have been in a car accident with a young man who speaks only Spanish. Can you come and help the police translate?" The elderly couple was just as frightened as the young man driving the truck.

God's timing is always perfect. I heard loud and clear, "This is my new church family."

Within a month, Robert, Dee, and I asked to become Catholics. We joined the group already in session of the RCIA, Religious Catholic Initiation for Adults.

After five months' preparation, on Easter morning 2009, I received the sacrament of confirmation as a member of the one, holy Catholic faith. What a glorious experience it was to become a part of this ancient heritage.

The church members embraced, encouraged, and have walked with me through this journey out of Community.

I remain overwhelmed by their love and care. I am no longer known as the nonthinking, sick woman that Evelyn believed me to be. Rather, I am known as someone who has a smile on her face, always ready to pitch in and help others. I have been able to take my love of cake decorating and turn it into a job, teaching classes at a nearby store. God took my love of children, and after learning how to assist at Mass, I am now responsible for a team of forty altar servers.

I remain close to several families from the Community. I have chosen to have no contact with Darren and Evelyn whatsoever, even though they live nearby. The story they tell about their time as Community elders is, as you can imagine, quite different from mine.

I work as a live-in caregiver. I own a car, thanks to Gary and Danielle. I am finally living the life of a successful, productive adult—a life that had been denied me for decades.

Only God knows what the future holds; whatever it is, I will be part of his plan.

*Community Recipes

Olga Przybyz' Russian Torte

Pound cake mix to make two 8-inch round cakes
4 cups heavy whipping cream
1 tablespoon powdered sugar
One 12.8-ounce jar chocolate fudge ice cream topping
1 cup chopped walnuts
One 18-ounce jar raspberry jam

Bake two 8-inch round pound cakes. When cakes are cool, divide each cake into 4 layers; place each layer on a paper plate. It will make it easier to stack if each layer is frozen.

Beat until almost stiff 4 cups whipping cream with 1 tablespoon powdered sugar.

Place first layer of cake on cake plate, cover with 1/2 cup chocolate fudge ice cream topping, and sprinkle with 1/2 cup chopped walnuts. Place next layer of cake on top and cover with 1/2 cup whipped cream.

Place next layer of cake on top and spread with 1/2 cup raspberry jam.

Place next layer of cake on top and cover with another 1/2 cup whipped cream.

Repeat the same procedure with the next 4 layers of cake, ending with cake on top.

Spread remaining whipped cream on top and sides. Can be frozen.

<u>Two-Tone Bread</u>

24 servings
Preparation: 35 minutes + rising
Bake: 35 minutes + cooling

White Dough

1 package (1/4-ounce) active dry yeast
1 1/2 cups warm 2 percent milk (110°F to 115°F)
1 1/2 teaspoons salt
2 tablespoons plus 1 1/2 teaspoons sugar
2 tablespoons plus 1 1/2 teaspoons shortening
3 1/4 to 4 cups flour, divided

Molasses Dough

1 package (1/4-ounce) active dry yeast
1 1/2 cups warm 2 percent milk
3 tablespoons molasses
2 tablespoons plus 1 1/2 teaspoons shortening
2 tablespoons plus 1 1/2 teaspoons sugar
1 1/2 teaspoons salt
2 cups all-purpose flour
2 cups to 2 ¼ cups whole wheat flour

In large bowl, dissolve yeast in warm milk. Add the sugar, shortening, salt, and 2 cups flour. Beat on medium speed for 3 minutes. Stir in enough remaining flour to form a soft dough (dough will be sticky).

Turn onto a floured surface; knead until smooth and elastic, about 6–8 minutes. Place in a large bowl coated with cooking spray, turning once to coat top. Cover and let rise in a warm place until doubled, about 1 hour.

For molasses dough, in a large bowl, dissolve yeast in warm milk. Add the molasses, shortening, sugar, salt, and all-purpose flour. Beat until smooth. Stir in enough whole wheat flour to form a soft ball (dough will be sticky).

Turn onto a floured surface; knead until smooth and elastic, about 6–8 minutes. Place in a bowl coated with cooking spray, turning once to coat top. Cover and let rise in a warm place until doubled, about 1 hour.

Punch doughs down; divide each dough in half. On a lightly floured surface, roll one portion of each dough into a 12 x 8–inch rectangle. Place the rectangle of molasses dough on the rectangle of plain dough. Roll up jelly-roll style, starting with a short side; pinch seam to seal and tuck ends under.

Place seam side down in an 8 x 4–inch loaf pan coated with cooking spray. Repeat with remaining dough. Cover and let rise in a warm place until doubled, about 30 minutes.

Bake at 375°F for 35–40 minutes or until browned. Cool for 10 minutes before removing from pans to wire racks to cool completely.

Yield: 2 loaves (12 slices each).

Souper Chicken/Rabbit
    1 can cream of mushroom soup
    1 can cream of chicken soup
    1 soup can of milk
    1 cup Minute Rice
    1 chicken cut into 8 pieces or 8 rabbit pieces
    1 package dry onion soup mix

Preheat oven to 350°F. Butter an 8 x 8–inch casserole.

Combine cream of mushroom soup, cream of chicken soup, milk, and Minute Rice. Put in casserole.

Arrange cut-up chicken or rabbit pieces over combined soup-rice mixture; salt and pepper to taste. Sprinkle dry onion soup mix over all pieces.

Cover tightly with foil. Bake for 1 1/2 hours at 400°F, then uncover and bake another 30 minutes. Make sure all the meat is cooked.

Crazy Pancakes
3 servings
    3 eggs
    1/2 cup flour
    1/4 teaspoon salt
    1/2 cup milk
    2 tablespoons melted butter

Beat eggs with fork.
Slowly add flour, beating constantly.
Add salt, milk, and melted butter.

Grease 8 x 8–inch square casserole dish. Pour batter in cold dish. Bake at 450°F for 15 minutes, then reduce temperature to 350°F for 10 minutes.

Serve immediately with bacon or sausages and syrup.

<u>Corn Patch Casserole</u>
8 servings
> 2 (16-ounce) cans cream-style corn
> 4 eggs, beaten
> 1 cup cornmeal
> 4 cups diced cooked chicken
> 1/2 cup chopped green chilies
> 1/2 cup melted butter
> 1 teaspoon salt
> 2 cups sour cream
> 2 cups shredded cheddar cheese

Combine all ingredients together. Grease a 3-quart, 8 x 8–inch casserole and place combined ingredients in it, then cover with foil. Bake for 30 minutes, then uncover and bake an additional 30 minutes until center is mostly solid.

<u>Grandma Merle's Strawberry Jam</u>

> 4 cups strawberries, cut-up
> 3 cups sugar, divided

Put strawberries into pan. Cook on medium heat, stirring constantly until comes to a boil. Then add 1 cup of sugar slowly, stirring constantly. When that comes to a boil, add 1 cup of sugar slowly, stirring constantly until it comes to a boil. Repeat with last cup of sugar. When it comes to a boil, remove from heat and let cool to enjoy. Or immediately put in jars for waxing.

Baked Chayote with Cheese

4 chayote squash, cut in half	1/4 cup grated Parmesan cheese
1 tablespoon unsalted butter	2 tablespoons shredded cheddar cheese
1 egg, beaten	1 1/4 cup cheddar cheese
1/4 cup heavy cream	1/2 cup dry bread crumbs

Place the chayote into a large pot and cover with water. Bring to a boil over high heat, then reduce heat to medium-low, cover, and simmer until very tender, 45–50 minutes. Drain and allow to steam dry for a minute or two.

Preheat an oven to 375°F (190°C).

Remove the seed and seed membrane from the chayote using a spoon; discard. Scoop out as much of the remaining pulp as possible into a bowl without puncturing the shell. Pat the shell dry with a paper towel and place in a baking dish; set aside. Squeeze the excess water from the reserved pulp. Stir in the butter, egg, heavy cream, Parmesan cheese, and shredded cheddar cheese until well blended. Fill each of the chayote shells with the pulp/cheese mixture. Sprinkle the remaining cheddar cheese on top, followed by the bread crumbs.

Bake in the preheated oven until heated through and the cheese has melted, 35–45 minutes.

Kraft Peanut Butter & Swirl Pie
Used by permission from Kraft Foods, www.kraftfoods.com

1 package (8-ounce) cream cheese, softened

1/2 cup sugar

1/4 cup creamy peanut butter

2 cups thawed Cool Whip

1 Oreo pie crust (6 ounce)

1/4 cup hot fudge ice cream topping, warmed

Beat cream cheese, sugar, and peanut butter in large bowl with mixer until well blended. Whisk in Cool Whip.
Spoon into pie crust. Drizzle with fudge topping; swirl gently with knife.
Refrigerate 4 hours or until firm.

Persimmon Pudding with Secret Butter Sauce

Pudding

1 cup sugar

1 cup persimmon pulp

1 egg

1 cup flour

1 teaspoon baking powder

1 teaspoon cinnamon

1/2 teaspoon salt

1 teaspoon baking soda

1 cup chopped nuts

1 cup raisins

1 teaspoon vanilla

1/2 cup milk
1 tablespoon melted butter

Sauce
    1 cup sugar
    1 cup butter
    1 cup whipping cream

Beat well sugar, persimmon pulp, and egg.
In separate large bowl put flour, baking powder, cinnamon, salt, and baking soda; mix well.
Add to above dry ingredients chopped nuts and raisins.
Stir dry ingredients to wet in large bowl; mix well with vanilla, milk, and melted butter. Blend well and pour into greased and floured shallow 8 x 8–inch pan. Cover with foil and bake 1 hour at 350°F; do not use extra heavy-duty foil. Uncover and serve warm with sauce.

To make sauce
Cream sugar and butter together; add cream and put in saucepan to boil until thick, stirring constantly until softball stage on candy thermometer, 234–240°F.

Frozen Strawberry Yogurt Pie
Used with permission of Kraft Foods, www.kraftfoods.com
8 servings

8 ounces strawberry yogurt	8- or 9-inch graham cracker crust
1/2 cup mashed strawberries	
8 ounces Cool Whip	

Mix together yogurt and strawberries. Fold in whipped Cool Whip until thoroughly combined. Pour into graham cracker crust. Freeze about 4 hours. Place in refrigerator 30 minutes before serving. Store leftover pie in freezer.

Poke and Pour Jell-O Cake
Used with permission of Kraft Foods, www.kraftfoods.com

One cake mix
3-ounce package of desired flavor of Jell-O

Frosting
1 package Dream Whip
1 small package instant pudding mix
1 1/2 cups cold milk
1 teaspoon vanilla flavoring

Make cake according to directions on package, in greased and floured 13 x 9–inch pan.
Bake according to directions for pan.
Cool 15 minutes in pan.
Dissolve gelatin as directed on package. Poke holes in cake all over top with fork. Pour warm gelatin all over cake. Chill 4 hours.

Frosting
In chilled bowl, blend Dream Whip, instant pudding, cold milk, and vanilla until stiff, 3–8 minutes. Frost cake immediately.

Scalloped Chayote Casserole
4 large chayotes

5 cups grated cheddar cheese, divided
1/2 cup butter, divided
4 tablespoons of flour
1/2 teaspoon of salt
2 cups warm milk

Slice 4 large chayotes in 1/2-inch slices; if the skin is tough, you will need to peel it off.

Parboil chayote slices for 4 minutes. Drain.

Grease 13 x 9-inch casserole dish and put a layer of sliced chayote on bottom. Sprinkle with 2 cups grated cheddar cheese, put small pieces of 1/4 cup butter over cheese, then sprinkle 2 tablespoons of flour and 1/4 teaspoon of salt.

Repeat layering the same way, ending with salt.

Pour warm milk over all until vegetables are covered. Bake at 350°F for 1 hour. In last 15 minutes, cover with another cup sprinkling of cheese.

Bobbie Jean's Kahlua Balls

1 pound Oreo cookies
1 cup walnuts
2 tablespoons cocoa powder
2 tablespoons shredded coconut
1/2–3/4 cup Kahlua
1/2 powdered sugar

In a food processor or blender, crumble Oreo cookies, walnuts, cocoa powder, and shredded coconut. Add Kahlua so mixture can be formed into balls.

Shape into balls and place on cookie sheet lined with wax paper. Refrigerate. When chilled, dust with powdered sugar and serve.

<u>Blitz Torte</u>
6–8 servings

Cake

1/2 cup butter	3 tablespoons milk
1/2 cup sugar	1 cup flour
4 egg yolks, beaten	1 teaspoon baking powder
1 teaspoon vanilla	

Topping

4 egg whites	1/2 cup sliced almonds
1 cup sugar	1 teaspoon cinnamon

Pastry cream filling

1/3 cup sugar	2 egg yolks, slightly beaten
2 tablespoons cornstarch	
1/8 teaspoon salt	2 teaspoons vanilla
11/2 cup whole milk	dash of nutmeg

Cake

Cream butter; add sugar, egg yolks, and vanilla. Add milk, flour, and baking powder. Spread into two 8-inch round pans lined with parchment circles, greased, and floured.

Topping

Whip egg whites in grease-free bowl until stiff and dry, adding sugar by tablespoons. Spread on unbaked batter. Sprinkle almonds and cinnamon. Bake in a preheated oven at 350°F for 30 minutes. Run a knife around sides of pan to keep from sticking, cool 10 minutes in pan, then invert to remove cakes and cool completely.

Pastry cream filling
Mix thoroughly sugar, cornstarch, and salt in medium saucepan. Stir milk into egg yolks; gradually stir liquids into dry ingredients. Cook on medium heat, stirring constantly until mixture begins to boil; continue to stir for 1 minute. Remove from heat, adding vanilla and nutmeg. Cool completely before filling cake.

Place one cake on plate, meringue side up, then cream filling, ending with other cake meringue side up.

Trane's Casserole
8–10 servings

>   2 pounds ground beef
>   1 minced onion
>   2 small cans black olives, drained
>   1 large can tomato sauce
>   1 pint sour cream
>   1 pint cottage cheese
>   1 small can diced green chilies
>   One large bag of tortilla chips
>   1 pound Monterey Jack cheese

Brown in a skillet ground beef and onion. Add black olives, drained, and tomato sauce; salt and pepper to taste.
Combine in a separate bowl sour cream, cottage cheese, and diced green chilies. Crush tortilla chips and set aside.
Grate Monterey Jack cheese.
Spray with Pam one 13 x 9–inch casserole dish. Place one layer of crushed tortilla chips, about 1/4 inch thick. Layer

on top 1/2 of ground beef mixture, then 1/2 sour cream mixture. Sprinkle with 1/2 grated cheese.

Repeat the 4 layers.

Bake uncovered at 350°F for 35 minutes if it is at room temperature; if cold, 15 minutes longer or until bubbly.

Bunny Kaplafka's Enchiladas

1 dozen flour tortillas
1 large onion, chopped
2 cups grated Jack cheese
2 cups grated cheddar cheese
2 cups medium white sauce

1 cup chopped green chilies
1 cup sour cream
1 cup mixed grated cheese for topping

White sauce
4 tablespoons butter, melted
1/4 cup flour
2 cups warm milk

Preheat oven to 350°F.

Sauté onion until soft; spread on tortillas. Mix the cheeses and divide between tortillas. Roll up the tortillas burrito style. Place in greased 9 x 13–inch casserole dish.

Make white sauce. Place melted butter in saucepan.

Add flour and mix until smooth. Remove from heat. Add warm milk, and mix until smooth. Place pan over medium heat, and cook until bubbly, approximately 1 minute. Remove from heat.

Add chilies and sour cream. Spread 1/3 of sauce on tortillas. Bake for 10 minutes. Then baste with 1/3 more sauce. Bake 10 minutes. Baste with rest of sauce. Bake 15 minutes. Sprinkle cheese on top. Bake 5 minutes.

Zucchini Relish

10 cups ground zucchini
4 cups ground onions
5 tablespoons salt
2 1/2 cups cider vinegar
6 cups sugar
1 tablespoon nutmeg
1 tablespoon dry mustard
1 tablespoon turmeric
2 teaspoons celery seeds
1/2 teaspoon black pepper
2 green and 1 red bell pepper, ground

Mix zucchini, onions, and salt together, and let stand overnight.
In the morning, drain, rinse, and drain again.

Place remaining ingredients together in large stew pot. Bring to boil, then turn down to simmer 30 minutes, stirring occasionally to prevent sticking on the bottom and to incorporate the flavorings. Divide relish between approximately five sterilized quarts, canning them using the water-bath method.

Four-Layer Pistachio Dessert

Dessert Crust
1 1/2 cups flour
10 tablespoons butter

1/4 cup chopped nuts

Filling

8 ounces cream cheese
1 cup powdered sugar
3 cups Cool Whip, divided
6 ounces instant pistachio pudding (may substitute lemon or chocolate)
3 cups milk

Make dessert crust by crumbling flour and butter until thoroughly mixed. Blend in nuts. Pat into 9 x 13–inch pan. Bake at 350°F for 15 minutes. Cool thoroughly.

Mix softened cream cheese and sugar. Blend well and add 2 cups Cool Whip. Spread over cooled dessert crust. Mix pudding with milk, and pour over cream cheese layer. When set, frost with remaining Cool Whip. Chill 4 hours before serving.

<u>Halloween Pumpkin Cookies</u>

2 cups flour	1 egg
1 cup quick oats	1 teaspoon vanilla
1 teaspoon baking soda	15-ounce can pumpkin
1 teaspoon cinnamon	1 cup chocolate chips
1/2 teaspoon salt	1 cup peanut butter
1 cup butter, softened	chips
1 cup brown sugar	1 cup raisins
1 cup sugar	

Preheat oven to 350°F. Combine flour, oats, baking soda, cinnamon, and salt. Cream butter; gradually add sugars, beating until light and fluffy. Add egg and vanilla; mix well. Alternate additions of dry ingredients and pumpkin, mixing well after each addition. Stir in morsels. For each cookie, drop 1/4 cup dough onto lightly greased cookie sheet. Spread into pumpkin shape. Bake 20–25 minutes. Cool 10 minutes. Remove from cookie sheet. Finish cooling. When cool, decorate with frosting and assorted Halloween candies.

St. Nicolaus Speculatius (Kris Kringle) Cookies (German Spice Cookies)

1 cup butter
1 cup shortening
2 cups brown sugar
1/2 cup sour cream
4 1/2 cups sifted all-purpose flour
1/2 teaspoon baking soda

3 teaspoons cinnamon
1 teaspoon allspice
1/2 teaspoon cloves
1/2 teaspoon nutmeg
1/2 cup finely chopped walnuts

Cream butter, shortening, and brown sugar; blend in sour cream. Mix and sift dry ingredients; add slowly to creamed mixture. (Do not use electric mixer if dough is too stiff.) Stir in walnuts. Divide into 4 portions; wrap each portion in aluminum foil; chill several hours or overnight. Work with one portion of dough at a time, leaving the others in the refrigerator. Roll out very thin, and cut with St. Nicholas cutters. Bake at 350°F for 10 minutes. Roll scraps into a ball; refrigerate briefly before rerolling. Frost and decorate as desired.

Printed in the United States
By Bookmasters